THE
FORFEIT

THE
FORFEIT

Florence
GILLAN

POOLBEG
CRIMSON

Published 2023 by Crimson
an imprint of Poolbeg Press Ltd.
123 Grange Hill, Baldoyle,
Dublin 13, Ireland
Email: poolbeg@poolbeg.com

A catalogue record for this book is available from the British Library.

ISBN 978178199-694-2

www.poolbeg.com

About the Author

Florence Gillan is a retired teacher originally from Sligo but now residing in Newry, County Down. She lives with her husband Eugene, two dogs and a cat with no name. Her childhood passion for reading encouraged her to write and tell stories at a young age. Her debut novel, *Let Them Lie*, was set in her native Sligo. *The Forfeit*, a dark psychological thriller, is set in Sligo and Dundalk.

Acknowledgements

Paula Campbell turned my life upside down when she agreed to publish my first novel, and now, thanks to her, I'm no longer a retiree but a full-time writer. She made this crazy adventure possible. I will always be grateful and appreciative of all her help and encouragement.

Gaye Shortland, my amazing editor, has helped me make this book the best version possible. She has taught me so much and has been patient with me as I stumbled through the editing process. Thank you, Gaye, for all your hard work, encouragement and advice. I appreciated it.

My gratitude to David Prendergast and all the team at Poolbeg who worked on this book and designed the beautiful cover.

Thanks to Paul Maddern at the River Mill writers retreat for his amazing hospitality and five-star cuisine.

Once again, my team of first readers encouraged me, calmed me down and listened to me when I struggled with plot issues. Thank you, Eugene Hanna, Mo Gillan, Martina Hamilton, Madeleine Skoronski and Fiona Ó Murchú.

Special thanks are due to Madeleine Skoronski and Fiona Ó Murchú, who read and reread the book with a forensic eye for mistakes. You are both legendary friends.

My two brothers, Seán and Aidan, offered me advice on farming issues. Any mistakes of a farming nature are purely my own.

My wonderful extended family of brothers, sisters, sisters in-laws, brothers-in-law, nieces, nephews, cousins and my fabulous and witty godmother Annie Kilfeather Walker have all been a chorus of love and encouragement.

To my wonderful parents, Mark and Mary, and my lovely brother and sister, Frank and Helen – you are all very much alive in my thought and memories. I treasure the time we had together. I just wish it had been longer.

Thanks to all my loyal friends for cheering me on and letting me drone for Ireland about how hard I was working.

My four lovely children, Rachel, David, Mark and Sarah, have supported me, encouraging me to keep going when I was getting weary of it all. They are at the heart of everything – my love and appreciation I send to you.

Finally, Eugene, thank you for keeping me fed and watered and bearing the brunt of my meltdowns with patience.

Dedication

Eugene, all my love and thanks

PROLOGUE

When Brenna opened her eyes, she shivered as though a dark cloud had enveloped the room. As she dragged herself out of bed, her skin swarmed with goosebumps despite the blaze of morning sunshine. A feeling of doom settled over her even before she saw the small envelope peeking out from the pocket of her summer cardigan. It mocked her with the malignancy she knew it contained. Her heart thudded and felt too heavy for her chest.

Staring at the envelope, she was afraid to open it but even more terrified not to. She dreaded the instructions awaiting within. Yet if she refused or failed the test, the forfeit would be even more terrifying. The room seemed to be closing in on her, her breath was trapped in her throat, and her head swam. Whimpering, she held the envelope in her hand. Once she opened it, the Game began, and there was nothing she could do to stop it.

CHAPTER 1

BREE

Dundalk

1992

She had opened a letter from a dead man. How was this possible? The white envelope had seemed so innocent when she'd noticed it on her doormat. An ordinary letter postmarked Dublin. When she'd torn it open, she'd been surprised to see it contained another much smaller envelope. She'd shook it out onto the table, and that was when her stomach flipped and her heart thumped painfully against the walls of her chest.

The small envelope, bordered in black, lay on the table. With trembling fingers, she turned it over, and there on the front was scrawled the name *Brenna*.

She slumped onto a kitchen chair, her blood pounding in her ears. It couldn't be. She stared, mesmerised, at the small envelope. Afraid to open it. It had to be some weird coincidence. But no one except Rory had ever sent her tiny envelopes bordered in black, and he was dead. She continued to stare helplessly. All the memories she had pushed to the deepest recesses of her mind surged agitatedly to the surface. They mustn't escape. She didn't want to think about the past. She *wouldn't* think about the past. She had spent thirty years building up a hard scab to hold it back.

She sat frozen in her seat, unable – no, unwilling to open the envelope. But she knew that she had to. It was nearly thirty years since she had last seen Rory. After her father got the transfer to Louth, she begged her mother not to invite her cousin to stay again. Her mother, seeing she was still traumatised after the events of the previous summer, hadn't forced the issue. Bree didn't know how she explained it to Rory's mother, and never asked. Once they moved, she refused to speak about Rory again. Now here was the past preparing to devour her once more. But how? Rory was dead. Her mother had told her about his death, but she had never asked her for details. It was enough to know that he was gone – hopefully to hell. Her overwhelming feeling had been one of relief. He might invade her dreams, but she was safe from ever having to encounter him again. But now his menacing presence was reaching out to her as she stared at the little envelope.

She had been so contented only a little while ago as she strolled to her car, enjoying the lovely late September evening. Summer warmth still lingered in the air, diluted by a slight autumn breeze, and she carried her jacket over her arm. Her spirits were high at the thought of Amy coming home from college for the weekend. She had cajoled Colm into letting her leave work early because she wanted to cook Amy's favourite meal – chicken curry and chips. Parking her car, she had done a quick flit around the shops, eager to get home and have everything perfect for her daughter.

Blissfully unaware of the minefield ahead. She had no sixth sense, no foreboding that her life was about to shift on its axis.

Now, she desperately wished to turn back time and recapture that earlier sense of contentment. She wasn't sure how long she had sat, lost in a swamp of painful memories. She glanced at the clock on the wall and shook herself free of the past, at least for the moment. Amy would be here soon, ravenous after her bus journey home, and she hadn't even started dinner. Leaving the envelope on the table, she struggled to her feet and unpacked the groceries, grateful for the opportunity to be busy. She chopped up the chicken breasts and sliced onions and vegetables. Soon she had the meat and veg sautéed, and the chicken curry was bubbling gently in the sauce she had made from scratch.

Amy was doing psychology through Arts at UCD. She had fallen in love with the subject, but had needed to excel in her first year to continue with it as her major. Unfortunately, she'd initially found it difficult to meet the standards required. Her tutor had suggested that she work with a colleague who occasionally coached students needing a little direction. It had worked out brilliantly. Amy said that he was a miracle worker. He restored her confidence and helped iron out the problems she had, so now she was a full-time second-year psychology student and was thriving. She still got occasional support from the helpful lecturer. It was lovely to see Amy happy, energised, and with her confidence back.

When she'd first moved away to college, Bree had felt bereft. She had missed her desperately. Her friend Anita had consoled her by saying she would now be free to pursue her interests and hobbies. The trouble was finding interests to pursue. It was a sad truth that Amy was her world, and friends and hobbies played second fiddle. She took on more overtime at work to fill up the vacuum left by her daughter's absence. At one time, she thought about doing a cookery course. But who to cook for? Amy came home fairly frequently now, but Bree knew that would change the more friends she made and the more fun opportunities that came her way. So, a cookery course might be a bit of a waste.

These last few years, Bree had been very happy. She was financially secure and, ten years before, with her mother's help, she had bought her own home. She loved her little house. It was at the end of her estate, so it had a larger if oddly shaped garden, perfect for Amy when she was young but a bit of a wilderness now. It was a typical three-bedroom house but she had converted the attic to a den for Amy and her mates, where they could listen to music and have a little privacy. Now that Amy was away, Bree used it to house her rowing machine and as a spare bedroom for those rare occasions when she had visitors. The smallest bedroom she used as an office.

Her mother lived locally, so although she didn't stay overnight she did visit regularly and once a fortnight came for dinner. Mary O'Hagan was still a sprightly woman at sixty-five, a widow now for many years, but Bree could see the vulnerability on her mother's face when she thought no one was looking. She still missed Sligo. Her husband's promotion had necessitated the move to Dundalk and, although they had settled happily there, Mary still liked to visit her friends and neighbours in Sligo. She was away on one of her little pilgrimages there this weekend. Bree didn't go with her. Her mother accepted that she never would. A long time ago, Mary had given up trying to persuade her to go, and for that Bree was truly grateful.

Thoughts of her mother brought the trauma of the past and the envelope once more to the forefront of her mind. She continued to work on autopilot, peeling potatoes and slicing them into chips to cook in the deep-fat fryer but, all the time, her mind clamoured with questions. Who could have sent the envelope? Could Rory have told someone about the Game? Why, thirty years since that awful time in Sligo, was she receiving another one of those sick things?

Enough! She wouldn't sully her time with Amy by twisting herself in knots about the envelope. She picked it up by its edge and shoved it into her shoulder bag which was hanging from a chairback, but it seemed to her that its toxicity permeated through the bag, taunting her with cowardice. Furiously, she pulled it out again and tore it open, not allowing herself time to think. Inside was a small sheet of paper folded over. Again, just like the notes Rory had sent her all those years ago. Her guts twisting, she unfolded the note. She stared at the typed words: **Miss Me?** And there was a little smiley face with one eye open and one closed, winking at her. Shivering, she felt Rory's corrupting presence contaminating her home.

Staring at the note, her mind piled on all the memories she had fought so hard to stifle. Like peas removed from the freezer, the memories were as fresh as when she first froze them in a deep part of her mind that she had refused to access. But now the defrosting had begun and she was unravelling. Could this be someone's idea of a sick joke? But she had never told a soul about the envelopes with their instructions or the events of that awful time when she was a child. There was no one alive to play this trick, and only a man dead for over twenty years could. It was impossible. And yet, here was the proof, her past had come back to haunt her. Someone else must know.

She heard a key in the door and then Amy's voice calling, '*Mam, I'm home!*'

She jumped up, shoved the note and envelope in the kitchen drawer, and shouted, '*I'm here, love!*'

Amy bounced into the room. That was her Amy. She didn't walk – she bounded, all her movements full of energy and fizzing with expectations. Bree was reminded of Amy's father, Joe. He filled every space with energy and enthusiasm too. His daughter looked like him and had much of his character and intelligence. No wonder they got on so well. They must find her very dull. The irony of the thought suddenly hit her. No, she wasn't dull, or at least her past wasn't, and she never intended to let either of them be privy to that information.

It was her need for secrecy which frustrated Joe. He felt shut out by her emotional distance and refusal to marry him when she got pregnant. Keeping up a reserved front was her best protection and the armour she was unable to surrender.

Amy flung her backpack on the nearest chair, pulled the scrunchy from her head, liberating her curly brown hair, and began telling Bree all about her week at college. Being the only child of a single parent, Amy had confided in Bree from an early age. She shared information about friends, boys she fancied, teachers she liked, and those she disliked. She was as open as Bree was closed off.

'I joined a mountain climbing group in college. We had a few easy climbs, but we plan to tackle something more challenging next week.'

'Is that safe, Amy? You've never climbed anything before. I wish you'd picked a less dangerous activity.'

'Oh, Mam, don't be a goose! I've got all the gear – Daddy gave me the money, and don't worry, I plan to pay him back when I get a part-time job. I'm sure the coffee shop on campus will give me hours. They're always looking for staff – the pay is brutal, but at least it'll keep me in booze and fags.' At her mother's horrified gaze, she grinned. 'Relax, Mam, only kidding. I'm not going to smoke, not after seeing you puffing away for years. Watching you give them up was enough to put me off for life – you were that cranky.'

They chatted for a while, and then Amy said she'd take her stuff upstairs and put her dirty laundry in the machine.

'Dinner will be ready in twenty minutes. I'm just heating the oil for the chips.'

'Great, I'm hungry like a shark. There was a lad on the train eating chips, and I was nearly desperate enough to ask him for one, but he looked the type to get notions, and I didn't want him to think I had any interest.'

'Did you? Have any interest?' Bree asked, smiling.

'Well, he wasn't bad-looking, but he had BO, so that's a no-no for me.' Amy headed off to get her dirty laundry sorted.

They ate at the small table in the kitchen. It could just about fit four people but, as this rarely happened, it was usually wedged out of the way against a wall, and there was room for just the two of them.

After dinner, Amy announced she was heading to the pub to catch up with her pals from school, and Bree told her to tell them all she was asking for them.

'What time will you be home, love?'

'Not sure, Mam, but don't wait up. Is it OK if one of the girls wants to stay over?'

'Of course. See you later then.'

The door slammed shut, and Bree was left alone with nothing but her thoughts and the little envelope and its cryptic message to keep her company.

CHAPTER 2

After Amy left, Bree went and sat in the living room with a cup of coffee, the past invading her mind. Should she ring her mother and find out about Rory's death? She tried to remember whether her parents had gone to his funeral, but she had buried so much from that time that her memories were slippery. Mary was staying with her cousin in Sligo and had left a contact number, but Bree was reluctant to call her.

She tried to remember exactly what her mother had said about Rory's death. It was twenty-five years ago, a time when she had been desperately unhappy at school. She shuddered as she remembered her stint in the hospital. She shook her head to block out the memories of that time – she couldn't let herself go back there; the pain was too visceral. Life hadn't been easy, but after the news of Rory's death something had opened in her. The crushing fear abated, if not the guilt. His death had been a rebirth for her. She had persuaded her parents to allow her to move schools. It was her reset time, her transformation into a different person. Her parents were relieved to see her coming out of the dark place she was in, and that was when she told them she wanted to be called Bree. Brenna was part of the past, buried in a dark recess of her mind and somewhere she refused to visit.

Her parents were thrilled when she went to college in Dublin to study law, but their joy was shortlived as she got pregnant less than a year after starting her college career. She was desperate to keep her baby and dropped out of college. Her mother had pleaded with her to finish her degree, but Bree knew that she would have found it impossible even with her parents' financial help. Having a baby outside of marriage in the 1970s was frowned upon. Mammy had been good about it. She was a religious woman, but she never uttered words of condemnation. The idea of putting the child up for adoption was never discussed. They would find a way to make it work. Mammy told her about the many miscarriages and stillbirths she had experienced as a young woman. There was never a chance either of her parents would have wanted Bree to put her baby, their beloved grandchild, up for adoption. They had a waterfall of love to shower on the new little person coming into their world.

For the first few years of Amy's life, they had lived in Bree's parents' house, two miles outside Dundalk. Her dad died of a heart attack shortly after Amy was born. He was only fifty. It was devastating, but they were consoled by the fact that he had met his grandchild. They had lovely memories of him cuddling Amy and singing little songs to amuse her. After his death, they created a shrine of photographs, mainly featuring Amy and him.

Bree set about applying for jobs. She needed to be able to provide for her daughter and wanted to be financially independent. Mary provided free childcare, which gave Bree the freedom to work, and shared her car, enabling her to work in the local solicitor's office. Bree settled into a routine of work and motherhood, aware of how lucky she was to have such a supportive mother. The two women doted on Amy. Mary was respectful of Bree and allowed her the freedom to mother Amy the best way she knew, but she was always on hand to offer advice and support.

Amy's father, another law student, was her first serious relationship. They got on great and had many friends in common. Maybe if things had been different, they might have lasted, but six months into their relationship she got pregnant. Joe had been terrified. His parents were extremely strict Catholics and he dreaded telling them. However, he never tried to avoid his responsibilities. He made an obligatory offer of marriage, even sounding as though he meant it. But their romantic relationship ended. Bree realised she had only spare room in her heart for this new little being she had brought into the world. Joe accepted that they would never be together and she knew he was relieved, whatever words of denial issued from his mouth. Bree knew it wouldn't work. He was just starting out, and his parents struggled to pay for his expenses at UCD. She didn't want to force him to drop out of college – and she knew he would help when he was able to.

It worked out well. Joe's parents got over their suspicion of her and came to love their little grandchild and respect her mother. They lived in Mayo. As a child, Amy stayed with them and her father for a weekend every month. Joe was a great dad. He worked as a solicitor in Dublin and, when Amy started college, he organised an apartment for her to live in and helped with her rent. Father and daughter had a close bond, which survived Amy's decision to study psychology instead of law.

Joe got married when Amy was six, and she was a flower girl at his wedding. Once he and Nora, his wife, had children, Amy was made to feel integral to the family. For that, Bree felt a debt of gratitude to Nora. The women were friendly but not close, and they coordinated family celebrations seamlessly. But Joe's new family's financial and emotional demands made it difficult for him to prioritise Amy. A year ago, he had moved to Cork, and the occasions when he and Amy met had dwindled.

All these memories surging up from the past made Bree uncomfortable, and she knew that the best way to avoid thinking was through work or exercise. She couldn't afford the gym, but the sea was free and, whenever her head disturbed her, she jumped in the water, and the cold drove everything from her mind. It was too late to head to the beach, the tide would be out, but she had purchased a rowing machine as a present for her birthday, and tonight it was going to be put to good use.

She changed into sweatpants and climbed the stairs to the attic. Everything was neat and tidy. A couch that could double as a bed was pushed against the wall under the window, and a small bookcase leaned against another. The rowing machine was placed at the back of the room so it wouldn't be in the way when she needed to convert the couch into a bed. She positioned herself and began. She started slowly, getting her limbs used to the rhythm, but soon she built up speed. She upped her speed and resistance whenever her thoughts drifted to the envelope or her childhood. Soon her body was bathed in sweat. She worked out for an hour and then went for a brisk walk around the estate.

When she returned to the house, she decided to have a bath to pass the long night but, once ensconced in the bubble-filled tub, she knew it was a mistake. Baths and reflection were a marriage made in heaven but not tonight. She emptied the water out and stood under the shower. The water was cold as she had used up so much in the bath, but she welcomed the chill. She dried off and dressed in her pyjamas. Intrusive thoughts kept tormenting her.

At eleven, she went to bed with a hot drink and a novel that she had been struggling to finish. She hoped the lengthy descriptions of sea scenes and nature might make her bored and sleepy, but her mind kept drifting backward in time, and she soon gave up the effort.

At midnight Amy came in and hopped into bed beside her for a chat. Bree loved when Amy did that. She was reminded of when she cuddled next to her as a little girl, and the closeness filled her mind with warmth and peace. Amy chatted about her friends and how they were getting on in college. She was a little tipsy and had a bout of hiccups. She kissed her mother and went downstairs to drink a glass of water to cure them. A few minutes later, Bree heard her going into her own bedroom.

After an hour of staring at the ceiling, Bree remembered the muscle-relaxing tablets her doctor had given her when she had a sore back last winter. She had never finished the pack. To her relief, they worked their magic, and she fell into a deep, dreamless sleep.

CHAPTER 3

BRENNA

1960

School was finished for the summer holidays, and Brenna glowed with happiness. Her feet barely touched the ground as she jumped off the bus. Two glorious months – eight weeks – fifty-six days, or 1,344 hours of freedom. The immensity of the number awed her. She didn't hate school, but the monotony of getting up and going there five days a week was a pain. Brenna remembered, back when she was a little four-year-old and had finished her first week at school, she told her mother that while school was OK, she'd rather not go for the next few days. She was shocked when her mother explained that school wasn't an option and that she would have to keep going until she was as old as the big girls she saw at Mass on Sunday. It was hard for the four-year-old Brenna to process. Those girls were sixteen or even more. She remembered counting out the number of birthdays before she could leave school forever. Twelve or thirteen birthdays, the number hurt her head to think about. Now as a big nine-year-old facing up to starting big school in another couple of years, the number still scared

15

her. Who would she be then? When she looked at the big girls and boys in their school uniforms in town, it seemed impossible to her that she could be like them.

But, today, freedom lay ahead for 1,344 glorious hours. She wouldn't have to do homework. No maths. No more fractions, decimal points, or percentages. Her heart was full, and she danced her way home.

Mammy was at the door to welcome her and shared her happiness at the weeks of freedom ahead. They did a little jig around the kitchen table to celebrate the start of the holidays. The piping hot cottage pie that Mammy placed before her was devoured hungrily. She chattered happily about all the things she planned to do with her freedom. They boiled down to reading her books, climbing trees, and going off exploring with her friend Coleen. Mammy reminded her that Daddy might need some help on the farm too, but that was fine with Brenna. She loved spending time with Daddy. He was a garda, and she loved when he put on his smart uniform every day and headed off to work – he looked so important. But he also worked on the farm. He had a man, Barry, who helped him, and every morning before heading off to work he and Barry would milk the cows.

She was expected to help on the family farm, like all her friends except for Coleen from next door who, as the youngest in her family, escaped most of the farm work. Coleen had four brothers to do all the hard jobs. As she was the much-petted only girl, her workload was light. Occasionally, she helped her mammy bake buns or do a bit of hoovering. Brenna was expected to help out a lot more. Every evening she fetched the cows from the high field and helped her daddy and Barry with the milking. Daddy had these machines that sucked the milk out of the cows, and he let Brenna attach the suckers to the friendly cows that didn't kick. She also helped with planting potatoes

16

and picking them when they grew. She hated this job as sometimes it rained, and her fingers and back ached. Every evening Mammy sent her to collect the hens' eggs. Brenna loved this job. The clucking and squawking of the little brown hens amused her, and she loved picking up the still-warm eggs and carrying them into the house, where Mammy would cook nice brown boiled eggs for their evening tea. Once, she found an egg with no shell. It was just a membrane sack, and she enjoyed squishing it in her hand, except when it burst and she ended up covered in sticky egg yolk.

Brenna was naturally a happy child. Sometimes, when bored, she would seek out the company of Coleen, who lived just across the road. Coleen was nice but, at times, she could be a bit clingy and whingy. Still, she was the only friend who lived nearby, and beggars can't be choosers. It would have been nice to have a sister or brother. Once, Brenna asked her mammy why she had no brothers or sisters like all her friends had. She was sorry she asked because Mammy's eyes filled with tears. She wiped them on a tea towel and said it was God's will. Brenna thought it was very unfair of God not to let her and Daddy have more babies, and she prayed every night that God would give them some. She worried too that she wouldn't be as much help as a brother would have been. She had been praying about this since she was eight, and still God hadn't answered her prayers.

But, now, the long golden days of summer stretched ahead, and she was planning to enjoy every moment. That night in bed, she planned all the things she was going to do. She fell asleep reading her latest Famous Five book and dreamed she was having adventures with George, Anne, Julian, Dick, and Timmy the dog. She wished something exciting would happen and she could solve a mystery like her fictional heroes. Closing her eyes and crossing her fingers, she wished with all her might for her own mysterious adventure.

* * *

The next day a letter from England arrived. It lay propped against the sugar bowl when Daddy came in from work. When Mammy drew his attention to it, he was eating his hard-boiled egg.

'Patrick, I got a letter from Julie.'

Daddy, a man of few words, just grunted, his mouth full of yellow egg yolk and brown bread.

'You know how hard it's been for her since Daniel passed.'

Again, Daddy grunted.

'She has no one to mind the young fellow Rory this summer, and she has to work.'

'Oh aye,' said Daddy looking a bit apprehensive.

'Well, she was wondering if we'd take him for the summer. He's a strong lad, and I'm sure he'd be a great help saving the hay and generally helping, and he'd be great company for our Brenna.'

Again, Daddy grunted.

'Well, Patrick, what do you say? Can he come?'

If Brenna had known how important his reply would be, she would have paid more attention, but she was stuck in the Famous Five adventure.

'Whatever you want, Mary. I just hope it won't mean more work for you.'

'Sure, what extra work will the lad be, and it would be nice to have Daniel's child here. I miss him so much.'

Daddy reached across the table and squeezed Mammy's hand. 'I know, Mary. I miss your brother too. Of course we'll take the boy and welcome he'll be.'

The next day Mammy cleared out the little box room that was used for storage. She got Brenna to hoover and dust, and together they made up the bed. The cover was pink.

'I hope the wee lad doesn't mind the colour, but it's all I have.'

Brenna couldn't see what the problem was. She never minded what cover was on her bed, so long as she was warm. Some nights during the winter when it got very cold, Mammy threw a few coats over her to keep her nice and toasty.

Rory was arriving in Ireland on the boat from Holyhead, and a relative of her mother was going to meet him and put him on the Sligo train the next day. On Friday, Daddy drove into town to the train station, and Brenna went along with him to meet her cousin. She was thrilled to get to sit in the front seat. Usually, when Mammy was on board, she had to sit in the back on a cushion, and every time Daddy braked or went over a pothole, she went sliding around. It was much nicer in the front, and she could see everything. Brenna and Daddy chatted about what she learned in history class. Sometimes he contradicted her teacher and said that she knew nothing. Brenna was shocked as Mrs Hardy was so smart that her eyes bulged out of her head which showed that her brain had filled up all the space inside. But she said nothing because Daddy was very clever too.

Soon they pulled up at the train station, and Daddy parked at the back of the building. He sent her on to meet her cousin, telling her, 'He'll be the only young fella on his tod, so you'll know him.'

Feeling a little shy, Brenna went into the station. She wandered into the waiting room with its plush red chairs and sat there with a few old people who were also waiting for the train to arrive. The room was thick with tobacco smoke, and she passed the time by making up stories in her head.

Absentmindedly she picked at an old scab on her knee, which was just beginning to come away from her skin. An old woman sitting clutching an enormous black bag glared at her, saying, 'You'll leave a scar if you keep picking at your scabs. Leave it be.'

Flushing, Brenna stopped what she was doing, and her face flamed as she saw the adults smirking at each other. Brenna hated having attention drawn to herself. It was with relief that she heard the screeching rumble of the train engine and the metallic sound of brakes. She wandered slowly outside.

As the people exited the train, some hurrying, some carrying heavy cases or rucksacks, she couldn't see any boy. She had started to turn away when she was tapped on the shoulder. She spun around to be confronted by a gangly boy, much taller than her, dressed in blue jeans and a dazzling white T-shirt and carrying a battered brown suitcase. His hair was jet-black, except for a strip of white at the front. She was mesmerised by his T-shirt. None of her T-shirts stayed that white for long. She wondered idly if it was new. She felt shabby in her old shorts and well-worn jumper.

'Are you my cousin Brenna?' His voice sounded strange, an English voice.

Conscious that she was staring dumbly, she nodded quickly. 'Are you Rory Brown?'

He grinned and smiled crookedly at her with big, white, even teeth.

'What age are you, gel?' he asked.

'Nine,' she answered shyly. 'Mammy says that you're twelve.'

The boy acknowledged this and once again smiled a big crooked smile as she led him out to the car. Daddy shook hands with him and asked after his mother. He told him to get in the front seat, and Brenna sat in the back, listening to her daddy ask the boy about life in England and whether he liked school and was good at his lessons. She couldn't hear his answers. The trip back to the house took about half an hour, and wasn't disturbed by any more conversation. Rory spent the time staring out the window. Brenna wondered whether he found the countryside very different from his home in England.

They pulled up in the yard and Daddy lifted Rory's case out and handed it to him.

Mammy ran outside to welcome her young nephew and gave him a quick hug.

'I'll call your mammy to say you've arrived safely.'

'Don't bother, Auntie Mary. We don't have a phone.'

'Oh, sure, that's right, I was forgetting. We only have one because of your uncle's job. He must be contactable. Maybe she can use a neighbour's phone and give me a call. I'm sure she's anxious to know that you've arrived safely.'

Mammy was telling the truth because no sooner had she sat Rory down for his tea than Auntie Julie rang. She spoke to her son for a couple of minutes, and then they hung up as calls from England cost a fortune.

Mammy asked Brenna to show Rory up to his bedroom. He looked all around him and then wandered over to the window.

'Are all those fields belonging to your father?'

Brenna joined him at the window. 'Yes, those you can see are ours, and beyond them are Mr Cullen's.'

'So, you can wander off anywhere you like, even on yon man's land?'

Brenna nodded. The boy seemed pleased by this.

A few minutes later, Daddy carried his case upstairs. Brenna showed him where he could put his things and went downstairs.

Mammy was in the kitchen. 'Well, Brenna, what do you make of your cousin Rory?'

Brenna shrugged. 'He seems OK,' and then added, 'For a boy,' and Mammy laughed.

Rory joined them in the kitchen, and Mammy told Brenna to call Daddy in for his tea. In honour of their visitor, Mammy had made drop scones and fried crispy bacon and sliced her homemade brown bread into thick slices.

She passed Rory his plate. 'That'll put hair on your chest, son.'

Rory laughed politely, and over tea Mammy interrogated him about his life in Northampton town. Brenna zoned out. The scab she picked at earlier was throbbing a bit. She worried about what the woman in the station said about scars – she was always picking at her scabs. At this rate, she'd be a mass of scars by the time she was big.

'Well, what are you waiting for?'

Brenna looked up, startled by her mother's voice.

'Brenna, you're off in a dream world again. I told you to take your cousin outside and show him around. I'm sure he's never seen cows or hens close up.'

Rory got to his feet, lifted his plate, and carried it to the sink. 'Thanks for a lovely tea, Auntie Mary.'

'You're more than welcome, Rory. You have great manners. I can see that you'll be a credit to your mammy while you stay with us. Off you go now and enjoy a bit of time outside before bed.'

Brenna led the way out through the little back kitchen and opened the back door. She was starting to walk across the yard when she realised he wasn't following her. Instead, he was staring at the wooden box with its mesh door hanging on the house gable.

'What's that?' he asked.

She looked puzzled. 'That's the safe.'

He stared at her. 'Why would you keep your safe outside? Won't the thieves get it?'

Then Brenna understood his confusion. 'Oh no – it's a food safe. It's for keeping milk, butter and meat cool and fresh. Daddy hung it in the corner of the gable so the sun doesn't get at it, and the breeze keeps the food cool. Don't you have one?'

Rory stared at her. 'Why don't you use a refrigerator?'

Brenna remembered hearing about refrigerators from the dentist's daughter at school. Her family had one, and she was always boasting about it. Brenna had never stopped to think about why her parents didn't have one. A wave of embarrassment washed over her, and she didn't know what to say.

'We have a small one in our flat,' Rory said. 'It's fierce handy for keeping the milk from going off. But I suppose you don't have to worry about milk going off when you have all those cows. Come on, show me everything.'

Brenna showed him the milking parlour, the two machines for sucking the milk out of the cows, and the little outhouse that was used to store the bright yellow oats. She told him she and her friend Coleen liked burying themselves underneath the oats when they played hide and seek. But it would be August before the oats would be ready for harvesting. Then she brought him to the hayshed. It was empty, waiting for the first cut of grass to dry out. Daddy said that soon it would be full of hay now that a spell of good weather had come.

She led him into the big shed where the young calves were. He put out his hand, and she giggled at the panic that swept over his face when the calf sucked his hand into its mouth.

He pulled it out, looking disgusted. 'His tongue is like sandpaper, yuck!'

Brenna hid her smile and showed him around the back garden with all the trees. She pointed out the ones that were good to climb and the ones that were easy to clamber up but the branches were spindly and might not hold your weight.

Rory seemed interested at first but, later, sitting on the wall that split the front and back gardens, he asked, 'Where're the shops?'

'Well, O'Gorman's is about a mile away.'

'A mile? Do you have to walk there?

'Well, I usually walk, but Coleen's brothers have bikes, and she lets me use one sometimes. Daddy said he'd get me a bike for my next birthday.' Brenna had felt proud showing off all the aspects of the farmyard, but now she felt like she was letting Rory down. Then she said, 'Daddy goes to the creamery on a Saturday, and there's a shop there. He buys me barley rock from there.'

Rory seemed suddenly bored. 'Let's go watch television?'

'We haven't got a television.'

Rory stared at her, his eyes wide. 'What, no television? What do you do of an evening?'

Brenna flushed, once more embarrassed. 'What do you watch on the television, Rory?'

'There's loads of brilliant shows, and I can't believe you've never seen *Crackerjack* or *Blue Peter* or *Robin Hood*.'

'We have the radio,' Brenna said, but the look Rory gave her made her cheeks burn. Instead of feeling proud of home, she now felt like apologising for it.

'What do your parents do to pass the time, Brenna?'

'Well, they listen to news programmes on the radio, and Daddy reads the paper every night, and Mammy knits or reads her books.'

'But what do you do? You must be bored out of your head.'

Brenna had never felt bored. She loved her jigsaws, her colouring pencils, and especially her books, and when the summer holidays came she never wanted to come inside. But suddenly she felt cheated, as though all her pleasures were childish, and she was envious of the glamour of all those television programmes.

She stood gazing at him blankly, not knowing what to say. 'Maybe

Coleen knows those programmes you're talking about. Her cousin Margaret in Dublin has a television and sometimes she goes to stay with her.'

'Who's this Coleen gel?'

'She lives next door. All her brothers are old. Cal, the youngest, is sixteen and is doing an apprenticeship. Coleen says he's going to be a plumber.' Brenna had only a vague idea of what a plumber did, but it sounded impressive.

They wandered around a bit more, and then Mammy told them to come in and get ready for bed.

Rory looked shocked. 'But it can't be bedtime already!'

When they went inside, Mammy asked Rory what his usual bedtime was. He told her it was about eleven. He didn't have a set time.

Mammy looked surprised. 'During the school term, Brenna goes to bed at half past eight, but in the summer she stays up until half nine. I suppose being older and a boy, your mammy lets you stay up a bit later. But I think you'll find out that running about in the countryside, with all the fresh air, will tire you out. How about you head upstairs with Brenna, and I'll bring you up a cup of cocoa and a biscuit, and you can read until you get sleepy. But, of course, tomorrow you can stay up a bit later as you're older than Brenna.'

Rory agreed and once again politely thanked Mammy for inviting him to stay and for the lovely tea. Brenna could see that Mammy was delighted with him.

After Mammy brought in her cocoa, Brenna got out her book and was soon lost in her exciting story. But all too soon her mother returned to collect her empty cocoa cup. Dropping a kiss on Brenna's forehead Mammy turned out the lights and told Brenna it was time to sleep. When she heard Mammy's footsteps going downstairs, she slipped her hand under her pillow where she had hidden her flashlight and lay under the bed covers reading her book. But soon the cocoa did its job and her eyes grew heavy with sleep and she turned off her flashlight and slipped her book under her pillow.

Before she dropped off, she thought it was lovely to have her cousin Rory stay for the holidays. Maybe he'd tell her all about Northampton and England. She had never been. It sounded exciting and very different from here. She was getting used to his funny accent too. She was excited for the morning to come and for all the lovely adventures ahead.

CHAPTER 4

BREE

Amy slept in on Saturday, so Bree went upstairs to the spare room and worked at her desk. She caught up on some work for Colm and around midday she heard Amy rattling dishes in the kitchen. She went downstairs.

Amy had piled her dark-brown hair into a messy bun and was still in her PJs.

'I'm making myself a bacon buttie. Will I fix you one too?' she asked.

Bree nodded. 'I'd love one. I didn't have breakfast yet, so I'm starving.'

The sandwich that Amy gave her was heavy on bacon and slathered in ketchup. It wasn't Bree's usual morning fare but, nonetheless, it was very appetising.

'I knew you'd like it,' Amy said, topping up her tea. 'Ketchup is the crucial ingredient in all food.'

Bree laughed. 'I agree this is delicious, but I think you'd find a lot of chefs would be outraged if you anointed their dishes in thick red sauce.'

'Well, we'll agree to disagree,' Amy mumbled, her mouth full of food.

'Do you fancy going for a swim today?' Bree suggested. 'The tide will be in around three, and we could get a decent dip at Shelling Hill.'

To her delight, Amy agreed. They both loved the water and swam every chance they got.

The beach was deserted, and they pulled off their clothes quickly. They were wearing their togs underneath. Amy was a good swimmer. Bree had ensured that she got lessons from an early age. Bree too had learned to swim when she was a child – she supposed she had to thank Rory for that –– and she had taken more lessons when she moved to Dundalk. She was a strong swimmer and loved tiring her body out in the water. Putting her head underwater always put things in perspective. The cold and the feel of the water against her skin acted as a stress-reliever.

'*Come on, Mam, let's have a race!*' called Amy.

They spent the next half hour pounding over and back until they were so tired they barely could make the shore. They raced up and down the beach to warm up and then, after towelling themselves roughly, got dressed. It was the least pleasant part of the outing as their still-damp bodies resisted their efforts, and they felt the damp stickiness glue the clothes to their skin.

On the way home, they picked up two takeaway coffees and ate a doughnut each. After exercise, the food tasted extra good. It was a lovely way to spend the day.

Back at the house, Amy had some work to prepare for college and Bree made a list of what she needed for dinner that night. Amy wouldn't be staying for Sunday lunch, so she wanted to cook something special tonight, and maybe they could share a nice bottle of wine. Amy had recently developed a taste for wine, and it was nice to have someone to share a bottle with. She shopped in Dunnes and picked up two steaks, a head of broccoli, and some nice rooster potatoes. She chose a bottle of wine and headed to the checkout. She was lucky. Usually, Saturday afternoon was busy and the queue long, but the gods were kind, and she was soon out of the shop and on the road for home. Thoughts of Rory and his time living with her family in Sligo intruded. No, not this weekend. She wouldn't think about it until Amy left in the morning.

Dinner was a success and, after eating, they sat on the sofa and watched a video Amy had rented, called *Field of Dreams*. Bree had dozed off before it was over, and Amy laughingly refused to tell her how it ended.

They went to bed at midnight, and Bree slept well. She figured the few glasses of wine helped to send her off.

The following day, after a full Irish breakfast, Amy said she wanted to catch the 1 o'clock train. She accepted a lift to the station, and Bree waved her off.

As she headed home, she knew she would have to deal with the envelope and its contents. But first she had to find out who was playing sick games. Her heart lurched as she wondered – did whoever it was know what happened all those years ago?

Her mother lived just out past the hotel. Usually, on a Sunday, Mary read the papers, watched TV and relaxed. She played golf most weekdays, and Saturdays were for catching up with the girls. The girls were the friends she had made in the Irish Countrywomen's Association and from her bridge-playing days. Mary met them every Saturday for lunch and often didn't make it home until late afternoon.

Mary was a creature of habit and Bree reckoned that her mother had made twelve-clock Mass in the cathedral and was probably sitting down to read the Sunday paper around now.

On impulse, instead of heading home, she took the road to her mother's place. Mary O'Hagan had moved to the large bungalow after her husband Patrick got his transfer and promotion. More gardaí were needed due to the proximity of the border and, although Patrick loved his home and farm in Sligo, he believed the move was the best thing for his family. But he was never happy in Dundalk. He pined for his farm and the familiar places that had formed much of his life. He was in his late forties when they moved and, although he enjoyed the work, he missed contact with the land. True, he had a large garden and grew vegetables, but he missed the livestock and that strong connection with nature.

For Mary, the move was happier. She learned to drive, and they could afford labour-saving devices for the home. She had more neighbours, and soon they turned into friends. She liked the town and often took Bree as a child on trips to the library, leaving her there while she met her friends for coffee and cake on a Saturday morning.

Bree treasured those long mornings in the library, and the librarian soon recognised that she loved books and helped her choose new titles. Although her first love was Enid Blyton, soon she was reading *Anne of Green Gables*, *Pollyanna*, *Little Women*, and countless other children's classics. Those were her only happy memories from that time, as she was a lost and lonely child, unable to make friends. But in books she was able to lose herself at least for a time.

Bree was very grateful to her mother. Keeping Amy would have been impossible without her, and she did it all without complaint. When her father passed away, her mother was able to continue to support them with the help of his pension. They were very different people, and yet they got on well, both united in their determination to give Amy the best life possible.

Mary must have heard Bree drive up because she was standing at the door, beaming.

'Well, look who it is! I was just thinking about you. I have the picture album out so we can reminisce.'

Bree thought about how well her mother was looking. Her hair was a soft white colour and contrasted with her face and arms, darkened brown by exposure to the sun during the summer and still lingering. Her eyes were blue and clear, surrounded by laughter lines. She looked robust and indomitable.

Bree followed her into the kitchen. The kitchen table where she ate and did her homework as a child was still the same. It was now covered with photograph albums and a sea of loose photos.

Bree picked up one of her parents and herself at the beach. They were smiling for the camera. Their eyes crinkled up because the sun was catching their eyes. Bree was sitting on her daddy's shoulders.

'Where was that taken, Mammy?' she asked.

Her mother took the picture from her. 'I'd say you're about five there, and we're probably at Streedagh Beach,' she said.

'Who's taking the photo?'

'That would be your Uncle Daniel. He died a few years after that picture was taken. Only forty-two, far too young! Cancer is a terrible curse.' Mary smiled sadly as she put the picture down. 'I've got so many of you. Being an only child, we doted on you.' She looked thoughtful. 'I was pregnant when he took that picture, about three months. I lost it soon after that day.'

Bree squeezed her mother's hand. 'That's awful, Mammy. You had a lot of miscarriages, didn't you?' She knew that her mother had three stillbirths before she was born and two miscarriages after.

Mary sighed. 'I did, indeed. Do you know that back then miscarriages were called abortions?' Shaking her head, she smiled and added, 'But, although it was hard, we felt lucky to have had you. Come on, sit down and let's have a cup of tea. Would you like a scone?'

'No, Mammy, I cooked a massive breakfast for myself and Amy, and I'm still full.'

'*Aww*, the pet, tell her to call to see me next time she's down, or there'll be trouble.'

'I will surely. She wants you to come up and visit her in her new flat in Blackrock when you fancy a skite up to Dublin again.'

Mary made tea and for a while they looked at pictures and reminisced about the past.

'It's nice to see you taking an interest in looking at photographs, Bree,' said Mary. 'I know you don't like too many reminders of the farm. I sometimes think we should have encouraged you to talk about that time more. You know, part of the reason Daddy accepted the transfer here was because of what happened. Maybe we should have stayed and got more help for you, but back in the '60s counselling was something the Americans did. It wasn't until you were a little older that we finally got you the help you needed.'

'I'm glad we moved but, Mammy, I did want to ask you about something that happened around the time I was still at my old school. Rory died and you and Dad were so upset. I'm a bit hazy about what happened to him. Wasn't it some kind of car accident?'

'Oh God, Bree, it was so sad! Such a lovely lad. It was a terrible tragedy. I remember you had just turned fifteen and were home on a visit from –' Mary paused.

'Yeah, I know, I was home from the hospital for the weekend. Go on with what happened. I wasn't able to take it in at the time.' Bree spoke rapidly, not wanting to dwell on her time in the hospital.

'We were delighted to have you home again with us and then I got a call from Julie. She said that Rory had gone missing, and then his body was found in a burnt-out car. The poor lad had started hanging out with a rough crowd, and Julie found it hard to manage him, especially after she remarried. I don't think he cared for his stepfather. Philip, her new husband, identified the body as the poor love couldn't face it. *Aww*, Bree, it was so tragic! All the bodies were badly burnt, but luckily Philip could identify Rory from the watch he was wearing. It had been his own watch and, I'm sorry to say, Rory had taken it without permission. It's so sad to think that the lovely young fellow that stayed with us turned out to be such a trial to his mother. She was heartbroken but, in a way, perhaps she was relieved too.' Mary put her hand over her mouth. 'No, what am I saying? To lose a child is always a tragedy. But he had her heart scalded by his brushes with the law and his anger. Julie was always a bit too soft, she didn't know how to handle the lad after Daniel died. A boy needs a good role model, and Daniel had been a great father.' Mary sighed. 'I stayed with her for a few weeks after the funeral. I can't say I took to her new husband but, then, I suppose I kept comparing him to Daniel, which wasn't fair. But I do think he tried to do his best by Julie.'

'Are you sure Rory's dead, Mammy?'

Her mother looked at her, puzzled. 'Of course he's dead. I was at the funeral, for God's sake. I wanted you to come, but you refused. I suppose he was a reminder of that summer. You were so unhappy, and I was at a loss. I didn't know what to do. Your dad and I stopped talking to you about Rory and his death because you got upset whenever I mentioned his name.'

'Mammy, do you ever hear from Aunt Julie now? I mean, when was the last time you spoke to her?'

'I lost touch with her over the years. I still send Christmas cards, but I stopped ringing her and, well, apart from Daniel, we have nothing in common. I think she moved away to London. Philip has family there, and I suppose she wanted to get away from the sad associations of Northampton after Rory died. Bree, why are you bringing this up? You've never wanted to speak about Rory before now.'

'No special reason. He just popped into my mind, that's all. Anyway, I'd better run. I have a few things to get finished for work in the morning. How about you come around for dinner next weekend? I'll call and fix something up.'

She got to her feet and gave her mother a quick hug.

'Oh, by the way, do you have any pictures of Rory?'

Her mother looked at her, puzzled by her sudden interest in her cousin. She rooted through her albums and took out two pictures.

'This is the one that went on his memorial card. Actually, I have the card here for you too, if you like – and here's one from when he stayed with us."

Bree took the photos and memorial card without looking at them and stuffed them in her bag. Waving goodbye, she walked out to her car.

Later that evening, Bree took out the photographs and card. The first was taken the summer he arrived in Sligo. Two children, all ready to have a lovely summer break. The irony was heart-breaking. She peered at their faces. They were sitting on the garden wall, her skinny legs dangling down, no doubt covered in scrapes and bruises, for she was an active child. Her hair was tied in a high ponytail, and the boy beside her had his arm around her shoulder. He was taller but just as skinny, smiling his bright crooked smile. Even in the picture, his eyes looked very blue, and the white streak of hair was like a halo around his head. They both looked happy but a bit self-conscious because of the camera. It hurt to look at the picture, seeing the innocence and happiness on her face was like seeing the before-image of a tragic accident. She stared at Rory's face. It looked open and happy, with no secrets, no darkness.

The second picture was of Rory on his eighteenth birthday. He was standing in front of a table with a large birthday cake. He was looking straight at the camera. He still had the same crooked grin, but he looked like a man, a handsome young man with nothing to hide and everything to live for. She couldn't bear to look at him.

Next, she examined the memorial card. It was in a little white envelope, and she remembered him telling her how he came by his stash of envelopes, and now he was inside one. The memorial card was the usual Catholic one, with a sentiment about death not being the end and an entreaty to pray for the deceased. She shuddered. Aunt Julie must have used the photograph from the birthday celebration, just the headshot.

She took out the little envelope that came in the post and compared it with Rory's memorial-card envelope. They were identical. Both had an embossed watermark on the right-hand corner: a little bunch of forget-me-nots.

CHAPTER 5

BRENNA

Brenna was still fizzing with the elation of being on holiday from school. This was Monday morning. Last Monday, she'd have been keeping her eyes firmly shut, dreading her mother's step on the stair and her shout to get ready for school. All the morning sounds, the radio playing its early-morning opening jingle, the beeps for the news, the sounds of Mammy setting the table, and the smell of toast in the air now filled her with happiness and not dread.

She didn't dislike school, but she wasn't good at many of her subjects, especially maths and Irish, and she knew her homework was untidy and poorly done. On Sunday nights, that didn't seem to matter, but on Monday mornings her stomach churned with nerves. She feared getting her sums wrong. Mr Casey, the master, scared her. Even a year after moving to his classroom, she still felt her stomach churn with fear. She was lucky because he didn't go in for hitting much – but sometimes she had to stand in the corner for not having her homework completed properly. He liked her essays, though, and often read them to the class. So, he wasn't all bad. And today he was far away, and she didn't have to see him for two glorious months.

She jumped out of bed and threw on her clothes, safe in the knowledge that Mammy would not nag her for not having washed properly. During the summer holidays, she was more easy-going about everything.

In the kitchen, Rory was sitting and chatting with her parents. Daddy, who had already milked the cows, was in for his breakfast of boiled eggs and toast. He always ate two brown eggs. Rory and Daddy were talking about politics. Brenna was amazed – none of her friends at school cared about the government or what was happening in the world. Mr Casey made them learn the ministers' names for all the different government departments. But no sooner had she learned them than she forgot them. But Rory seemed to know what to say, although Daddy was doing most of the talking. They looked up when she came in and sat down.

'Good morning, sleepyhead,' said Mammy as she shook cornflakes in a bowl for her.

'Now then, Rory, what would you like to do today?' asked Daddy.

'Well, I'd be happy to help on the farm. Mum said I was to make myself useful and not be lazing around making work for you and Auntie Mary.'

'Well said, young fella, but I think we'll give you a day or two to settle down before we put you to work. Brenna, why don't you and Rory go off on a ramble around the place? I'm sure Rory has lots of questions about farm life, seeing as he's a city slicker. Then after tea this evening I'll drive you to the sea for a swim. Do you have togs with you, Rory?'

Rory shook his head.

Daddy laughed. 'No problem – you can swim in your underwear – there'll be no one around to see.'

Rory looked horrified and Mammy, seeing his face, made a '*tisch*' sound.

'Stop teasing the lad, Patrick,' she said.

'I never thought to bring a cozzie, Auntie Mary,' Rory said.

Mammy patted his shoulder. 'Don't be worrying, Rory. The Foleys will be sure to have spare ones. The youngest lad, Cal, will have a few ones that don't fit him anymore.'

After breakfast, Brenna and Rory wandered into the garden. Usually, if she were on her own, Brenna would have played her imaginary games. Her favourite was standing on a low-hanging branch over the stream bordering their garden and pretending to be a pirate ship's captain. But she thought Rory would think it a childish game. Instead, she suggested they climb a tree. He watched as she scrambled up to the top of her favourite one, which gave her lovely views of the whole farm. Reluctantly he joined her at the top. He didn't seem too impressed by the tree or the view.

'Do you like stories?' he asked.

'Of course. I've read most of the Famous Five stories and the Secret Seven.'

Rory looked at her pityingly. 'Those are for kids. I mean proper scary stories. Would you like me to tell you one?'

Brenna nodded.

They slid down the tree and sat, resting their backs against the treetrunk.

She listened to Rory spellbound. He had a wonderful way with storytelling, and soon she was lost in a trance of excitement and enjoyable terror.

Abruptly, he broke off. 'That's all for now. I'll tell you the ending tonight.'

No amount of pleading on her behalf would change his mind.

She wondered what to do to entertain him next. She thought about taking him over to meet Coleen but, before she could suggest it, he said, 'Let's go to the shop. Do you have any money?'

'Well, I do have some in my money box, but I'm saving that for Daddy's birthday.'

'Come on, loan me some. My mother will send me a postal order during the week, but I'm broke until then.'

In her room, Brenna reluctantly opened her piggy bank, and he watched as she counted out her money. She had one pound and fifty-five pence in change. Before she could stop him, he swept it all up.

'Come on, we'll get loads of peps with this, and we can buy a few comics too.'

Puzzled, Brenna asked him what 'peps' were. He explained they were what he and his mates called sweets.

The weather was fine as they walked the mile to the shop. Rory talked about all his friends in England and the places they went. The pictures featured a lot, and Brenna felt a bit sad as she had never been to the pictures and didn't know any of the films he mentioned. She was beginning to think him very swanky.

At the shop, Rory asked her what sweets she liked, and he bought them and picked up copies of the *Beano* and the *Dandy*. He also bought two ice lollies. They licked them contentedly as they walked along.

'Do I have any change, Rory?' she asked, suddenly regretting she had spent so much money. He handed her back four shillings and some coppers.

'Is that all that's left?'

'Look, stop worrying. I'll pay you back when my mother sends me the postal order.'

So Brenna let it go.

As they crossed over the fields, she pointed to the glimpse of the sea ahead. 'Daddy will take us further along the coast this evening where it's safe to swim. He usually takes me after teatime. But, for now, we could walk up to the old henhouse in the next field. It's got a flat roof, and we could sit on it and have some of the sweets you bought.'

Rory agreed and, when they reached the henhouse, they clambered onto the flat roof. The tin roofing felt warm on their bottoms as they sat eating sweets while Rory talked of his school and the daily beatings he and his friends got from the masters. It didn't seem to bother him, though. She wondered whether he missed his mother and his friends. She couldn't imagine being away from her mammy for such a long time, and she felt very sorry for him.

In the distance, she heard her mother calling *cooee* and saw her waving a red tea towel.

'It must be dinnertime. That's Mammy calling us.'

'You have dinner in the middle of the day?' Rory asked, puzzled.

'Yes, of course, don't you?'

'I have dinner after Mum comes in from work at six.'

Once again, Brenna felt how exotic and different Rory's life was from hers.

'Best not tell Mammy we ate sweets before dinner, or she'll be raging,' she whispered to him as they washed their hands in the scullery.

After dinner, Brenna took Rory over to meet Coleen. She could see that Coleen was a little in awe of Rory. She was a slight girl. Once Brenna heard her mother and Mrs Foley talking, and Mrs Foley said that Coleen was delicate and had just about survived her infancy. Coleen had bright, brown eyes and a rash of freckles across her nose.

Her hair was shiny and curly. It bounced when she talked, which she did rather a lot. Brenna could see that she was trying hard to impress Rory by telling silly stories and showing him all her toys. In fairness, she did have a lot. They went out the back, and they played on her swing and seesaw. But Brenna could see that Rory was getting bored. She suggested they head back home. In truth, she was desperate to get back to her book. She had never read so little during the day before.

'Your friend is an awful dose, isn't she?' Rory said as they walked down the road. 'How do ya stick her?'

Brenna flushed. It was true that Coleen could be a bit of a show-off, but she was her only close friend in the area, and she felt she ought to stick up for her.

'She's all right. She can be good fun – it's just that she tries too hard. Give her a chance.'

'OK, if you say so. Race you home!'

He took off like the clappers, and she raced after him. They were almost neck and neck by the end, but he held the lead by a head.

'You cheated,' she said, laughing. 'You started running first.'

Winded, they sat on the garden wall and played 'I Spy' until it was time for evening tea.

After, Rory impressed the grown-ups by asking if he could sit with them to listen to the news and the current affairs programme on the radio. Bored, Brenna went upstairs to read.

There seemed to be a lot of laughing going on downstairs for people watching boring news stuff.

Mammy arrived with her cocoa.

'Where's Rory?' she asked as her mother set the warm drink on her bedside locker.

'Oh, himself and your daddy are listening to some sports programme on the radio. Bad enough having to listen to live coverage but they have to do a roundup of everything that happens in sport as well. My head is addled with the noise of the commentator, so I'll take a book to bed soon too. Night-night and God bless, love.' Her mother flicked some Holy Water at her from the bottle on her dressing table. And shut the bedroom door.

Brenna read for a while until she felt sleepy. She put her book away and went to the bathroom. Her feet were cold on the tiled floor, but she never could be bothered to wear her slippers. Yawning, she got back into bed and turned her lamp off. She lay in the darkness planning all the fun things she would do in the morning. Then, her heart thumping, she heard a noise in the darkness. It sounded like heavy breathing. Oh God, it seemed to be coming from underneath her bed. Then something crept out from underneath, a monster with glowing eyes. She opened her mouth to scream, and a hand roughly clamped over it.

Struggling in terror, she heard Rory whisper, 'It's only me, silly! What a baby!' He took the torch away from his face so he didn't look like a monster any more.

Brenna thumped him as hard as she could on his arm. '*I hate you!*' she hissed.

Rory giggled. 'I thought that you wanted to hear the rest of my story.'

Torn between rage and curiosity, curiosity won, and she asked him to finish the story he had started earlier. She lay propped up by her pillows as she listened, and the images from the story combined with the darkness, mitigated only by the torchlight, increased her terror. When he finished, she lay in the darkness, convinced she would never sleep. She asked him to stay, but he laughed, yawned, and went off to his room.

Brenna tossed and turned, her nervous imagination preventing her from closing her eyes, but eventually she drifted off.

CHAPTER 6

BREE

Colm was in great humour on Monday morning. He regaled her with an account of a date he had on Saturday night. They had got on like a house on fire, and he was hoping this might be the 'one'. Bree was unconvinced. Colm was always falling in love, convinced that he had finally met his life partner. The women were perfectly nice but all completely unsuitable for him. For a start, they tended to be actresses, musicians, and once a comedian. They had no interest in settling down to quiet domesticity, which was what Colm craved. He just kept choosing the wrong woman to do it with. But she hadn't the heart to dampen down his hopes and just let him chatter on. She owed a lot to Colm Dolan. When she dropped out of college, he gave her a job, even though she was pregnant and had no real experience in office work. Her year as a of law student wasn't much use when what he really needed was a secretary. But he was kind, patient, and understanding on those days that Amy was sick and Bree couldn't make it in to work. In return, she rewarded him with loyalty and her willingness to work hard.

She was busy all morning, doing research for one of their long-standing clients and handling the paperwork for a house sale. The morning flew by, and at lunchtime she ate her sandwich in the little back room which served as a primitive kitchenette. Then she took a brisk walk around the town to clear her head for the afternoon.

She had just returned to work when the office phone rang, and Colm, with a look of desperation in his eyes, said, 'Bree, it's bound to be Pat O'Brien about the conveyancing. He has my head addled. If you can talk him down, get me out of having to deal with him, you can take the afternoon off.'

Grinning, Bree nodded, picked up the receiver and poured soothing words into the client's ears. Then after finishing off a few items she had been working on, she took Colm up on his offer and left work early.

It was lovely to have the afternoon to self-indulge. She treated herself to coffee and cake in the Imperial Hotel and spent a pleasant hour reading her book and relaxing. She was reluctant to go home. The hotel and her book provided a peaceful oasis. Now, being alone in her house offered neither peace nor relaxation. But, eventually, she realised it was time to shift herself and head home. On her way back, she picked up a takeaway pizza which she ate while watching the TV. It was an indulgent afternoon and evening, which she finished off with a warm bath and then went to bed, where she fell into a blissfully dreamless sleep.

The strident ring of the telephone dragged her back to consciousness. She glanced at her bedside clock. It was two in the morning. Who the hell was ringing her? Oh, God, something must be wrong. No one called at that time of night unless something bad had happened. She raced downstairs and grabbed the phone.

'Is this Ms O'Hagan, Amy O'Hagan's mother?'

Her heart thudding, she said, 'Yes, it is. Is something wrong? Is Amy all right?' She could hear the panic in her voice.

'I'm Susan, Amy's flatmate.'

Bree flashed an image of the tall redhead who shared with Amy. 'Yes, Susan, is something the matter with Amy?'

'Please don't be worried – Amy is fine. She just had a bit of an accident.'

Bree became aware that Susan was speaking in the slow, careful tones of someone drunk.

'Really, she's fine. The hospital just wants to keep her in.'

'*Oh God, she's in hospital!*' By now, Bree was conscious that she was shrieking.

The girl started to sob and dropped the phone.

Another voice spoke, 'Mrs O'Hagan, this is Leah. We haven't met, but I'm Amy's other flatmate. Please don't panic. Amy was out for the night with some girls on her course, and she managed to fall down some steps. She banged her head, and someone from the group called an ambulance. She's at St James's Hospital. Really, I don't think it's anything serious.'

Her hands shaking, Bree thanked her, replaced the receiver, and dressed rapidly.

The drive to Dublin felt interminable. Was Leah telling her everything? Was Amy really OK? Finding a parking spot took a while, but eventually she found a space.

At the reception, she got directions to the room where Amy was being monitored. She saw her daughter, a large plaster on her forehead, lying on a bed. Her eyes were closed, and for a heart-stopping moment, looking at her white, still face, she feared the worst. Then Amy opened her eyes.

'Mam,' she said, smiling weakly, 'why are you here? I told them not to bother you. I'm fine, as you can see.'

'But Amy, what happened? They said you fell down some stairs.'

'Relax, it wasn't a big deal. I was out celebrating with my friends, and I swear I wasn't drunk, but suddenly I started feeling strange and badly needed air. I decided to get out of the pub, and somehow I lost my balance and fell down the stairs. The next thing I remember was being put on a stretcher.'

'Where's the doctor? I need to speak to someone about you.'

Eventually, Bree found a nurse and was told that Amy was fine, apart from a slightly sprained ankle and a cut on her forehead. But they were keeping her in just in case.

Then a doctor, with huge dark circles around her eyes, drew her aside. 'Mrs O'Hagan, we were a bit concerned because when she first came in Amy appeared very confused. We suspected that she may have taken something. Have you any concerns that she may be taking drugs?'

Bree stared at her in disbelief. 'No way! Amy enjoys a drink certainly, but I can't believe she's taking drugs.'

'Often, parents are the last to know. Anyway, she seems much better now. But we'll monitor her for the next few hours and then she can go home later on today.'

When she arrived back at Amy's bedside, her daughter looked pale and wan. She took the chair beside her bed.

'Amy, I spoke to the doctor, and she suggested that you took some drugs. Is that true? Were you high?' She watched Amy closely – years of living with her daughter made her recognise the signs when she was lying. She had studied all her subtle tells over the difficult teenage years.

Amy struggled to sit up. 'I knew it!' she said triumphantly. 'I knew I wasn't drunk. OK, I had a few pints, but I wasn't in a bad way. I wanted to be sharp for Rigney's lecture in the morning. So someone put something in my drink!'

Bree stared at her. Amy's reaction looked genuine. Could someone have spiked her drink? Suddenly, she felt exhausted.

'Look, love, I'm going to get a coffee from the vending machine. I'll be back in a few minutes, and you can tell me everything that happened then.'

While she waited for the coffee, she got herself a bar of chocolate and broke off a large chunk and ate it. The sugar hit worked, and she felt energy course through her tired body again.

On her way back to the room, she finished off the chocolate and sipped the coffee. It worked its magic, and she felt capable of dealing with everything. She decided to go home, now that she could see that Amy was OK. Colm would need her in the morning. She'd ask Bill, Joe's brother, to collect Amy whenever she was discharged. He lived in Drumcondra, so it wasn't a big ask. Bill was an obliging soul and would be happy to help his niece. She'd sit with Amy until she fell asleep and then head off. She wasn't looking forward to the drive home, but if she left soon at least she'd have time for a shower and breakfast before work.

As she walked back to Amy's room, she heard laughter. Amy was sitting up, grinning at the man sitting on the chair next to the bed. She waved when she saw Bree.

'Oh, there you are! Come and meet my tutor.'

The man stood up, turned towards her, and her heart collided painfully against her chest. She stopped short.

He was much older than she remembered, but his hair still had that brilliant white streak in front, and his blue eyes still pierced like lasers. The cup of hot coffee slipped through her fingers and splattered all over the floor.

47

Amy called to a passing nurse as Bree stared with a sick fascination at a dead man. She was dimly aware of someone mopping up the mess and felt foolishly incapable of moving out of the way. Amy had to hiss at her to move.

Her mouth was dry, but she finally managed to croak. 'Rory!'

Amy looked puzzled. 'Do you two know each other?'

Bree couldn't speak. She continued to stare as though hypnotised at the man facing her.

Rory beamed at her. 'I wondered when we checked Amy's next of kin and saw your name, but I thought it was a coincidence. When I knew you, you went by Brenna. Amy, this is an amazing coincidence. Your mother and I go way back. I knew her when she was a little girl back in Sligo.'

Bree stared, mesmerised, unable to pull words out of her mouth.

'Really? Mam never mentioned you,' said Amy.

Rory smiled. 'Well, it was a long time ago. Your mother and I are first cousins, and one summer her parents took me in for a whole glorious six weeks so that my mother could continue to work. It was a magical time, wasn't it, Brenna?'

Bree felt a sickness in the pit of her stomach. This couldn't be happening. Her legs had turned to jelly, and she wasn't sure they would support her much longer. She couldn't take her eyes off him.

He chattered away delightedly, acting as though this was a happy meeting. This was impossible. And he was Amy's tutor, but he was dead. The feeling of nausea in her stomach intensified. This was a waking nightmare. Nothing made sense.

She desperately wanted to flee the room but didn't want to leave Rory alone with her daughter.

Amy was looking at her with concern. 'Are you OK? You look as white as my sheets.'

Pulling herself together, she forced herself to smile. 'I'm fine, Amy. I'm very tired – it's been such a shock and I probably need to eat.' She avoided Rory's eyes as he beamed at her.

'Why don't you join me for something to eat, and we can catch up on old times?' he said. 'We have lots to reminisce about. What do you say?'

Bree, suffocated by the walls that seemed to be closing in on her, was finding it hard to breathe. The thought of spending any time with Rory horrified her. She forced herself to speak.

'Thanks, that would be great, but I've got to get back to Dundalk for work, and I'll be late if I don't leave now.'

'Oh Mam, Colm won't mind if you don't make it today. Tell him what happened to me. He's a softy and will tell you to take the day off.'

Trying to steady her breathing, Bree leaned over her daughter. 'I'll ring Uncle Bill and I'm sure he'll be able to pick you up when they discharge you.'

Rory smiled his crooked smile and moved close to her. It took all her resolve not to flinch as he took her hand in his.

'Well, Brenna, now that we've met up again, we mustn't lose touch.'

She pulled her hand away and kissed her daughter's cheek. 'Ring me tomorrow, OK?'

Amy nodded. She looked tired and very young, and Bree was overwhelmed by a fierce wave of protectiveness. She turned to Rory.

'I'm sure we'll meet again, Rory. But Amy needs her rest.' It was a dismissal. She stood guard at the end of Amy's bed, determined not to move until he left.

'You can count on it,' he replied.

To her ears, it sounded like a threat.

Rory smiled at her and blew Amy a kiss.

Then he was gone. Bree, her legs wobbly, sat down on the edge of the bed,

Amy grinned at her mother. 'You never told me about your hunky cousin, Mam. He looks really distinguished with that white quiff.' She laughed. 'Hey, were you kissing cousins?'

'Don't be ridiculous, Amy. He was my aunt's son, and I barely remember him.'

Bree got to her feet abruptly.

'Sorry, Mam, I was only joking. The very idea of kissing cousins is creepy. I get the feeling you didn't get on when you were kids all those years ago in Sligo?'

Bree sat back down. 'You know what, I barely remember him. It was so long ago. But, Amy, if you like I can stay. I'm sure you're right and Colm will be OK with me taking the day off.'

'No way, Mam. I'm getting tired of talking, and I'm hoping the cute registrar will come back to check on me.' She grinned up at her mother.

Bree bent to give Amy a quick kiss and then left.

Outside the room, she debated how she could leave the hospital without meeting Rory. She was worried that he was lying in wait for her. Rory was back from the dead and haunting her again. She decided not to leave by the main entrance. Instead, she walked through A&E. She asked a passing nurse where the public phone was, and she rang Bill. She knew it was early but hoped he'd be up. She told him what had happened and he agreed to pick Amy up later that morning or whenever she was discharged.

Then she left the hospital and walked rapidly to the car park. Stressed and distracted, at first she couldn't locate her Ford Fiesta. She had left it at the far end of the car park.

When she reached it, she stopped short. A small white envelope was wedged into her windscreen wiper. Rory must have been watching her when she first arrived. Her skin tingled, and she looked around her. Was he still watching her? Her hands trembling, she picked up the envelope. She got into the driver's seat, holding it. The thought of opening it made her flesh creep and every memory she had worked for thirty years to suppress overwhelmed her.

She tore the envelope open. The note was neatly folded. She unwrapped it and stared at the typed message: **Let The Fun Begin!**

CHAPTER 7

BRENNA

The summer drifted along gloriously. On warm days, if Daddy didn't need help on the farm, Rory and Brenna, with Coleen tagging along, roamed the countryside, revelling in their freedom. They climbed trees, went on picnics and played chasing games. Most evenings, Daddy brought them to the seaside and watched to ensure they didn't go out of their depth. Rory was a good swimmer and, with his coaching, Brenna became more assured in the water. Coleen was scared of the sea. She preferred to make sandcastles and paddle close to the shore. Rory teased her for being a coward, and Brenna felt guilty for not standing up for her friend, but it was such fun to be with Rory. He told her wonderful stories, and he had great ideas for adventures.

One Monday morning when they felt uncharacteristically bored, they tried to think up ideas to enjoy the day. They lay on their backs on top of the henhouse, staring up at the sky and making up silly names for the passing clouds. Rory convinced them that a plump cloud resembled Father Higgins, the parish priest. It certainly had his little round tummy. They giggled as they imagined various neighbours floating by and bumping into each other.

They were silent for a while then until Brenna exclaimed, 'That one looks just like Mr Cullen! See, it has a stick like the one he carries poking out.'

'I love his apples. I wish we had apple and pear trees in our garden,' Coleen said wistfully.

'He gave me a few apples when I called to give him our newspaper on Saturday. They were tasty, but I did find a worm in one,' said Brenna.

'*Yuck*, I hate it when that happens! One time my brother Peter ate a worm in his by mistake. He was puking for ages afterwards." Coleen giggled. 'It put him off apples for a while, I'm telling you!'

'Brenna, you never told me Patsy Cullen has an orchard,' Rory said as he sat up.

'Oh, I thought you knew. All the apples in our fruit bowl are from it.'

'Hey, I have a great idea! Why don't we rob his orchard?'

Brenna and Coleen were shocked.

'Come on, Brenna, it will be a laugh. We won't take much, but it will be an adventure. Come on, it'll be great fun.'

Brenna looked at him uncertainly. She hated the thought of robbing Mr Cullen, but she loved the idea of an adventure.

Rory could see she was wavering. 'Come on, we needn't take much – it's just for the challenge of getting in and out without being seen. What do you say?'

Brenna, caught up in the romance of the adventure, soon agreed. Coleen bit her lip and shook her head but, when she saw that her two friends were set on going, she reluctantly agreed.

They arranged to start their adventure early the next day. Brenna knew that Mr Cullen liked to head up his fields to feed his old donkey every day around ten o'clock, so in the morning before ten the three friends ran down the road and ducked down behind a hedge across from his house to keep watch. They didn't have long to wait. They heard the creak of his gate as Mr Cullen set off at a fair clip.

Giggling with excitement, they ran across the road and hopped the garden wall. Brenna led the way through the yard at the back. They had to pass Lucifer, the dog Mr Cullen kept chained up beside his kennel.

When the dog saw them, he started barking dementedly.

Coleen shrank back in terror.

'It's OK, Col, he's tied up and can't get near us. Come on!' Brenna said.

Rory strode past them and swung his leg over the low wall separating the orchard from the yard. The girls followed, keeping an eye out to make sure the coast was clear and then, with hearts pounding, they slipped into Patsy Cullen's orchard.

The orchard was a sea of apple and pear trees, listing with the weight of fruit. Brenna had never been there before. Mr Cullen often sent apples home with her daddy when he visited on Sundays to listen to the football on the radio. She felt torn between excitement and shame at being in the orchard.

Rory grabbed at the apples while Brenna held the sack they had brought.

Coleen, clearly terrified, kept saying they should go. Rory snapped at her to clear off and be a baby somewhere else. When Brenna didn't defend her, Coleen ran off crying that it was a mortal sin to be stealing. Rory just laughed.

'Look, we have enough, Rory – let's go!' Brenna begged. Coleen's anxiety was contagious. But Rory was tempted by a clump of apples just beyond his reach, and he shook the branch hard.

Just then Brenna looked over her shoulder and saw Mr Cullen striding into the orchard. She froze, but Rory had already started to run.

'Ya needn't mind running off and leaving your wee cousin to face the music. Come here, ya coward!'

Rory stopped and then sauntered back, acting as though he hadn't a care in the world.

Brenna could see this was making Mr Cullen furious.

'Come here, ya wee English gurrier! You should be ashamed of yourself for getting your cousin to be stealing. That class of thing might be OK in England but not here, my boy!'

Rory, instead of apologising, just smirked, and before either of them knew what happened, Mr Cullen's arm shot out and he gave him a shove. Rory wasn't expecting it, lost his balance and fell on his behind, banging his cheek against an apple tree.

Mr Cullen seemed as shocked as Rory. He offered him a hand up, but Rory ignored the outstreached hand and got to his feet, glaring at the old man.

Mr Cullen glared back at him. 'Away with you two now and, mind, Brenna, I'll not say anything to your parents this time, but I don't want to see you sneaking in here again.'

Rory turned on his heel and legged it to the road.

Brenna hung her head. 'I'm so sorry, Mr Cullen.'

'Brenna, you know that you only have to ask if you want my apples. It's not like you to be stealing.'

She stood staring at the ground, her eyes pooled with tears of shame, and then she slunk off after her cousin, who had stood waiting for her on the other side of the hedge.

Rory, raging, spent the whole walk home telling her exactly what he thought of Patsy Cullen. Brenna had never heard such words before, and she was shocked. Rory's cheek had a red mark from when he banged it and, at dinner, he told Mammy when she enquired that he tripped over his shoelaces and fell.

After dinner, as they lay on the henhouse roof, Rory continued to rant about Mr Cullen and how he meant to get him back. Brenna said nothing. She felt ashamed. Mr Cullen had always been nice to her and lived alone, so he probably was nervous about people sneaking into his garden.

'I bet Coleen told him we were in the orchard,' Rory said, sitting up. 'Funny how he appeared just after she left.'

'*Aww*, Rory, don't be daft. Coleen wouldn't do that. She's a bit of a scaredy-cat, but she's not a tattletale.'

But it made no difference – he was set in his view that Coleen had warned Mr Cullen that they were robbing his apples.

The next day, when Coleen called around, he accused her of telling on them.

Poor Coleen sobbed. 'I never did, Rory! I wouldn't tell on you, I swear!'

Brenna wanted to stand up for her, but Rory had set a seed of doubt in her mind. Coleen looked at her beseechingly, but Brenna didn't say anything, and she didn't go after Coleen when she ran away, crying.

That night when she was saying her prayers, she felt a wash of shame as she thought about her friend's heartbroken face.

Coleen didn't call around for a while after that. Meanwhile, Daddy had roped Bree and Rory into jobs. It was perfect weather for saving the hay and then they were sent off picking the early potatoes. Daddy was impressed with Rory's work and paid him a few shillings for his efforts. He gave Brenna some money for her money box too. It was quite full. When she shook it, there was barely enough space for the coins to rattle, and she was pleased as she weighed it in her hands.

Aunt Julie had come good, and Rory was able to pay Brenna back the money he had borrowed. Brenna was saving hard for Daddy's birthday, and she planned to get him a nice tie. Mammy was taking her into the shops on Saturday to buy it. She was looking forward to the day out in town with her mother.

On Friday, after he came home from work, Daddy took them for their evening swim. He asked why Coleen hadn't been joining them lately and suggested that Brenna call over and get her. Brenna looked at Rory, and he shook his head. Maybe it would be better if Coleen kept away for a bit longer until things blew over and Rory forgave her. She promised herself that she would make it up to Coleen and invite her along in a few days and, in the meantime, she'd work on persuading Rory that he was being too hard on her friend. After all, everyone deserved a second chance, that's what Daddy always said. She told Daddy a lie and said that Coleen didn't want to come when she asked her earlier in the day. She hated telling lies. It was another sin to confess to Father Higgins when Mammy took them to Confession.

Daddy took them to Cloonagh and, although it didn't have a sandy beach, she loved the rich scent of it. The rack the sea had stacked up in piles against the stones gave off a pungent, heady smell. Rory wrinkled his nose in distaste, but he was like a fish once they got in the water. Daddy watched nervously from the shore, his trousers rolled up. He signalled every so often if he thought they had gone too far out. After their swim, they headed home and had their supper. The sea air always made them feel ravenous, and Mammy usually had a nice treat for them when they arrived back. Tonight it was buttered scones still warm from the oven.

Later that evening, Rory pushed Brenna as she sat on the swing in the front garden. He pushed her very high, and at times she was scared but held on tight and didn't let on that she was bothered. She didn't want him to think her a scaredy-cat too, like Coleen. It was still very bright even though it was nearly nine at night. She asked him if he had another story to tell her, but he shook his head moodily and after a while he went off and sat on the garden wall.

She wandered over to him. 'Do you want to play Snap?'

'God, Brenna, that's a kiddies' game!'

'Well, what do you want to play now?'

Rory looked thoughtful. 'Well, there is a game I know – it's called Game Master – but I don't think you'd like it. It's a bit grown-up and, after all, you're only nine.'

Brenna felt insulted. 'Come on, Rory, let's play it. I really want to.'

'OK, well, if you're sure. It works this way. I will give you a little envelope and inside will be a piece of paper. On the paper will be a task. You get a reward if you complete the task, but if you fail, you get a forfeit.'

'I don't know, Rory . . .' She wasn't sure she liked the idea of a test. She hated them at school.

'I told you that you're too little for it. I play it with my mates all the time. Look, we'll start with something easy. Are you game?'

Brenna nodded uncertainly.

'OK. Now, it's important you never see me deliver the envelopes. They will pop up somewhere unexpected, and you have twenty-four hours to complete the task. So, we'll start in a few days' time. '

Brenna felt both excited and nervous about this mysterious game. She hoped she wouldn't fail to complete the tasks. The idea of a forfeit made her nervous.

Two days later, when putting on her wellington boots, Brenna saw a small envelope wedged at the bottom of one. It wasn't at all like the big envelopes that came in the post. Her name was neatly printed on it. She noticed a little bunch of flowers embossed on the left-hand corner of the envelope. Hardly daring to breathe, she pulled it open. Inside was a note folded over several times. Her heart thumping with pleasurable excitement, she read it.

It said: *Your Task is to catch three butterflies, all of different colours. Your reward is a treasure hunt. Don't Fail!*

Well, that seemed easy. But it still took her the greater part of the afternoon to catch the butterflies. The real challenge was to find three different ones. She tried her best not to hurt them as she trapped them with her hands and popped them into a paper bag. Triumphantly, she handed them over. Rory was impressed. He shook the bag to release them, but sadly one had died. Grinning broadly, he gave her a clue for the treasure hunt he had planned for her reward, and she spent the rest of the day running back and forth around the farm in search of clues. Mammy thought Rory was such a nice boy to organise a lovely treat for his cousin. She didn't know that Brenna had earned it.

After an hour of following clues, Brenna found the treasure hidden in the very wellington where the letter had been placed. It was a large bar of milk chocolate, her favourite. She offered Rory some, but he refused, saying she had earned it. She told him she loved the Game and asked when they could play again.

'Maybe,' she suggested, 'I could leave you a letter?'

But Rory said no. He was the Game Master. Brenna found she was in fact relieved because she didn't think she could come up with clever tasks or treats.

'Where did you get such tiny envelopes?' she asked.

'After my dad died, my mum got stacks of memorial cards, and she had loads left over after she gave them to family and friends. I took the envelopes. I thought they looked weird, but I liked them, and then

I invented the Game, and I thought it would be cool to use them for the tasks.'

Brenna wasn't sure how she felt about the idea of using envelopes that were for a dead person's picture.

A week later, when she was settling down to read, she found another envelope under her pillow. Eagerly she opened it and read: *Your task is to throw an egg at Patsy Cullen's window. Your reward is a special treat. Do not Fail!*

She went into Rory's room, where he was reading a comic on his bed.

'Hey, Rory, I'm not doing that test. It's mean.'

'OK, Brenna,' he said with a shrug.

Relieved at his attitude, she went back to her room.

On Saturday, Mammy shouted that she was heading into town and to hurry up if Brenna wanted to choose Daddy's gift.

Brenna ran to her money box. It was empty. She heard Mammy coming upstairs.

'Hurry up, love, I have lots to do, and I don't want to miss the bus into town. What's keeping you?'

Seeing her daughter's stricken face, she asked, 'What's the matter, Brenna?'

'My money's gone,' Brenna sobbed.

'What do you mean it's gone? Did you spend it all on sweets?'

'No, I didn't – I don't know where it went.'

Rory came in and, seeing how upset everyone was, asked what was up.

'Brenna has no money in her money box for her daddy's present. She says she didn't spend it, but it can't have disappeared. Really, Brenna, this is so thoughtless of you. Well, I don't have time to wait.'

'Auntie Mary, look, my mother sent me money, and I really don't need it. How about I lend some to Brenna so she can buy her dad a present?'

Mammy beamed at him. Then she glared at Brenna. 'Well, thank your cousin,' she said.

Brenna mumbled thanks as Rory counted out three pounds into her hand.

After Mammy left the room, he smirked at her. 'I told you there are consequences to failure.'

Brenna shoved past him, her face red with anger.

She picked out a tie in town, but all her pleasure in the day was gone and even the birthday cake tasted like ashes in her mouth. Mammy had been very cold towards her in town and full of praise for Rory. She longed to tell her mammy about the test Rory had set her, but she wasn't a tattletale.

Rory was nice to her all evening, but she ignored him.

At bedtime, when she was drinking her cocoa, he carried his cup into her room.

'I don't want to talk to you,' she said, turning her head away.

He sat down on the end of the bed and smiled at her. 'Come on now, Brenna, you knew the tasks came with rewards or forfeits. You agreed to it. You can't just back out when it gets hard. Games have rules.'

'Well, I don't want to play anymore.'

'It doesn't work that way. We made a deal.'

Brenna put her cup down, lay down, and turned on her side away from him.

Rory gave up trying to make her talk and left.

A few days later, she found another envelope within the pages of a book she was reading. At first, she contemplated tearing it up unread, but curiosity got the better of her. She opened it up.

Your task is to answer every question you are asked with another question from breakfast until midday. If you complete this task, you will be well rewarded. Don't Fail!

Brenna was intrigued by this task. It challenged her, and she loved the idea of showing Rory that she was up for anything. But she wouldn't accept any reward, and it would be the last game.

She started that morning at breakfast. Mammy asked her if she would like orange juice, and she replied. 'Do you think I'd like orange juice?' Mammy looked puzzled at first, and then got irritated as the morning wore on and all her questions were met with other questions. Luckily Daddy was busy on the farm and it was only Mammy she had to deal with, and somehow she got through the morning and fulfilled her task.

'See!' she said triumphantly to Rory.

He grinned at her. 'Well done! Are you ready for your reward?'

Brenna shook her head. 'I don't want a reward. I only did the task because it was fun.'

'OK, but don't you want to see it?'

Brenna stubbornly shook her head.

'Why not come and see it anyway? Then you can decide if you don't want it.'

Brenna was full of resolve to resist sweet treats or other inducements and to stick to her guns. She followed him into the hayshed.

He pointed to a small cardboard box on the ground. To her amazement, it was rocking from side to side.

'What is it?' she asked, her mouth dry with excitement.

'Open it and see,' he answered.

Swiftly she opened the box and inside, mewing, was a small black-and-white kitten.

'Oh Rory, she's beautiful! Is she really mine?' She buried her nose in the kitten's soft fur.

'Does that mean you'll accept it as your reward?'

'God, is Mammy OK with it?'

'Of course – she helped me pick it out from Mr O'Connor's litter. I had a hard job persuading her to let you have a kitten.'

Delirious with happiness, Brenna hugged the kitten gently. 'How did you persuade Mammy? She's not keen on pets.'

'I just told her how much you'd love a little kitten, and she agreed to let you have one. And I told her that you'd keep it outside.'

'But how did you know I'd pass the test?'

Rory smiled. 'I have faith in you. I knew that you'd come through."

Brenna was so happy she thought Rory was the best cousin ever, and she forgave him for the trick he played on her.

Two days later, she awoke to find another envelope poking out from the pocket of her cardigan. This time she felt afraid.

CHAPTER 8

BREE

After leaving the hospital, Bree's heart raced uncontrollably. How was Rory alive, and how did he end up tutoring Amy? She felt sick at the thought of his games, and she didn't want his malign influence corrupting her daughter's life.

She arrived at the office just as the Angelus bell was ringing from the nearby church. She told Colm what had delayed her and, as he was very fond of Amy, Bree hastened to reassure him that she was on the mend.

At lunchtime, Amy rang to say she was out of the hospital and back at her flat.

'Rory arrived before I saw the doctor and offered to drive me back to the flat. So I called Uncle Bill and told him I had a lift home. Rory's such a sound guy. We had a nice chat, and he told me all about your adventures in Sligo.'

Bree, her skin prickling, sat up straight. 'He took you home, Amy? Why did he do that? What did he want?'

The sharpness in her voice caused Amy to snap. 'Mam, what's wrong? He's your cousin, for God's sake! What's the problem?'

Taking a breath, Bree forced her voice to sound casual. 'Nothing's wrong. It's just that I didn't particularly like him and didn't enjoy that summer.'

'Well, he was full of your praise and told me about all the adventures you guys got up to. He said that you were a total tomboy and led raids on the neighbour's orchard.'

Bree clenched her teeth. 'That's not how I remember it. But, Amy, I wouldn't spend too much time with him. He wasn't nice as a boy, and I'm not sure if he's changed all that much. You don't have many dealings with him, do you?'

'Mam, don't you ever listen? I told you last April that I was struggling with my work. I had no chance of continuing with psychology until one of my lecturers put me in touch with Rory. He coaches me for free. He works in the college but doesn't teach me, so he can give me advice. And he has a practice as a clinical psychologist too. It's what I want to do eventually, so he's a brilliant help. He told me that when he was a kid he felt lost, as though no one cared, but eventually he found his way and wanted to make the road easier for others, so he does the coaching to help out. He said that he agreed to help me because I was the child of a single mother. He never realised that we were related. Mam, whatever little squabbles you two had as kids, he's been good to me. If I keep working with him, I'm on the path to getting a 2:1, and Rory thinks I could even make a first.'

'Amy, I thought you said a man called Straffen was helping you.'

'Yeah, Rory Straffen. Why?'

'It's just that I knew him as Rory Brown.'

'You'll have to ask him about that.'

Bree sat in silence. She found it hard to believe that Rory chanced on Amy by accident. This was just one of his sick games.

'Look, Amy, I'm sure that he's been a great help to you, but I want you to stop working with him. I'll pay for a different tutor to help you.'

'Mam, why are you being so weird? I don't want a different tutor, and I can't believe that just because of some ridiculous childhood grudge you expect me to stop working with Rory. Maybe you should let go of the past. Rory clearly has. He spoke fondly of you. I think he wants to get in touch.'

'Why does he want to?' Once again, Bree was conscious that her voice was sharp and loud.

'Don't know, Mam. I'm sure he'll forget all about it.' Amy now sounded bored. 'Look, I have a pile of work to catch up on. I'll give you a call later in the week. OK, bye."

Colm insisted on taking her out to lunch. They went to a pub and had a bowl of soup and brown bread. Bree couldn't taste anything. She struggled to keep up with his conversation. Luckily, he was so engrossed in telling her all about his new girlfriend that he never noticed how distracted she was.

The afternoon was very busy, and she was able to avoid thinking about Rory. But on the journey home, with nothing to distract her mind, her head churned. She knew that if she headed for home, it would be more of the same useless speculation about Rory's resurrection from the dead. She needed answers, and only one person could help her with them. So, instead of taking the road home, she changed direction and pulled up outside her mother's house.

Her mother's little Mini sat outside. Bree went to the back door, and Mary waved to her from the kitchen window. She went in and Mary, who was washing dishes, smiled delightedly at her.

'Well, this is a nice surprise, two visits in two days. Come on in, and I'll make you a cuppa.'

Bree refused tea and waited patiently for her mother to sit down.

'Rory's alive!' she said.

Mary raised her eyebrows. 'What did you say?'

'He's alive. Rory's alive.'

'But that's impossible. Shure, I gave you his memorial card. You must be mistaken.'

'I had to go to St James's yesterday. I met him there. Amy had an accident. She took a tumble and ended up in the hospital.' As Mary's eyes widened, she hastened to reassure her. 'It's fine, Mammy. She slipped on some stairs, banged her head, and hurt her ankle. They just kept her in overnight for observation. She was let out this morning. You won't believe this, but Rory is her tutor. He calls himself Straffen now, not Brown.'

Mary looked shocked. 'I can't believe it. Look, are you sure it's him? Maybe with all the talk of him yesterday, it's confused you.'

'Mammy, it's no mistake. He knew me and spoke about spending that summer with us.'

Mary shook her head. 'I don't understand this at all. Why change his name?'

Bree shrugged.

'Maybe he took his stepfather's name,' said Mary. 'I didn't think his surname was Straffen, but I may be wrong. Oh my God, Rory is alive! I can't credit it. I wonder why Julie never let me know.'

The two women sat in silence.

'Whose funeral did I go to then?' said Mary.

They stared at each other, puzzled.

'Should I ring Julie? I mean, does she still think her son is dead?' Mary wrinkled her forehead. 'Bree, what do I do? Surely she must know.'

'Maybe give her a call and bring the conversation around to me seeing someone in the street who's a dead ringer for Rory. What do they call it when you see someone's double? It's a German word . . . I can't remember.'

'I'll give her a call tonight and get back to you. But, Bree, this is great news. I was always fond of Rory and, despite what happened that summer, I have lovely memories of the two of you playing. Do you remember the little kitten he got you? He was that fond of you, Brenna.'

Bree's jaw clenched. 'I remember, Mammy. Let me know as soon as you've spoken to Aunt Julie.'

When she got home, she made herself tea and toast, but it lay untasted on her plate. Her appetite was gone, and television was no distraction. She did some unnecessary laundry, emptied out her kitchen cupboards, and scrubbed out the yard bin, but the evening passed unbearably slowly. She both longed and dreaded hearing back from her mother. She debated ringing a friend and going to the cinema but didn't want to miss her mother's call. She checked the phone several times to make sure it was working. She wondered whether she should get herself one of those mobile phones. Amy got one when she started college. It would be a good idea if she had one too and she could contact Amy more easily.

What was Rory up to? She knew what he was capable of and didn't want him anywhere near her daughter.

The shrill ring of her telephone jerked her back to the present.

It was her mother.

'Well, what did Julie say? Does she know?'

'Slow down, Bree. I managed to get talking to Philip, Rory's stepfather. Julie has been unwell for the last few years. He said she had a breakdown a few years ago and has been in and out of the hospital. She didn't want anyone to know. I think the poor love is ashamed.'

'But what about Rory? Do they know that Rory is alive and living in Ireland?' Bree demanded.

There was a pause.

'*Mammy?*'

'Bree, they do know. They discovered it about a year after they had supposedly buried him. They got a phone call from the police in London. They arrested a boy for something or other, and it turns out it was Rory. The whole story came out. It seems that Rory hadn't been in the car, but he had sold one of the boys his stepdad's watch to buy drugs, and when the boy died and was identified because of the watch, Rory decided to clear off. The police wanted to bring charges against him for letting the other boy be misidentified. But as the dead lad had been in the care system his whole life, there were no parents to claim the poor fellow, and so the police decided to let things drop.'

'My God, this is like something out of a film. What happened then?'

'Well, initially Rory had no interest in going back home. Seemingly he had caused a lot of trouble to Julie over the years, and he resented it when she married Philip. But Philip persuaded him to come home and be reunited with his mother. According to him, at first everything went well. Julie was over the moon to have her son back. It seemed as though they could all make a fresh start. Rory got a place at university studying psychology and he was excelling. He had a bright future ahead of him. Mind you, he always was a bright boy – your dad was very impressed with his grasp of politics and history when he was a young chap. They used to have lovely chats about everything under the sun.'

Impatiently Bree interrupted. 'Never mind that. What happened next?'

'Philip isn't sure, but he noticed an increase in tension between Rory and his mother. Julie got upset whenever he came to stay and began to be very agitated and depressed. She had another breakdown and was hospitalised. Rory stopped visiting. Philip didn't know he had moved to Ireland. To be honest, he didn't want any more involvement with Rory and felt it would be better that I didn't mention it to Julie, not that I'd have much contact with her nowadays. But it's so sad to think of the poor boy being disowned like that.'

After they finished speaking on the phone, Bree's head ached. She swallowed some painkillers and sat staring into space. What was Rory up to? Why had he come back into her life? Above all, she worried about him having anything to do with Amy.

CHAPTER 9

BRENNA

Your Task is to take a pound from your mother's purse. You will be well rewarded. Don't Fail!

Brenna raced to find Rory. 'I'm not doing it. I'm not stealing from my mother.'

'Fine, Brenna, you don't have to do anything you don't want to.'

He smiled at her, and she shivered.

Twenty-four hours passed, and the next morning she looked anxiously at Rory. But he seemed in great form, joking with Mammy and offering to help Barry, the farm worker, fix the broken fences in the top field to stop the cattle from breaking out onto the road.

Breakfast over, she went out to feed Daisy, her little kitten. Usually, when she opened the shed door she came rushing out to be fed and petted, but there was no sign of her.

Bree ran into the kitchen.

'*What have you done with Daisy?*' she shouted at Rory.

Mammy glared at her. 'Keep a civil tongue in your head! Why are you accusing poor Rory of taking your kitten? He's the one who persuaded me against my better judgment to give you the silly creature.'

Furiously Brenna ran out of the kitchen and went upstairs to fetch the little envelope to show Mammy, but it was gone. Rory followed her into the room.

'Now stop being silly. You weren't planning to tell Auntie Mary about the little task I set you, were you? I'm not sure she'd believe you, Brenna. You have been behaving oddly lately, and well, I've been a perfect gent. Now do you want kitty back or not?'

'Yes,' she muttered furiously.

'Well, you know what you have to do, don't you?'

'I can't,' Brenna whispered.

'Fine, I just hope the poor little thing doesn't meet with a nasty accident. There are so many dangers out there for a little kitty.' He winked as he turned to go.

She grabbed his arm. 'OK, I'll do it, but you need to get Mammy out of the kitchen.'

'No problem. I'll tell her I think I heard mewing coming from the garden and get her to come and look. Good gel – be quick about it!'

Brenna waited until she heard Mammy and Rory going out the back door. She darted into the kitchen and saw the black handbag hanging on the chairback. She opened the clasp with trembling fingers and rooted inside until she found the little brown-leather purse. She was pulling the pound note out when Mammy and Rory walked in.

She froze.

Mammy looked shocked and, behind her, Rory, smirking, was holding the kitten.

'Brenna, what do you think you're doing?' said Mammy, her lips thin.

Appalled, Brenna could only open and close her mouth foolishly.

Mammy strode over to her and took the purse from her hand. 'Give me the money,' she snapped.

Feeling sick, Brenna handed it to her. Her mother was looking at her with a mixture of shock and disappointment.

'Brenna, I've been noticing small amounts of money disappearing from my purse recently and, God forgive me, I was suspicious of your poor cousin. I never dreamed my own daughter would steal from me.'

Brenna rushed into speech. 'I never took money before, Mammy – honestly, I didn't.'

'I don't think the word *honest* falls easily from your lips. I thought I brought you up to be trustworthy. Why in the name of God would you be stealing from me?'

'It was Rory. He told me to.'

Mammy's face was creased with her disgust. She pushed Brenna away from her. 'Now you have sunk even lower, blaming your cousin. The cousin who persuaded me against my better judgment to get you a kitten and who now has found it for you! And you reward him by blaming him. What has happened to you? You used to be such a straightforward, honest girl.'

Brenna started crying, big gulping sobs.

Rory interrupted them, still holding the mewing little kitten. 'Auntie Mary, I'm sure Brenna just panicked and thought she should put up a reward for the return of the kitten. Isn't that right, Brenna?'

Brenna could only sob. All words had deserted her.

'Well, you've got it back now. I hope that you're happy.' Mammy reached out to the kitten struggling in Rory's arms. She tore it from his grasp and practically threw it at Brenna who managed to catch it before it fell. The little creature, terrified by all the raised voices, struggled to get away and scrabbled at Brenna. 'Well, my girl, you'll not be short of sins to tell Father Higgins in Confession next Saturday. Now get out of my sight. And, Rory, take that animal off your cousin and put it outside.'

Brenna slunk outside, where Rory joined her.

'Why did you do that?'

'Do what, coz?'

He grinned at her, and she longed to turn on him, hitting and spitting, but she knew that Mammy was watching from the kitchen.

'Why did you let Mammy catch me, and why did you let me take the blame?'

'Brenna, I warned you what would happen if you broke the rules of the Game.'

'But I was doing what you told me. I was taking the money. Why did you let me be caught?'

Rory's blue eyes darkened and hardened. 'You have to learn your lessons, Brenna, accept the consequences of breaking the rules – but look at the bright side – at least the kitty is safe.' Then he grinned at her. 'For now!'

He reached into his pocket, pulled out a packet of sweets, and offered her one. She pushed his hand away.

'I'm not playing your Game anymore. *I hate you!*'

'I'd be careful, Brenna, if you won't play the Game. Who knows how I might amuse myself? Let me think, there's fun to have with kitty, and maybe silly little Coleen might offer me a bit of amusement. What do you think?'

Grinning and whistling, he wandered across the yard. She saw him heading across the fields towards Barry.

For the rest of the morning, sick in her tummy, Brenna had no heart for her usual pleasures. She couldn't read, climb trees, or wander over the fields. Everything was spoilt. She tried to talk to Mammy and offered to help in the house, but Mammy said that she didn't want to look at her. Miserable, she waited outside until dinnertime.

When she was called inside to eat, the tension at the table was awful. Mammy must have told Daddy what happened because he looked at her with such disappointment in his eyes that her insides ached. The lump in her throat made it almost impossible to swallow her food.

Rory, in the meantime, chatted away as though he hadn't a care in the world. She hated him with every fibre of her body. Eventually, the torment of the meal ended, and Mammy told her to help her wash and dry the dishes. They worked in silence. Then, when the kitchen was clean, she told Brenna to sit at the table as she wanted to discuss her behaviour.

Sick to her stomach, she slumped onto a chair, and Mammy sat beside her. 'Brenna, your father and I are so disappointed by your behaviour. I can't believe a daughter of ours would steal. I still can't credit it.'

As Brenna tried to interrupt, her mother shushed her. 'There's no point in trying to put the blame on your cousin. To his credit, he even tried to take the blame. He's a good boy. He stood up for you and, to think, after all the nice things that he's done for you, you reward him by trying to get him into trouble. In fact, when I told him I wanted to give back the kitten as your punishment, he begged me not to and, lucky for you, I relented. So, your punishment is no money for jobs for the remainder of the summer, and you have to go to bed an hour earlier every day for a week. I'm very disappointed in you. You know that stealing is always wrong. It's a sin, Brenna. Haven't you learned that in your catechism?'

Brenna nodded as she listened, her heart dissolving in pain as her mother spoke.

'Well, have you anything to say to me?'

'No, Mammy, just that I'm sorry.' With those words, she burst out into loud sobs.

Her mother gathered her in her arms and hugged her. 'I love you, Brenna,' she whispered in her ear and then, releasing her, added, 'We'll say no more about it. Off with you, and mind, be nice to your cousin.'

The afternoon dragged out, and she avoided Rory. Around four o'clock, she saw him and Coleen playing on the swings in the front garden. He beckoned her over, but she turned on her heel, ran down the back garden and climbed her favourite tree. She sat up there until she was called for her tea. She ate silently, and Daddy looked at her kindly and asked if she was reading a good book now. She couldn't answer and just shook her head. Daddy and Mammy looked at each other, and she could see they were worried.

Rory looked at them brightly. 'I know what will cheer her up. Why don't I tell her one of my stories later tonight? You always enjoy them, don't you, Brenna?'

She longed to scream at him to leave her alone, but she was afraid. Instead, she muttered. 'Thanks, but I'm too tired tonight. Mammy, can I go to bed after I finish helping you clean?'

Her mother looked concerned. 'Are you not feeling well, love? Do you need something to settle your tummy?'

Brenna accepted a tablespoon of milky medicine to keep her mother happy and was sent immediately to bed.

She wasn't left in peace for long. Rory sauntered in, his face was full of fake concern.

'*Get out!*' she snarled at him.

'That's a nice way to greet your favourite cousin.'

'*I hate you. You're wicked. I hope you die.*'

'Now, now, little coz, don't be so rude. There I was, trying to be nice to your little friend Coleen. She's very sad because she thinks you've been avoiding her. The poor wee thing thinks you don't like her anymore. Of course, I stood up for you, but I may have let slip some of the mean things you've said about her.'

Brenna sat bolt upright in the bed. 'What things? I've never said a bad word about her!'

Rory giggled. 'Well, maybe it was me who said the mean things, but I may have told Coleen you said them. *Oops*, silly me!'

Brenna stared at him in horror. 'Why are you being so horrible, Rory? Please leave Coleen alone – she hasn't done anything to harm you.'

'Well, Brenna, I did tell you that if I got bored I'd have to think of a new game, and Coleen, although a bit stupid, does have possibilities. I'm afraid that she's very cross with you, so I'd be careful if I were you.'

Patting her hand gently, Rory left the room.

She stared at the ceiling until she eventually drifted off, but sleep held no rest, only nightmares.

CHAPTER 10

BREE

All night, memories of that summer in Sligo churned around her head. The memories she had spent over thirty years squashing down could no longer be held back. They didn't seep back, they poured like torrents, overwhelming her. In desperation, she took two of her muscle relaxants, and they worked so well that she fell into a deep sleep, but her nightmares tortured her awake, bathed in sweat, at five in the morning. Desperate to get out of the house, she decided to go for a run.

Her route took her around her estate and out onto the main road. She raced as hard as she could, anything to force thoughts from her head. Eventually, her lungs bursting, she arrived back at her house, exhausted in mind and body. She took a long cold shower. The sting of the water helped with the tiredness, and she felt, if not rested, reinvigorated and able to face a day of work.

Colm was out of the office all day meeting clients. He had left a large chunk of paperwork for her to deal with and, between answering calls and filing, she hadn't time to think. Her friend Anita called, inviting her to the pictures. She was going to refuse but, in the end, decided it would be better than staring at the beige walls in her house.

They arranged to have a bite to eat after work and then decide what picture to see. Anita was a good friend. They had known each other since their school days and the friendship continued when they went to college. Anita worked as a barrister in Dublin but she sometimes had cases in her hometown, and when it suited her schedule they would meet up. Bree was grateful that Anita had kept in touch with her. When she dropped out of college and had Amy, she slowly lost touch with all her friends from Dublin. Their lives were so different and perhaps Bree resenting their freedom and prospects, had unconsciously shut them out. But Anita hung in there. Despite all the times Bree had backed out of arrangements, Anita never held it against her. She was Amy's godmother, never forgot her birthday and was there for all the key events: First Holy Communion and Confirmation and her Debs. Bree valued their friendship and realised that her life would be diminished without it.

They met in the Imperial Hotel and then headed over to the Roma, where they ate fish and chips, washed down with tea. Anita looked sharp. She had been dressed for court in a black skirt and crisp white shirt. Her copper hair was cut in a sharp bob. She looked intimidatingly smart, especially when she wore her glasses – she once confessed that she didn't really need them, but she found that when she wore them she was more effective. Her intelligence impressed the criminals, and her colleagues were deterred from patronising her. The fact that she had a razor-sharp line in put-downs helped too. No one would mess with Anita Lennon.

They ate quickly, both hungry.

'Bree, you've circles the size of saucers under your eyes. I hope Colm hasn't been working you too hard,' said Anita and then, nudging her friend and winking, added, 'Maybe something else is keeping you up at night?'

Despite the temptation to talk about the resurrection of Rory, Bree knew she wouldn't. The habit of secrecy was engrained for too long. For decades she had kept her past hidden, and she didn't trust anyone with the secret she carried.

Instead, she grinned. 'I'm just not sleeping well, Anita – I think I'll have to go easy on the coffee at bedtime. Now, what movie do you fancy?'

They examined the local paper's movie listings. There wasn't much choice, *Wayne's World* or *Single White Female*. Anita said she had heard that *Single White Female* was a good thriller, and Bree was game to give it a go.

The movie certainly proved a mixed blessing. The dark, obsessive story with its homicidal protagonist felt too close for comfort to Bree's life. Rory and Hedy from the movie had a lot in common. Why was Rory so fixated on messing with her head? Hadn't he done her enough harm?

Afterwards, they went for a drink in the Fane bar and discussed the film. Anita loved it and planned to recommend it to all her friends.

They met a few old schoolmates on a night out, drunk and full of nostalgic good cheer, and Bree ended up staying later than she had planned.

When she arrived home, she could see from the driveway that all the lights in her house were switched on. She turned the key in the door and wondered whether Amy had returned from college. Maybe she was still suffering the effects of her fall. But why light up the house like a bloody Christmas tree? She walked inside, calling out to Amy. There wasn't a sound in the house.

Puzzled, she began turning off the lights, starting in her little attic room and working her way downstairs. Where the hell was Amy, and why had she switched on all the lights? It was true that Amy could not turn a light off when she left a room, but this was ridiculous. A troubling thought assailed her. What if it wasn't Amy? But no one else had a key to her house. Maybe Amy had left a note in the kitchen explaining why she had come home.

The kitchen was just as she had left it, with no note or sign that Amy had been home. Amy was a messy eater, leaving a trail of dishes and spilt food wherever she went. But the kitchen was spotless.

The only odd thing, apart from the blazing lights, was that every framed photograph she had was turned face down. She stood stock still, the hair rising on her arms as her nerve endings tingled. Someone had come into her house. Should she call the gardaí? And say what? That someone had broken into her home and turned all the lights on. They'd laugh her out of it.

Was Rory up to his tricks? But he lived in Dublin and, although her address was on file in the college, he wasn't likely to have access to it, was he? Anyway, she doubted if he'd come down to her house in Dundalk and turn all the lights on. Besides, how did he know she wouldn't be here, and how could he get in? Her stomach clenched and she felt in need of a drink. She wished she had some alcohol in the house but, unless she was expecting visitors, she rarely kept it in the house. Then she remembered Colm had brought her a bottle of Rioja from Spain last summer. He went on his holidays there every year. She opened it and poured herself a glass. As she sipped the fruity wine, she felt a little tension ease from her body.

Then a disturbing thought intruded. What if there was someone still in the house? Should she ask someone to come and help her check? Colm would come, but it was after twelve now, and he was probably long in his bed.

81

She rooted in her cutlery drawer and found a sharp carving knife. Her heart pounding, she went into every room, opening wardrobes and checking under cupboards and behind doors.

There was nobody in the house but her. Her body sagged with relief but her heart still hammered uncomfortably in her chest. She returned to the small living room with her drink, but she couldn't relax. feeling hyper-alert.

At two in the morning she was exhausted but, unable to face sleeping in her bedroom, she took the duvet off Amy's bed and carried it downstairs. She dumped the rest of the Rioja, made herself a mug of drinking chocolate, and got comfortable on the couch. It took a while, but eventually she dozed off.

The phone woke her. How long had it been ringing? She checked her watch. It was after three. Oh, God, maybe it was Amy. Was she ill? She raced out to the hall, colliding with the door frame. She grabbed the phone, afraid it would ring off.

'Hello!' she shouted, sick with anxiety.

There was no answer.

'Hello,' she repeated.

Again silence, but there was someone there. She caught the faint sound of a breath and then the sound of the receiver being replaced. She stood stock still.

It was Rory. It had to be. She lay on the sofa, wide awake, exhausted.

CHAPTER 11

BRENNA

The next morning, Brenna slept through all the usual morning sounds, unaware of the energetic crowing of Foleys' cockerels or the desperate lowing of the cows as they waited to have their bursting udders relieved of milk.

Her mother's voice awakened her from the doorway. 'Brenna, it's nearly ten o'clock. The morning will be gone if you don't get up soon. Are you feeling better?'

Brenna nodded, pulled her blankets off, and struggled out of bed.

'Good girl. I'm going over to Foleys' for a chat, so eat your breakfast and clear up afterwards.'

Sluggishly, Brenna sat on the bed, her limbs heavy, and she had to force herself to get moving. She washed quickly in the chilly bathroom, then filled the sink with cold water and sank her face into it, hoping to liven herself up. She pulled on her shorts and T-shirt and went down to breakfast. Thankfully there was no one around, and she ate her cornflakes in the quiet kitchen. She found she was hungry and ate two bowls of the crunchy cereal and then pulled on her wellingtons. She hoped to avoid Rory today, so she planned to take her book and head out to the rush field, where she had a secret spot that Rory didn't know about.

She enjoyed a quiet hour until she heard her name called. It was Rory, and he was with Coleen. She kept as still as she could, hoping they wouldn't find her. She was glad that her T-Shirt was green so it wouldn't stand out amidst the brambles and rushes, and she hunkered down in the hedge where she had kept an old stool for comfort. Eventually, the calls stopped, and she went back to her reading. Perhaps she could come here every day and avoid her cousin until he went back to England. He was here for over a month, so she only had to put up with him for another two weeks before his mother reclaimed him. Mammy said Aunt Julie had taken two weeks off work at the end of August to spend with her son. Only two more weeks, fourteen days, and she racked her brains to do the maths. In three hundred and thirty-six hours, she would be rid of him. The thought of him back in England made her feel lighter. He had poisoned everything in her world. Even her lovely kitten was tainted by him, and she felt sad when she fed her and played with her. But she worried about Rory coming back next summer. Her heart felt sore at the thought of him returning year after year. But at least she'd be free of him for a while.

Sometime later, her book finished, her tummy rumbled, and she knew it must be nearly dinnertime. She struggled to her feet, her body stiff and cramped from sitting in one position for so long, and she wandered slowly back to the house. Her timing was good because her mother was just coming out to call her and Rory. Daddy was scrubbing his stained hands with the nailbrush, and he smiled at her. That lifted her spirits. He didn't seem angry or disappointed in her anymore. It was unusual to see him about on a working day. Maybe he got time off from his Garda duties because he had worked a few late nights.

She took her seat at the table, and Mammy was serving the food when Rory came in. Brenna avoided his eyes. Daddy and Mammy chatted about the farm, and Rory asked questions about farming. Daddy teased him that, for a city boy, he was starting to pass for a real culchie. Rory laughed and said he could be worse things, and Daddy looking pleased, asked him if he'd like to go to the local mart with him tomorrow. Brenna was stung. Daddy had never taken her to the mart. She felt her eyes smart with stinging tears. But she consoled herself that at least Rory would be away all the next day. She only had to avoid him for the remainder of the day. Unfortunately, Daddy asked them both to weed the five ridges of carrots he had planted in the top field. Seeing the face she made, he misunderstood and thought she was angry about the work, not the presence of Rory and told her off for being lazy. Rory smirked at her, and choking rage weighed her down.

She pulled on her wellingtons and walked up to the field where the carrots poked out a sea of green with splashes of orange peeping through. She took her bucket, started at the opposite end to Rory, and pulled the weeds, imagining it was Rory's hair. She ignored all his attempts at conversation. Then, frustrated, he started throwing weeds at her head. His aim was sure, and she felt clay and weeds spatter over her and slide down her neck, making her skin itchy. He stopped for a while, and she worked in peace, but he started up again until she screamed at him to quit what he was doing. Once again, he stopped, but when he passed her to empty his bucket, he pulled out the back of her T-shirt and spilt a load of clay down her back. Furious, she got to her feet and threw the contents of her bucket at him.

It was at that exact moment that Mammy arrived in the field. She had a flask in her hand and two bags of crisps.

'*Brenna, why are you behaving like such a hooligan?*' she cried out.

'Auntie Mary, it's my fault – I was teasing her about her accent. I didn't mean to hurt her feelings, but I've maybe gone too far. Sorry, Brenna.'

Unbelievably, he held out his hand. She slapped it away. She could see from her mother's face that nothing she could say would convince her of the truth.

'Right, Rory, you can head off now. Miss Brenna can finish this on her own. It'll keep her busy when you are away tomorrow at the mart with your uncle. No arguments, Rory – here, take both bags of crisps and be off.'

Then Mammy glared at her and headed off to catch up with Rory.

Brenna gritted her teeth, barely able to see the weeds through the blur of her tears. She worked mechanically until teatime.

When she came into the scullery to pull off her wellingtons and wash her hands, she overheard her parents talking about her.

'I'm telling you, Patrick, I think she took against the boy because she's jealous. Maybe she sees how good he is on the farm and worries that, because she's a girl, she's not good enough.'

'Do you think I should take her to the mart with Rory tomorrow?'

'Maybe, Patrick, it can't hurt, and maybe she'll get back to her old self.'

Brenna turned on the kitchen tap so it gushed loudly, and her mother said, 'Whist, she's here.'

Silently she slid into her usual seat and buttered her bread. She saw Mammy nod to her daddy.

He coughed and said, 'Brenna, I was thinking maybe you'd like to come to the mart with your cousin and me tomorrow. What do you say?'

Brenna mumbled, 'I have to finish the carrots tomorrow, Mammy said.'

Her mother looked up and smiled. 'Now, Brenna, you were being a bit of a hooligan to Rory, but I'm willing to let you off carrot duty tomorrow if you'd like to have the day out.'

Brenna dropped her eyes to her plate. 'I'd rather stay here.'

Mammy looked puzzled. 'Well, you'll not lounge around if you stay. You'll still have to weed those carrots.'

'That's fine, Mammy, I don't mind.'

Her parents looked at each other questioningly.

Then Rory arrived full of fake friendliness. Brenna ignored him, never lifting her eyes from her plate.

She went to her room shortly after tea, even though it was bright outside.

Looking out the window, she saw Rory heading across the road to Coleen's house. Her stomach knotted, and her new book didn't distract her.

The next morning Daddy and Rory drove off to Manorhamilton to the mart after the milking was done.

Downstairs, Mammy was reading a magazine and sipping tea. Brenna poured herself a glass of orange juice and drowned a Weetabix in milk. She ate rapidly and then rinsed her glass and bowl at the sink. She dried them and put them away. Mammy was engrossed in her magazine and, impulsively, as Brenna was walking past, she put her arms around her neck, hugged her, and then ran out to the back kitchen and put her boots on.

A stiff breeze was blowing out in the field, and she was glad she had brought her jumper. She felt strangely happy as she weeded. For the first time in ages, she sang whilst she worked. It was with satisfaction that she saw that she was halfway through the drill.

At eleven o'clock, Mammy arrived up to her with a flask of tea and three chocolate biscuits. Mammy sat down beside her while she had her break.

'You've done great work there, Brenna. Daddy will be pleased. You know, I think you're a faster worker than your cousin. Those city lads are all right, but they'll never make farmers. Mind you, Rory's daddy, lord rest him, wasn't great on our farm either. He was always skiving off.' As she spoke, Mammy looked sad.

'What happened to Uncle Danny?' Brenna asked.

'When he and your Aunt Julie got married, they moved to England, and Danny got work at one of the shoe factories in Northampton. Unfortunately, one day he was involved in a car accident. It wasn't a bad accident, but they discovered he had cancer while he was in the hospital. He didn't last long. Auntie Julie had to get a job to support herself and Rory. She was lucky to get a good job in the post office. We visited her when we could, but she had her mother to help her, so she managed. Last winter, her mother died, and she's finding it hard to manage everything. Life hasn't been easy for the pair of them. That's why we took Rory for the summer.'

Brenna, munching on her last biscuit, tried to imagine life without Daddy or either of her grannies, and it made her ache inside. It was hard on Rory to lose his daddy, but she still hated him. She knew from her teacher and the priest that it was wrong to hate people, but she couldn't help it. Maybe he might change if she prayed for him, but she didn't think so. She couldn't forgive him for how he had tricked her and made her look bad in front of her parents.

She sat close to Mammy, shielded from the wind. She felt comforted and safe.

Mammy smiled at her. 'I think you've done enough work. How about you help me make some scones?'

Brenna nodded happily.

Mammy gathered up the flask, and Brenna emptied her bucket into the ditch.

Back at the house, she spent a lovely afternoon baking scones and learning how to make brown bread. Mammy turned the wireless on and picked a music programme.

'Come on, Brenna, I'll teach you how to jive,' she said.

She was so happy as her mother whirled her around the kitchen that she thought her heart would burst through her body. It was the last happy time for a very long time.

CHAPTER 12

BREE

Bree endured the week. Her eyes ached and itched, and she saw her bed each evening as a source of mockery. Tiredness made her irritable and, more than once, she had seen Colm look at her with hurt eyes, and he grew silent. She thought about making something up to explain her irritability, but the effort proved too much. So, they continued working silently.

After the break-in at her house, she had called a locksmith, and he rang the office to say her new keys were ready for collection. She picked them up on her way home. It made her feel more secure. But what if she gave Amy a key and Rory found some way of copying it? But Amy had to have her own key, so she'd just have to risk it. There was no way she could afford an alarm system. Perhaps she could set up one of those pretend alarms and hope it would deter any would-be burglar.

On Saturday, she took the bus to Dublin and met Amy for lunch at Bewley's on Westmorland Street. Its dark interior and the cacophony of voices and rattling plates always soothed her. She waited for Amy to arrive. Timekeeping was not Amy's forte, but she was only ten minutes late on this occasion. She swept in, hair flying and the mascara from the night before staining her skin. Being young, she looked dishevelled but somehow chic. Did I ever look like that? Bree wondered. In college in the early seventies, her uniform was jeans and tops. She wore what was clean and saved her money for going out and cigarettes.

Amy slung her bomber jacket over the back of her chair and, smiling brightly, said, 'Let's order, Mam, I'm starving.'

When the waitress arrived in her smart white-and-black uniform, they gave their order. Bree chose a cottage pie and Amy fish and chips.

While they waited for their food, Bree asked, 'Are you fully recovered from your fall, love?'

'Mam, I'm grand, honestly. Don't fuss!'

Clutching her napkin tightly in her hands, Bree asked, 'By the way, Amy, I was wondering if you'd seen Rory since your night in the hospital?'

'Your dishy cousin? Actually, I bumped into him on campus. He asked for you and wanted to know when you were free to meet up and catch up on the old days.'

The napkin in Bree's hands now resembled confetti. She took a breath. 'Amy, I'd be happier if you could avoid spending time with Rory. He's not a good guy.'

Amy speared her with a glance. 'What do you mean? Why? Did he do something bad? He didn't hit on you when you were kids? I mean, cousins, that's revolting.'

Bree coloured. 'Of course he didn't but, Amy, he's not a good person, and I'm asking you to keep away from him.'

She realised as soon as she spoke that she had made a mistake. Sure enough, Amy started to interrogate her for details of Rory's 'badness'.

Bree refused to say any more and knew that Amy's curiosity was aroused. Rory would now be a mystery to be solved. It would have been better if she had let her believe that Rory had made a pass at her. Shit, she should have kept her big mouth shut.

'By the way, I lost my keys to the house and had the locks changed. Here's a set for you.'

'Doesn't Colm have a spare set? Why did you need to change the lock?'

'He was away for a few days and, anyway, I changed it. The lock wasn't great, to be honest, and I didn't like the idea of my house keys lying around. I thought it safer to replace them.'

Bree changed the subject. 'Did you report that your drink may have been spiked?'

'I thought about it, but I never left my drink unattended,' Amy said, wrinkling up her forehead. 'There were always my mates and Rory around so that it couldn't have been spiked and, to tell the truth, maybe I had more than a few pints, and I hadn't had much to eat, so I probably have only myself to blame.'

Bree paled. 'Rory was out with you that night?'

'Mam, don't make a production out of it. I met Rory on the way to the pub and asked him to come along. I wanted to buy him a drink to thank him for all the help he's been giving me.'

'I see. Well, I still don't think it's appropriate for him to hang out with you. He's older than you, for God's sake!'

'Mam, I'm really fed up with this thing you have against Rory. Besides, he was great that night. He called the ambulance, and my friends said he insisted on going to the hospital. *He* told them to call you. Can't you see how unreasonable you're being?'

Bree started to speak, but Amy raised her hand.

'Mam, let's change the subject. What did you do during the week?'

Realising that arguing with Amy was pointless, Bree said, 'I met up with Anita, and we went to see *Single White Female*. Have you seen it?'

Amy had, and they chatted about it until the meal arrived. Where food was concerned, Amy couldn't multi-task. She focused on eating and didn't lift her head from her plate until it was clean. Neither of them wanted coffee, so they just sat feeling sated.

Amy was fiddling with her bag, and Bree wondered whether she had plans for the afternoon. She got to her feet.

'Look, I'm going to wander around the shops. Do you want to come?'

Amy grinned. 'Yes, if it means you'll buy me something nice.'

They spent a pleasant couple of hours shopping. Amy modelled some outfits, and Bree bought them all.

'Mam, you don't have to buy me all this stuff. One of the plaid shirts would do. I don't need three and the jeans too.'

'It's no problem, Amy. They look great on you.'

Amy looked coyly at her mother.

'What?' asked Bree, puzzled by her daughter's expression.

'It's just that I'm going to a party tonight, and I've met this cute guy. He's on the entertainment committee, and we were chatting about this gig that the committee were organising and, well, he mentioned that he was going to a party tonight and said I should come along.'

Bree was happy for her. Amy had her heart broken in her last year of school by a lad who two-timed on her, and her self-esteem was fractured badly. It was lovely to see her dipping her toe into the world of romance again.

She just wished that Rory wasn't hovering in the background like a sinister moth. She left her daughter after they had finished shopping and headed for her bus.

CHAPTER 13

BRENNA

Daddy and Rory tucked into a hearty tea when they came home and then, to Brenna's relief, there was a sports programme they both wanted to listen to on the radio. She was able to scuttle off to bed, secure in the knowledge that Rory wouldn't be annoying her that night. She was in bed so early that she even managed to finish her book. Mammy brought her cocoa, and she could barely finish it before she fell into a deep, dreamless sleep.

The usual morning sounds of a cockerel and the urgent lowing cows awoke her, and she sat up in bed feeling refreshed. It was a Sunday, and that meant Mass. She knew she needed to have a good wash because Mammy would check that her knees and neck weren't neglected. The water was cold, but she got out her facecloth and soap and washed her face and neck. Then she gave her knees a good scrub. Some of the mud from weeding the previous day had stained her them badly and they needed a bit of extra attention. Soon they were fit for inspection. Mammy would have nothing to complain about. She looked in her wardrobe for her Sunday clothes. She donned her navy dress, white socks, and a little white cardigan. Then she went downstairs. It felt strange to be wearing a dress instead of her usual shorts.

Everyone was sitting at the table. She ignored Rory and said good morning to her parents. Because it was so close to Mass time, she knew better than to eat breakfast. When she was preparing for her First Holy Communion, the teacher explained that it was against Church law to eat or drink anything except water an hour before Communion.

Daddy and Rory had been up early and had already eaten. It was annoying that Rory was spending so much time with Daddy. She knew that he was sucking up to him. The trouble was that he was better at lots of things on the farm, faster and stronger. Her tummy grumbled, so she poured herself a glass of water.

Mammy arrived downstairs in a rush and, glancing at the clock, hurried everyone out. Daddy wore a suit even though it was a hot day. He went out to start the car, and Rory followed him. Mammy got a white mantilla, pinned it to Brenna's hair, and put a black one on her own head. At first, Brenna liked wearing mantillas, thinking she looked like a bride or a princess, but the feeling had worn off and now she just felt silly wearing them.

The Mass was long. She tried to say her prayers, but she felt God was disappointed in her, and she couldn't concentrate. She tried to keep up with the responses recited in Latin. A trail of sweat ran from the base of her neck down to her spine. The dress felt prickly and uncomfortable. Her mother nudged her that it was time to go up for Communion. She knew that she shouldn't be receiving Communion, not after telling lies and stealing and hating Rory and saying she wished he was dead. Mammy must have forgotten about the stealing. It was too late to say anything. Mammy had left her seat. Wasn't it a terrible sin to receive Communion when you had committed a mortal sin? Stealing was definitely a mortal sin but maybe when it was only apples it wasn't as serious? And she didn't actually take the money from Mammy's purse. She felt panicked and unsure about what to do. Daddy tapped her shoulder, and she was swept up by the people leaving their seats and had to go with them. She thought of the picture in her religion book of a white heart-shaped soul. The teacher explained that when people committed venial sin it was like small black blots started to appear on their souls, but the mortal sins would turn the soul very black if they didn't go to Confession. Should she go back to her seat before she made things worse by receiving the Holy Communion when her soul was full of black dots? She noticed Coleen coming down the aisle as she went up it. Coleen gave her a very dirty look. Brenna shivered even though she was hot. The line for Communion was long, but Father Higgins was a quick priest and made short work of it. Feeling sick, she received the Blessed Sacrament and went back to her seat. She asked God to forgive her all her sins and promised she would go to Confession as soon as she could. She asked for help to be a good girl, and she asked that Rory would return to England soon and leave her in peace.

Then the priest said the final prayers, and they stood for the last hymn. The singing was terrible. The choir of children boosted by whatever adults could join in was off-key. She caught Rory sniggering out of the corner of her eye. She felt angry and suddenly protective of the choir. They were doing their best.

Then it was all over, and everyone headed for the church door, eager to catch up with friends.

Outside the church, she saw some of her school pals, and it was nice to talk to them and ask about what they were doing with themselves over the holidays. Mammy and Daddy met up with their friends too. Mammy was in the ICA and was busy exchanging recipes and planning their next day out. She saw Daddy and a gaggle of men laughing and guessed that they were talking about sports or politics. Only Rory looked a bit lost. He asked Daddy for the key to the car and went to sit in it. Mammy, feeling sorry for him, signalled to Daddy to come on. They stopped on the way home to pick up the *Sunday Independent* and a block of ice cream.

Sunday dinner was usually a bit later because of Mass. Mammy cooked a big chicken, and she did carrots, parsnips, and lovely roast spuds. Brenna loved it, and today they would have ice cream too. During the week, it was always tapioca or rice for dessert. But the presence of Rory darkened her mood. She didn't like the way he was smirking at her as though he knew something she didn't.

After dinner, everyone except Daddy cleared up and washed the dishes from dinner. Daddy went off to read the paper, and Mammy carried him in another cup of tea and a nice chocolate biscuit. Brenna heard him say, 'You spoil me, Mary.'

When the kitchen was clean, Mammy ran the two youngsters outside. Standing in the yard with Rory was the most difficult part of her day. She had managed to avoid him for the last two days. She left him and went off to her tree, wishing she had brought her book. Maybe if she were reading, he'd leave her in peace. She climbed as high as she dared and hoped that he'd find something to occupy himself. He wasn't a reader like her. In fact, he was always pulling her away from her stories to do stuff. Well, no more. She was going to keep well away from him. Maybe she could spend more time with Coleen. Rory despised Coleen so she'd be able to get away from him. But, then again, since they had fallen out, he seemed to be spending time with her friend. She had seen them down the fields once, and Rory called over to see her a couple of days ago. Come to think of it, Coleen had glared at her at Mass, and usually after Mass she was all over her like a rash, barely giving her an opportunity to chat with her friends from school. But this Sunday she had been different. She had glared at her and avoided going near her. Brenna felt sick at the thought of the lies that Rory was telling her. But would Coleen believe anything that Rory said? After all, he had been mean to her? But Rory was a demon. He could make anyone do anything, believe anything. He had her mammy and daddy eating out of his hand, thinking him such a great lad. Her skin prickled.

She decided to go and talk to Coleen. She walked the short distance to the Foleys' house.

Mrs Foley, her plump face flushed with exertion, was bustling around her kitchen. She looked up as Brenna tapped on the back door.

'Well, hello, Brenna! I suppose you're looking for Coleen. Sorry, but you're out of luck. She went off with young Rory this afternoon. I think they're planning to look at the new litter of pups that her uncle's dog Molly had. You only just missed them. I'm sure if you hurry, you'll catch up with them.'

'Thanks, Mrs Foley, I'll do that. Bye.'

Brenna had no intention of following Rory and Coleen. She felt hurt that Coleen had gone off with Rory. Why hadn't she told her about Molly's pups? She'd have loved to go and see them. But she didn't want to see them with Rory there. She wandered back to her house, feeling sad and lost. Usually, when she felt bored or lonely, she got stuck in a book, but today the world of make-believe held no appeal. She was on the brink of asking Mammy if she wanted any help when she remembered her kitten. She went into the barn and spent a happier half hour feeding Daisy and playing with her. Watching her chase a ball of wool made her laugh, and then the little creature bounced up to her, purring and demanding to be petted. She sat on an old tyre and allowed her to clamber all over her and rub her little nose in her face. She wished Mammy would let her bring her inside, but Mammy said she had enough to do without cleaning up cat poo.

She heard voices outside the barn. It was Rory and Coleen. They seemed as thick as thieves lately. What should she do? She felt miserable and wished Rory would go away and she could talk to Coleen on her own. She waited just inside the shed, hoping he'd go off somewhere. She listened, and she could hear Coleen's high bright laughter.

'Yes, Rory, let's do that! I'll not spoil things this time, really I won't!'

She couldn't hear Rory's reply but, whatever it was, they went off together. She put the kitten down and made sure she had fresh water and a clean litter box and decided to follow them. She'd be careful not to be seen. It felt like an adventure, and her spirits lifted.

Luckily, she was wearing her sandals, not wellies, so it would be easier to stalk them. She caught sight of Coleen's pink T-shirt in the distance and started to enjoy herself. She kept them in sight as she hid behind trees and under bushes. Once, Rory looked back and she was afraid he had seen her, but he forged on ahead. She was puzzled when they left the large overgrown garden to clamber over the ditch that in winter was a damp, muddy pool, but now was dry and covered in brambles. They came out on the road just across from Patsy Cullen's house. She watched as they clambered over his garden wall. Surely they couldn't be planning an apple raid after what happened last time? Again, keeping her distance, she saw they were heading for the house. What on earth? There was no sign of Mr Cullen, his battered van was missing, and the only sound was the incessant barking of Lucifer, his dog, attached by his long chain to a tree. The dog was supposed to scare away robbers, but everyone knew about him being tied up. He did look nasty, though, and Brenna had never wanted to go too close to him. Why were they heading towards the back of Mr Cullen's little house when he clearly wasn't there? Maybe they had planned to ask him for apples as he had suggested, rather than stealing them. But she doubted it. She watched as Rory wandered around the house, looking in windows. What was he doing? She looked at Coleen, who had started to back away. She had a scared face, and Brenna knew this was the face she usually made just before she cried. Could Rory be thinking of breaking into the cottage? She decided to stop hiding and find out what was going on.

Coleen looked startled when she came into view, but Rory didn't look at all surprised. So, he had seen her following them. It was just another of his games.

'Well, if it isn't Secret Agent Brenna, snooping around. What do you want?'

She ignored him and turned to Coleen. 'Come on, Col, let's get out of here before Mr Cullen comes back.'

Coleen glared at her, torn by her desire to stop trespassing and her suspicion of Brenna. 'What do you care?' she said.

'Come on, Coleen! Let's get away from here, and we can talk.'

Rory ambled over to Coleen. 'It's OK, Coleen, I wasn't really planning on breaking in. I just wanted to see what his house looked like on the inside. Let's grab a couple of apples and we can head. I got some sweets from the shop yesterday, and we can share them if you like.'

Gratefully, Coleen agreed and walked past Brenna as though she hadn't seen her.

Brenna chased after them. She caught up to them as they were about to and climb over the low wall into the orchard.

She caught Coleen's arm. 'Why are you so angry with me? What did I do to you?'

Coleen shook her arm off. 'Don't pretend – you told lies about me to all my friends – none of them would speak to me at Mass, and you told Rory that you hate me coming around to your place. He said you told him I smell and that I told Mr Cullen you were in his orchard just to get you in trouble. *I hate you, Brenna O'Hagan!*

Sickened at the scale of Rory's lies, Brenna could only stare at her. Coleen turned away, and Rory smiled his creepy smile and winked at her. Unable to bear any more, Brenna lunged at him and started hitting him, screaming that he was a liar.

Coleen stared, unable to move at first, and then she tried to pull Brenna away from Rory.

'He's lying to you, Coleen! He just wants you to stop being my friend. Everything got spoiled when he came here. You know I'd not tell lies about you. *He's* the one who doesn't want you coming around, and *he's* the one who blamed you for telling on us that day in the orchard!' Brenna paused to catch her breath, tears of frustration coursing down her face.

The drama was interrupted by the sound of laughter. Rory was shaking, his eyes wet with tears of mirth.

The girls stared at him, mouths agape.

'Oh, that was so worth putting up with all your whinging, Coleen, you eejit! Do you seriously think I liked your company, you spineless little girl? Fuck you, Brenna! I nearly had her climbing in the window and robbing the auld git's house. Why did you have to open your mouth?'

Brenna glared at him with hatred, then Coleen shocked her by propelling herself at Rory and almost knocking him off his feet. She scratched and kicked at him. Furious, Rory grabbed her and flung her with force towards the wall. There was a sickening crack as her head met unyielding stone, and Coleen lay in a crumpled heap. Her body was still, too still.

Brenna ran to her, but she wasn't moving. '*Help her!*' she screamed at Rory.

He looked dazed, frozen in place. She ran to him and shook him, sick with terror at his helplessness. He didn't respond, just stared at her blankly.

'*We have to get help!*' She ran back to Coleen and tried to lift her up, but she was like a giant floppy doll, and her eyes stared sightlessly at the sky.

Then Rory came to life.

'It's OK, Brenna. I'll tell them that it was an accident, that you didn't mean to hurt her. I'll say she followed you into the orchard, and you argued, but she was pushing you, and you shoved her, and she fell and cracked her head.'

Brenna stared at him in horror. '*You* shoved her, not me! *You* did it, not me! Why are you lying?'

'But, Brenna, who's going to believe you? You've been behaving oddly, stealing from your mother, and falling out with Coleen and me. I told your dad – the day we went to the mart – that you've been behaving strangely lately. Both of your folks are worried about you. I think they'll believe me, don't you? But it's OK, I don't think they send children to jail. But you'll probably be taken away from your parents and put in a reformatory. I have a mate who was put in one for thieving, and he never saw his folks again.'

'*No, no, Rory, stop it! We must get help!*'

'No, Brenna, I think I'll call the police and tell them all about the nasty things you've been saying about Coleen. I think they might even believe that you deliberately attacked her.'

Brenna sank to her knees, sobbing.

'I'll tell you what, Brenna, I'm willing to help you out. We can hide her in the garden and pretend we never saw her since she showed me the pups. We can just pretend none of this happened. Then we'll both be safe.'

Terrified, Brenna, barely aware of the hard stony ground poking into her knees, sobbed helplessly.

Rory pulled her to her feet. 'Come on, you need to help. I can't do it on my own.'

Rory made her help drag Coleen out to the orchard. Her body felt floppy and heavy as they half lifted and half dragged her over the low wall. Then they staggered towards the back of the orchard. Brenna saw that they were heading for the low ditch, that in the winter was filled with water but now was bone dry. Rory cursed at Brenna to hurry up and then he shouted to drop the body. Brenna watched with horror as he pushed Coleen with his foot over the edge into the ditch. She flinched as Coleen's soft body hit the hard ground. Rory threw branches over her.

Brenna watched, hearing the pounding of blood in her ears and her ragged breath.

'OK, that will do,' Rory said.

As Lucifer filled the air with his desperate barking, Rory grabbed her arm and dragged her out of the orchard, past Mr Cullen's house and across to the road. Then they ran the short distance to the safety of her garden.

He pulled her to a far corner out of sight of her house. 'Now listen, they are going to start looking for Coleen soon, and I don't want your mother seeing you looking like this – she'll get suspicious.'

Brenna, incapable of speech, stared at him mutely.

'OK, this is the plan. You say that you have a sick stomach. Put your fingers down your throat and make vomiting sounds in the bathroom. Then get into bed, and I'll take care of everything. OK?'

They walked back to the house and, avoiding her mother, she ran upstairs to make herself sick. She locked the door behind her. Once bent over the toilet, she found she didn't have to force herself. She looked at the bowl and started retching uncontrollably.

Rory must have said something to her mother because she could hear her rattling the bathroom door.

'Are you OK, Brenna, love?' She called from outside the door.

Eventually, Brenna knew that she would have to come out. She opened the door carefully, avoiding her mother's eyes. Her mammy placed cool fingers against her forehead and scanned her face anxiously.

'OK, off to bed with you, love. I don't suppose you'll be able to eat anything more today.'

Brenna shook her head and shuddered.

Mammy left her in her bedroom with a basin on the floor beside her in case she felt sick and couldn't make it to the bathroom. A glass of water was placed on her bedside locker, and Mammy drew the curtains. Brenna lay staring at the ceiling. Feeling thirsty, she drank from the glass and lay down, her stomach in knots and her head cloudy. Mercifully her brain shut down, and she stared at the dips and dimples in the pock-marked ceiling through the light filtered by a gap in the curtains. She didn't know how long she lay there.

Mammy came in, followed by Rory. 'Brenna, sorry to disturb your rest, but Mrs Foley was over. She was wondering if you saw Coleen at all. She hasn't shown up for her tea, and her mother is worried about her.'

Brenna stared at her mother stupidly.

'Well, have you seen her this afternoon?'

Rory glared at her from behind Mammy and shook his head.

'No, Mammy,' she whispered through dry lips.

'Well, not to worry, she probably went for a wander and lost track of time. You've done it often enough. Look, go back to sleep, and I'll look in on you in a wee while.' She went to the door, calling over her shoulder, 'Don't be chatting to Brenna for long, Rory. She needs her rest.'

'I won't, Auntie Mary,' he said.

He leaned over Brenna, his eyes bright with excitement. 'I think it's going to be all right. You may have got away with it.'

He patted her hand, and she opened her mouth to speak, but no sounds came, then he was gone, and she continued to lie there staring at the ceiling.

That evening Mammy came upstairs, her eyes red with tears. 'Brenna, love, I have some terrible news. They found poor little Coleen this evening, and I'm afraid . . . she's gone, love.'

Brenna sat bolt upright, her heart full of hope. Coleen was gone. She must have only been stunned. 'Oh, thank God, thank God!'

Seeing the relief on her daughter's face, Mammy took her hand. 'Love, I'm sorry . . . I mean, she passed away. The doctor couldn't do anything for her. She's dead.'

The word hung in the room, and it seemed to Brenna that it reverberated and boomeranged around the walls, a hideous echo . . . *dead, dead, dead.*

She struggled to get out of bed, and Mammy got the bowl to her face just in time as she dry-retched, bringing up only bile.

She got up later that night and sat hunched over the range. Mammy had spent some hours with Coleen's parents. When she returned, Brenna listened as she described how the Foley family was in bits, poor Alice Foley sitting frozen with shock, repeating the same sentence over and over: 'Why would someone want to hurt my girl?' And no one could answer her. Mammy described how Mr Foley and Coleen's brothers paced the floor, rage and pain etched on their faces.

'If they could get their hands on Patsy Cullen, he wouldn't be long for this world,' Mammy said to Rory.

Brenna half listened – the words made no sense. Why would the family be angry with Mr Cullen?

Rory and Mammy left the room. She dreaded them coming back. She desperately wanted to be alone, but Mammy wouldn't allow her outside and she couldn't face being alone in her room, she was afraid Rory would try to talk to her. She slid under the big kitchen table, just as she did when she was a small child and wanted to hide from the grown-ups when they were looking to put her to bed. She sat there quietly, knowing that she was safe from Rory.

Later, Daddy came in wearing his Garda uniform. He looked exhausted, and Mammy brought him a drink of whiskey from the high press. Daddy didn't ever take a drink in the house except when he had a cold.

'Patrick, sit down. You look terrible.'

Daddy sat, accepted the whiskey and downed it in one gulp.

Brenna found it hard to breathe. Her parents were caught up in their upset and unaware of her hiding place. She kept very still and listened.

'It makes no sense, Mary. The Patsy Cullen I know wouldn't hurt a fly. But the facts speak for themselves.'

'What did he have to say for himself, Patrick?'

'Not too much. He seemed incapable of saying a word and kept shaking his head and moaning. Shortly after we started questioning him at the station, he took a turn. The doctor arrived, and he had him brought to the hospital. The doctor isn't hopeful.'

'Maybe it's for the best, and it'll spare his family the heartbreak of a trial.'

'I know, Mary, you're right, but I just can't believe it of Patsy. Shure, look at how good he has always been to our Brenna.'

'What's happened, Mammy?' Brenna blurted out. 'What are you saying about Mr Cullen? What's happened?'

Her mother looked to where she was peering out from underneath the table. 'Oh love, you were that quiet I didn't know you were hiding there. Look, this is nothing for you to worry about, just grown-up business. You look done in – your eyes are tripping over with the want of sleep.'

But Brenna insisted, 'Why was Mr Cullen at the station?'

'Well, love, poor wee Coleen's body was found in his orchard and, of course, the gardaí had to ask him how she got there – and, well, he had a bad turn while he was being questioned. Try not to worry, pet.'

Brenna opened her mouth. She had to explain, to tell them. She couldn't let Mr Cullen get into trouble. She got to her feet and screamed, '*No, it's all wrong! Mr Cullen didn't do anything! Please, Mammy, don't lock him up!*' And she burst into hysterical sobs.

Mammy pulled her close but Brenna struggled and wailed. She had to make them understand but the words wouldn't come out right. Her shouts had brought Rory to the doorway. He stood frozen to the spot, his face white and scared, but she didn't care. She had to tell them. She couldn't let poor Mr Cullen take the blame.

'Patrick, we must fetch the doctor!'

Daddy carried her shouting and screaming to bed. Her mouth felt as thought it was filled with cotton wool, she couldn't form words, only inarticulate sobs. Eventually she cried herself to sleep but woke again to scream and struggle in Mammy's arms.

Then Dr Toner arrived, and she felt a prick in her arm, and a warm feeling swarmed over her body, and then there was nothing.

The following day, she heard that Mr Cullen was dead. She stopped speaking then.

CHAPTER 14

BREE

Bree finally managed a night's sleep and woke if not refreshed, at least not zombified. To charge herself up, she threw on her tracksuit and runners and took off into the grey misty morning. It was hard to see clearly, but she found herself at one with the dull monochrome world. It suited her to be in a fugue-like state, where nothing, not even nature, intruded. Maybe if the world were blander and colourless, there would be less ambition, greed and war. She managed to keep her thoughts at bay and felt at one with her breath and the rhythmic pounding of her feet on the hard pavement. The roads were quiet, and she left the residential area and ran towards the town. She stopped when she reached the end of Long Avenue and doubled back on herself. She arrived back at her house tired out, but her body felt relaxed for the first time in over a week.

She turned on the immersion and soon was revelling in the warm water as she showered. Then she dressed rapidly. Downstairs she boiled an egg, put a croissant in the oven to warm and brewed up a pot of coffee. As she ate and drank, she wished she had thought to pick up a Sunday paper. She wanted to keep her mind distracted.

She was just washing up when her phone rang. She stared distrustfully at the instrument. The call on Friday night had unnerved her, and she was reluctant to answer. She picked up the receiver cautiously.

'Yes,' she said.

'Morning, Mam,' said Amy.

'Wow, you're up early this morning. Did you have a good time last night?'

'Yeah, it was class.'

'Well, was the guy you fancied there?'

'No, Mam, but it was still a fun night. Look, the thing is, I was wondering if you could check my bedroom to see if I left an essay there. I thought I'd brought it back with me, but it's not in my bag. I need to submit it tomorrow, and I can't miss the deadline.'

Bree raced upstairs and looked in Amy's room. It was hard to find anything amidst all the clutter. But, although there was lots of paper with her daughter's sprawling handwriting on it, nothing looked like an essay.

'Sorry, Amy, I couldn't find it. Are you sure it's not in your room in college?'

'Of course not. I've torn the place apart.'

Bree detected a note of panic in Amy's voice. 'Is it very important?' she asked.

'Yes, I must get it to Professor Smyth tomorrow by midday or I'm going to lose marks. Mam, it's my second year, and all marks go towards my final degree. Smyth's a stickler, and he'll fail me.' Amy's voice cracked.

'Can you write it again?'

'Mam, it's five thousand words. I barely managed the first time, and I dumped all the early drafts I did.' By now, Amy sounded like she was struggling to control her tears.

Bree, helpless as to how to help her, could only mouth platitudes.

'Right, I have to go now, Mam.'

Abruptly Amy hung up, and Bree stood helplessly holding the receiver.

She wandered back to the kitchen table, feeling useless. What could she do? The answer was a big fat nothing.

She drove to the shops, bought herself the newspaper, and spent the afternoon trying to read and failed. She was worried about Amy. Should she drive up and see her? Of course not. Amy would be furious, and her presence would just get in her way.

At bedtime, the phone rang again. It was Amy, her voice vibrant and happy. 'Hey, Mam, brilliant news. I've got the essay.'

'Oh, thank God, where was it?'

'It was all thanks to that guy I was telling you about. The cute one that I hoped to meet at the party. Well, I may have dropped it in the ENT's office when I popped in to check out what was happening on campus. It must have fallen out of my bag. Well, he found it, and I could have kissed him.'

'Amy, that's the best news. I'm so delighted for you.'

'Even better, he asked me out, and we're going for a Chinese on Thursday.'

'Well, your day certainly came good. I'm so relieved.'

'Thanks, Mam. Sorry for stressing you out earlier.'

'No problem, love, now off and enjoy the rest of your day. Love you!'

They hung up, and Bree sat down to watch whatever the telly had to offer. She slept well that night.

* * *

For the next few weeks, it seemed like life had returned to normal. There were no more envelopes with cryptic words, and Amy had done well on her essay. Her new boyfriend seemed to be making her happy. At least, she gathered that from how she rarely came home for the weekend. There was always some new concert they were heading to or a party that she couldn't miss. Bree didn't mind. Yes, she missed her, but she was glad that she was happy. It seemed as though all her worries about Rory's malign influence seemed exaggerated and would not come to anything.

Then, when another long Saturday stretched ahead, she decided to pop up to Dublin to see her. After all, 'If the mountain didn't come to Mohammad, then . . .'

A few hours later, she parked her car outside her daughter's apartment. Both the girls Amy lived with came from Newry and travelled home most weekends. This pleased Amy as, although she liked the girls, she loved having the place to herself, especially now that she had a boyfriend. Bree wished she had let Amy know that she was calling but, at the time, she thought it would be fun to surprise her. Now she wasn't so sure. What if the boyfriend was there? It might be awkward. Well, it was too late now.

She entered the foyer of the building and pushed the buzzer for the first-floor flat. Amy answered and sounded slightly cagy but buzzed her in. She headed up the stairs.

Amy was waiting at the door, looking uncomfortable.

'Mam, this is a surprise. I wasn't expecting you.'

Bree, feeling defensive, forced herself to smile. 'I just decided on the spur of the moment to call to see you, but if you have plans that's grand. I have lots I can be doing in town.'

Amy ushered her in, and the bright kitchen faded into the background when she saw Rory sitting on the couch, drinking from a mug.

A tall young man with long hair tied in a ponytail was eating cereal at the kitchen counter.

'Mam, this is Jason.'

Bree barely acknowledged the young man who stood up to greet her. She was vaguely conscious that he had taken her hand before she snapped it away. Why was Rory here? Ignoring the boy, she glared at him.

Amy, seeing the dark looks directed at Rory, said defensively, 'Rory was giving me a hand with my course work, Mam.'

'Really, college life has changed since my day. I didn't realise faculty made house calls early on Saturday morning.'

Rory grinned up at her from his perch on the couch, '*Aww*, Brenna, Amy isn't just any student. She's family. Isn't that right, coz?'

Bree realised from the pain that her fingernails were impaled in her palms.

'And, besides, I don't teach Amy. I happened to be in the area and wanted to check on how she did in her last assignment. You know, the one that she mislaid.' He turned to Amy. 'I'm sure you didn't need that stress so close to your deadline. Anyway, Amy, I think I'd better head off now. I'm sure you and your mother have lots of plans for today. I'll say my goodbyes.'

He walked towards the door.

'Wait, Rory, I'll go down with you for a few minutes,' said Bree, 'and Amy, perhaps you and . . .' she stopped having forgotten the boy's name.

'Jason,' Amy said, glaring at her.

Bree was conscious that she wasn't making a good impression on

Amy's boyfriend. 'Perhaps you and Jason would like to have lunch with me?'

'Sorry, Mrs O'Hagan,' said Jason, 'but I have things to do, and I'll be heading soon.'

Amy looked frustrated, and Bree knew that she had messed up their plans for the day.

She followed Rory downstairs. He was waiting just outside the door. He grinned his crooked grin, and she wanted to hit him so hard he would fall over, but instantly the image of Coleen lying lifelessly on the ground filled her mind, and she stared at him, sickened.

'Why are you here?'

'I told you, Brenna, that I'm helping Amy out. She had some difficulties with aspects of the course, and I'm giving her some insights – you could say that I'm mentoring her.'

'I'm warning you to stay away from her.' Bree said, her voice rising.

Rory pulled a mock sad face.

'My mother told me you were dead,' she snapped.

'Well, you could say that was a bit of a misunderstanding and one that my dear mother and Philip decided to go along with for a while. To tell the truth, it suited me too. I needed a little time to let the dust settle and start anew.'

'You never told the truth in your life!' Bree glared at him.

'That's a bit harsh, Brenna. You mustn't be so hard. We had some good times, remember?'

'Stay away from my daughter, Rory. I'm warning you.'

Rory laughed. 'Or what, Brenna? What are you going to do?' He laughed again.

'Please, Rory, leave her out of whatever sick game you're playing.'

'*Aww*, but Brenna, you know the rules of the Game. If you want me to stay away from Amy, then *you* must play by the rules.'

113

'I'm not having anything to do with you or your games, Rory, so back off.'

Rory shook his head sadly. 'Cousin, you have become so difficult. But, you see, I make the rules and I say you must play.'

'Right, Rory, I'm going to the university authorities. I'll tell them you're harassing my daughter.'

Rory laughed delightedly. 'Oh goody, I'd love to sit in on that conversation. I wonder what Amy will say. Do you think she'll say I'm bothering her when I spent the morning coaching her for free?' He leaned back against the wall of the building, grinning. 'Besides, you wouldn't want Amy's grades to suffer, would you? Look how she mislaid her essay – who knows what other mishaps might occur.'

'*You bastard!* Did you take it or get that guy, Jason, to take it?'

'My, my, what paranoia you have, Brenna.'

Bree pushed past him and walked back up the stairs.

'Bye, coz, I'll be in touch.' Rory called after her. 'Soon.'

When she returned to the flat, Jason was heading out the door. He mumbled a quick goodbye and left.

Amy glared at her and accused her of meddling. Realising that staying to explain would just inflame Amy, she decided to leave.

She drove home too fast. That evening, the food she prepared to eat lay untasted, congealing on her plate. She dumped it in the bin and stared at the television screen.

Her phone rang in the middle of the night and, when she picked it up, the line went dead. Twisting and squirming all night left her sheets a tangled mess in the morning.

CHAPTER 15

On Monday, when she returned from work, a plain white envelope was lying on her mat. Inside there was another little envelope with *Brenna* neatly written across it. Should she just burn it unopened? She wasn't a child anymore; she didn't have to play his games. He couldn't manipulate her unless she allowed him to. She knew that she was going to open it eventually, but for now she couldn't face it. The evening ahead stretched long and lonely.

Television offered nothing to tempt her away from her sense of impending doom. She paced the floor, suddenly desperate for a cigarette. She hadn't smoked in years, but a visceral longing tormented her, making her skin crawl with anticipation. Unable to bear it anymore, she went to the local shop and bought a pack of Carrolls. She tore them open in the car and lit them up. The taste was poisonous, but she sucked the pale smoke in as though it had healing properties.

Back at the house, she chain-smoked in an orgy of self-hatred. Then unable to avoid it any longer, she took a deep breath and picked up the miniature envelope. She stared at the name *Brenna*, a name from another time. A time she had thought was in the past, locked away, never to be examined again. Images of Coleen's crumpled body flashed in technicolour across her mind and tortured her. The open sightless eyes stared at her through time. She should have told her parents what happened – surely they would have believed her. But Rory had set the seeds of distrust in their hearts, making them suspicious of her, and he had ruthlessly exploited her fear of losing them and being locked up. He wasn't much older than her. How had he dominated her so easily? He had succeeded in stripping away her confidence and destroying her parents' trust in her. How much else had he stolen? Poor Patsy Cullen lost his life and his good name. He died because she and Rory had kept silent and let everyone believe that he had harmed Coleen. Poor Patsy became a bogeyman for the community forevermore. A lifetime of being a decent human who was respected by all of his neighbours was brutally taken away. He was now a name to be spoken like a curse.

At least she hadn't had to stay, watch, and listen as his character was ripped apart. She had escaped to Dundalk but carried her misery like an invisible cloak, suffocating her and despoiling her childhood. But she wasn't a gullible child anymore. His sick games wouldn't work anymore. She opened the envelope.

Your Task: Locate the file belonging to Ryan Carty. Copy the document and hand over the file to an associate in the Whitehouse Bar on Tuesday evening at seven p.m. Don't Fail.

Bree shook her head. Rory was a lunatic. She wouldn't engage with him; she would just ignore his craziness.

The next day at work, she impressed Colm with her work ethic. She barely took a break and, when finished her tasks, she sorted out the filing cabinet. But she couldn't resist checking to see if there was a file for Ryan Carty. There was. She took calls from clients that Colm dreaded dealing with, soothed angry ones down and even managed to get a few to pay long-overdue bills.

That evening she went to the pictures on her own. She just wanted to get through the evening. The movie, *Lethal Weapon 3*, turned out to be a waste of money. It was background noise to her misery and, after a while, she gave up trying to follow the plot. Her head just wasn't capable of immersing itself in a fantasy world, however engaging the movie.

On the way home, she bought a takeaway and ate it while watching a comedy show on TV. She even managed to sleep, feeling satisfaction in having thwarted Rory. Now he would realise that she wasn't a helpless child anymore.

The phone dragged her awake. She staggered downstairs.

The message was terse. A hoarse voice whispered, '*You know what to expect.*'

She lay awake for the remainder of the night in a state of anxiety.

At eight in the morning, her mother rang, her voice panicked. 'Bree, my house has been broken into, and all my things wrecked.'

'Are you all right?'

'Yes, yes – just shocked.'

Her heart pounded as she said, 'I'm on my way.'

At her mother's house, there was a patrol car sitting in the drive. Hurrying inside, she had a look into the living room. It was a mess, with chairs overturned and drawers gaping. The floor was covered in items from the drawers, photo albums, and broken ornaments.

In the kitchen, Mary, still in her dressing gown, was sipping tea while a garda patted her hand.

Bree hugged her mother who assured her that she was unhurt.

'Mammy, I'm just going to have a word with the garda, and then we'll chat.'

She beckoned to the garda, who, after calling instructions to his colleague, who was checking windows at the back of the house, stepped into the garden to talk to Bree. He was middle-aged and had a shock of curly grey hair and chewed on well-bitten fingernails as he spoke. He introduced himself as Garda Jim O'Shaughnessy.

'This is a bad state of affairs, Miss. It's sad when the auld dears aren't safe in their homes.'

Bree wasn't sure her mother, who was still in her early sixties, would like to be referred to as an 'auld dear'.

He continued, 'I remember your dad when he was on the force. I was just a new chap, wet behind the ears, and he was sound to me. I'm that annoyed that this should have happened to your mammy.'

'Was there anything taken, Garda O'Shaughnessy?'

He pulled off his hat and ran his fingers through his grey crop of curls. 'Well, truth to tell, I've seen worse break-ins. They only took a few things – some bits of jewellery and a few electronics. They pulled things apart a bit, but no real damage was done. I think it looks worse than it is, although that's no comfort to your poor mother.'

When the gardaí were finished with their investigation, O'Shaughnessy offered to send someone around to talk to them about improving home security.

Bree helped her mother put the house back together. Her next-door neighbours on both sides insisted on cleaning the house from top to bottom and sprinkling Holy Water in all the rooms. Eventually, satisfied that Mary was feeling better, they left.

Bree made her mother a sandwich and tea, and they sat in the sitting room.

'Oh, Bree, I can't believe I didn't hear them come in.'

'Well, thank God you didn't. They might have attacked you. But, Mam, you left your window ajar. It was no bother to them to get in.'

Mary looked shamefaced. 'Don't be cross, Bree.' She held her hands up. 'I know you've warned me lots of times about shutting my windows, but the nice garda said that although I made it easy for them they'd have got in anyway. He said I needed to beef up my security and suggested getting an alarm in.' Then she started to cry.

'Oh, Mammy, you're OK now. I'm here, and I'll stay with you until we get all new locks on your house.'

'I'm grand, Bree. It's just that the brats have taken my favourite picture. You remember the one of the three of us, taken when you were only a little girl. I suppose they wanted the silver frame. But I wish they'd left the picture. You remember, I always kept it on the sideboard.'

Bree recalled the picture. It was kept in pride of place in the Living room. Mammy loved it because she had precious few photos of the three of them from when they lived on the farm in Sligo.

Later that day, a garda arrived to advise Mary on securing her home, and that afternoon Bree had a locksmith call to change the locks on all her mother's doors and put a deadlock on her front door. She also organised for an alarm company to call during the week.

That night, despite repeated offers, Mary refused to have her stay over.

'I'm not a child, Bree. I refuse to be scared in my own home. Now away with you and thank Colm for me for letting you keep me company today.'

Bree refused to leave until Mary agreed to have one of her friends from the golf club stay over with her until the alarm was fitted. Her mother muttered and complained but reluctantly agreed as it was the only way Bree would agree to go home.

Feeling satisfied that her mother would be safe, Bree drove home. It was dark when she entered her hallway, and on the mat was a letter. She tore it open, and inside was a torn-up photograph. Sickened, she saw it was the one missing from her mother's house. Examining the pieces, she saw that her image was missing. It was the work of Rory. The idea of him having a picture of her as a child sickened her.

The phone rang. It was Rory.

'I hear that you had a tough day, Brenna.'

'*You bastard!*' she spat.

'*Tut, tut*, little coz, you know there are rewards and consequences to the Game. You must take the rough with the smooth.'

'My mother has always been good to you, and this is how you reward her!'

'Well, it's true I was always fond of Auntie Mary, but, Brenna, you did this. I warned you. Perhaps in future you'll stick to the rules of the Game.'

'When I come off this phone, I'm calling the gardaí and telling them everything about how you bullied me as a child and how you are creating havoc for me now. *I'm* warning *you*.'

Rory was silent for a moment and then said, 'Yes, you could do that, Brenna, but I think it might rebound badly on you. Do you want your mother and sweet little Amy to know that you killed a little girl and let an innocent man be blamed for it?'

'I'll tell them what really happened, that you killed Coleen and forced me to hide her body.'

Rory laughed. 'I don't think so. Do you really think I haven't prepared for just such an eventuality?'

'I don't believe you!'

'OK, Brenna, why don't we meet tonight? I fancy a little trip to see my cousin, and perhaps I'll drop in on Auntie Mary too.'

'Keep away from my mother, I'm warning you!'

He gave a delighted chuckle. 'See you tonight after ten. Don't bother cooking for me.'

Bree slammed down the phone.

What should she do? The thought of telling the gardaí everything that happened terrified her, but she was more scared of what Rory was capable of. She smoked cigarette after cigarette, crushing them viciously on a saucer that now functioned as her ashtray.

Two hours later she saw the lights of a car draw up outside. She didn't wait for the bell to ring, pulling the door open as he slammed shut his car door.

'Eager to see me,' he said as he walked past her inside.

He sat on an armchair and glanced around.

'This looks cosy, Brenna. I've been trying to picture your home – really, it's charming.'

'Stop calling me Brenna, and don't get comfortable,' Bree snapped. 'I want you gone as soon as you've said your piece.'

'*Mmm*, techy you! I just thought that before you start telling tall tales to your friendly local garda, I should explain that you might find it causes you more trouble than it's worth. You see, I went to see a therapist when I lived in London. I had these strange, disturbing dreams, and my very helpful therapist suggested I use hypnosis to try to release what was plaguing me and causing me to dream about a dead child. We unearthed a vast store of repressed memories though not much detail. I told her that I thought that something awful had happened when I was in Ireland as a child. She urged me to do a little research, but she warned me that if I thought a crime had been committed, I had a duty to report it.'

'I don't care about your bloody therapist. I'm going to tell the truth. I don't care what happens to me.'

121

'*Ahh*, but the truth is I saw a little girl viciously attack another girl and hide the body. I knew the attacker and wanted to protect her, but she refused to own up, and it had tragic consequences. She threatened that she would tell everyone I had done the wicked deed. So, I returned home traumatised and buried the memory. My pattern of getting into trouble with the police in my youth, the therapist made me see, was a coping mechanism – acting out, she called it.'

'*You are fucking nuts!*' Bree shouted, clenching her fists.

'Very possibly, Brenna, but I think that my therapist, armed with those detailed notes, would make a compelling witness, especially when I explained that I confronted you with my memories and you became furious. Also, if you make accusations, my position as a respected Doctor of Psychology might just trump your story. But go ahead, I don't mind, and after they arrest you I'll look after dear Auntie Mary and our lovely Amy. I'm sure the sentence will be lenient, and I'll try to be there for you.'

Bree slumped onto the sofa. 'What do you want?'

'I want to play the Game with you, Brenna. I did try with others, but they were too easy to manipulate, and they lacked what you would call moral fibre. They were usually happy to do the naughty things I asked for. But with you, it was such fun, watching as you twisted in the wind, tormented by guilt but compelled to sin anyway.'

Bree sat unmoving. She longed to lunge at him, scream at him to leave her home, but her body felt curiously detached. She wasn't sure she had any control of it anymore.

'Right. So, Brenna, to business. You failed the last Task, so I'm giving you another opportunity. Copy the document for my associate and deliver it to the same place, at the same time tomorrow evening. Don't mess this up, Brenna. Amy is counting on it. We both want to keep her nice and safe, don't we?'

Electrified, Bree jumped to her feet. 'Keep away from Amy! I'm warning you, Rory. I'll *kill* you if you do anything to hurt her.'

'Now, now, calm down. I won't be touching a hair on the sweet girl's head, and hasn't she a big strong protector at her side? Sir Jason the Good, I call him. I must say he's a very handsome boy, a bit of a movie star in the looks department, and very athletic too. Did Amy tell you he plays for the college football team? In fact, I did wonder how they got together. He's a bit out of her league. I mean, Amy is a pretty girl, but she's more the girl-next-door type than the dolly birds he usually associates with, but then I did introduce them and, well, the mysterious power of attraction came into effect.' Rory got to his feet. 'Well, I must be off.' He looked at her, his blue eyes cold. 'Brenna, don't mess this one up.'

She sat slumped on the sofa as though all the vitality had been sucked out of her body. She listened to the front door slam and heard his car start. She shook her head to clear it. What was he implying about Jason? It was Jason who had returned the essay, and according to Rory, it was he who introduced them Was Jason a plant? Put into Amy's life by Rory to mess with her head. Was he going to do something to hurt Amy?

That night she didn't even try to sleep. She just sat in the dark, smoking and drinking coffee until the morning light infiltrated. Then she showered and dressed.

CHAPTER 16

The office was empty, with no sign of Colm. She opened the filing cabinet and found the file marked **Ryan Carty**. She hurried to the photocopier. It was early, but sometimes Colm came in to get a head start on his work. Working rapidly, she soon had all the documents copied and stored in a folder. She had just returned the Carty file when she heard Colm entering from the street. Hastily she shoved the folder into her bag.

'Are you OK?' Colm was staring at her, his brow furrowed.

'Yes, I'm fine, Colm. Why?'

'You look exhausted, and no wonder with Amy's mishap and then your poor mother being burgled.'

Smiling brightly, Bree said, 'I didn't get much sleep last night, but now that Mammy has agreed to update her security, I'll sleep better. One of her cronies from the golf club is staying with her so I feel better about leaving her.'

Bree was relieved when the phone rang and she could return to work. But work was no distraction from the folder in her shoulder bag. Every time she glanced at it, it seemed to her guilty eyes to emit radioactive pulses. If she delivered it tonight, then she would be playing Rory's game and the thought of what the endgame would be frightened her. She wondered if she could find out something about this Ryan Carty. Her head throbbed, and she both longed for the day to end and yet was terrified of it ending because then she would have to face her assignation with a stranger in a pub. She was handing over God knows what information, but she had to do it for Amy's sake. She had to protect Amy. Focusing on her daughter helped.

At five, she drove home and struggled to put in the hours before she had to go to the Whitehouse Bar. She tried to force some soup down, but her stomach, riddled with nerves, heaved as she drank it. Sighing, she gave up and chainsmoked. She stared at the folder, debating whether to destroy it or deliver it. She was afraid of breaking Rory's sick rules. But was it more dangerous to continue playing his games?

At a quarter to seven, she drove into town and parked a short distance from the pub. It was a dive. Although once painted dazzling white, hence its name, it had since discoloured into a dispiriting yellow shade. The interior was even worse. It stank of stale cigarettes and despair. It was not a place where she would have socialised because of its seediness and its dubious reputation. She doubted if she would meet anyone she knew. She ordered tonic water from a greasy-haired barman who didn't make eye contact. He was absently wiping the countertop. He grunted to let her know he heard, and she paid him and went to sit down.

The barman plonked her drink down on the stained table. She looked at her watch. She didn't know who was meeting her, but she reckoned that she would stand out as not being a regular customer.

She turned her head to stare at the door as an old boy entered and ordered Guinness with a side of Jameson. She was still staring intently when she felt a presence behind her. The hairs on her body rose and she turned around. Standing beside her was a stocky man in his early fifties. He sat down heavily on the seat next to her. The chair creaked its protest. Bree's nose wrinkled as she inhaled a mixture of stale sweat struggling to coexist with cologne.

He signalled to the barman, who hurried over with a whiskey.

'Do ya want one?' he asked Bree, his voice curiously high-pitched as though it had never broken when he was a boy.

She shook her head.

He took a slug of his whiskey, swirled it around in his mouth and sighed as it went down. *'Another one, Pascal!'* he shouted to the barman. His sleeves were rolled up, exposing arms covered in thick black hairs.

The barman hurried over with the drink.

The man smiled at her and took a sip from his second drink. 'Well, girlie, I believe you have something for me.'

She reached into her bag and placed the folder on the table.

Without warning, he caught her hand in his. His fingers felt hard and slippery with sweat. 'I'm assuming that everything is in there?'

She nodded, her flesh crawling from his proximity. She pulled her hand away.

'I hope you'll be a better timekeeper in future, pet. I don't like being kept waiting. I was here for over an hour on Tuesday. I'm a busy man,' he grunted.

She glared at him. 'There won't be a next time. This will never happen again.'

He grinned at her, displaying perfect teeth. Too perfect to be real. He reached into his pocket and slid a thick brown envelope towards her.

'What's that?' she demanded.

'That, girlie, is your reward. Now take it and fuck off.'

'I don't want your money.'

He grinned. 'Money is money – now take it.'

She jumped to her feet, left the envelope on the table, and walked away. She didn't look back.

Back at the house, she washed her hands furiously. She felt contaminated by the man's touch. He spoke of rewarding her, and she thought back to the rewards Rory had prepared for her before: treasure hunts, sweet treats, and the kitten – the little creature, Daisy, that she had left behind in Sligo. Her mother begged her to take it when they left to live in Dundalk, but she couldn't. It felt contaminated by its association with Rory. She gave it to a neighbour. The thought of a reward terrified her.

Flowers were delivered to her at work the next day. A pretty posy of dried flowers tied with a cream silk bow. She stared at them . . . forget-me-nots.

There was no card, and Colm teased her about a secret admirer. He wondered aloud why they were artificial. 'Perhaps he was being considerate, Bree, saving you the trouble of putting them in water. He sounds like a catch.'

Bree felt relieved. Flowers were a benign reward. She could cope with that. On the way home from work, she bought a bottle of wine, cigarettes, and a bag of chips. She dumped the flowers in a bin at the filling station.

When she opened her front door, a thick brown envelope lay on the floor. Someone had pushed it through her letterbox. She forced herself to carry it into the kitchen. She opened it. It was crammed with banknotes. Fivers, tenners and twenties. The flowers were just another one of Rory's jokes. He was forcing her to accept the money.

She counted the notes. A total of one thousand pounds. Each note looked as though it was specially chosen to be as battered and used as possible. Trembling, she stared at the cash. What should she do? Destroy them? Give them to charity? But one thing she knew: there was no way she could keep them. She scrubbed her hands until they stung and opened her windows, convinced the notes had left a stench in her kitchen. Then, wearing kitchen gloves, she wrapped the notes in tinfoil, hid them at the bottom of her kitchen bin, and placed a bag over them.

That evening she rang Amy. 'Hey, honey, haven't heard from you for a while. How have you been?'

Amy sighed, 'I'm OK.'

Concerned by her tone, Bree asked, 'Has anything happened?'

'No, Mother, nothing has happened, unless you mean how rude you were to Rory and Jason when you called the other day.'

'Amy, I'm sorry. I wasn't expecting to find Rory in your flat. I thought you agreed not to see too much of him.'

'Mam, I don't know what your problem is. Rory has been so good to me. If it weren't for him, I'd have failed my last essay.'

'Listen, Amy, I'd like it if you avoided him. He's not good news. I can get someone else to help you with your studies.'

'Look, Mam, Rory told me about when he came to stay with your family in Sligo. How you were jealous of his friendship with that kid, Coleen, from next door. He said you blamed him for the falling-out you and she had. Really, Mam, don't you think it's time to let all that kid stuff go?'

Bree licked dry lips. To hear Coleen's name in her daughter's mouth horrified her. But she wouldn't argue now. She lightened her tone. 'We'll agree to differ, Amy, but there are other sides to that story.'

'Mam, he was standing up for you. I was reading between the lines. He wasn't bad-mouthing you at all. He'd love you to be friends with him.'

Her flesh crawled and she tried to calm her breathing. 'OK, I'll think about it. By the way, what are you doing this weekend? I was hoping that you might come home.'

'No can do, Mam. I've got plans with Jason on Saturday night.'

'Well, how about I drive up in the morning, and we can go for a late breakfast?'

'No, Mam, I have work to do for college.'

'With Rory?' she asked.

Amy sighed. 'No, not with Rory. Look, I have to go.' Without saying goodbye, she hung up.

Bree stared at the receiver sadly. She and Amy never were off with each other. Their relationship was close, but now Rory was turning her daughter against her. Just as he had done with Coleen and with her own parents. He had the power to make people believe what he chose. What lies would he continue to spin? And was Jason his creature, ready to hurt Amy? She had to do something. The more she thought of Jason hurting Amy, the more tormented she felt. Rory would use him to betray Amy and dump her in the most humiliating way possible. She remembered how Amy had been so broken after her last relationship had soured. The boy had cheated on her and broken her heart. The thought that it would happen again, all controlled by the puppet master Rory, made her furious. He had more or less admitted that he had set them up and could control the relationship. Did he have some hold over Jason? Something to force him to do as he asked? Maybe he was bribing him. Her head hurt. She swallowed some painkillers and poured herself a glass of wine. She turned on the television and stared blankly at the screen.

The doorbell ringing jerked her from her trance, and she put her cigarette out.

Her mother stood on the doorstep. 'Well, are you going to let me in?' she asked, smiling.

Bree led the way inside.

Her mother wrinkled her nose. 'Bree, when did you start smoking again?'

Bree cracked open a window. 'Come into the kitchen, and I'll make tea,' she said.

As she put the kettle on, she was conscious of the unwashed dishes and takeaway detritus cluttering the countertops. She was aware of her mother's disapproval. Mary didn't need to say a word – her face spoke volumes of disgust.

'Bree, are you feeling well?' she asked.

'Of course I am!' she snapped. 'Why are you here?'

Her mother flushed, and Bree was contrite.

'Sorry for snapping, Mammy. I'm just not sleeping well.'

'Bree, it's not like before, is it?'

Hearing the anxiety in her mother's voice, Bree knew that she was thinking back to her childhood where she would lie awake for hours and then, when she did sleep, she'd wake drenched in sweat, crying out. Mammy had tried to get help for her, but she sat in the child psychologist's office, refusing to speak. The doctor suggested that perhaps it was too soon after the trauma of Coleen's death and to wait a while. But then Brenna became Bree and seemed happier, but she still refused to talk to her mother about Coleen, Rory, or anything to do with Sligo.

'No, Mammy, I just had a lot on lately. Look it should be me asking about you. Having your home burgled must have been awful. How are you feeling today?'

'Aww love, I'm grand, I had a grand few days with my guest. I think Una O'Shea was glad to get a break from her husband's snoring. But enough about me. Colm tells me that you look exhausted and have become very irritable at work. He's worried about you, and he isn't the only one. Amy called me to say that you're being very strange about Rory. Look, love, I think meeting Rory is bringing stuff up for you. Maybe it's time for you to deal with the past. Look, everyone is going to counselling now. It's practically trendy.'

'Will you give over, Mammy? I'm fine, really I am. I'm more concerned about you. Have you had the alarm system put in?'

'Yes, I have, and I keep forgetting the bloody code, though. I wanted to go 1,2,3,4, but the man from the company was shocked, so after a few goes I settled on using your birth year instead. But look, Bree, please take care of yourself. Why don't you come for dinner on Sunday?'

'I'd love to, Mammy, but I've made plans to go to Dublin with Anita,' she lied. 'We fancied a nice meal and maybe go to a matinee at the theatre.'

'I'm so glad that you have nice plans. We'll do dinner Sunday week.'

Desperate for her mother to leave, Bree agreed.

CHAPTER 17

On Sunday Bree, feeling bad about her conversation with Amy, decided to drive up to Dublin. This time she took the precaution of ringing Amy on her mobile phone and letting her know she was planning to visit. Amy sounded reluctant but she agreed that she could call to take her out for brunch. She arrived at half past eleven, a little early but she hoped Amy wouldn't mind. She buzzed the flat and heard the door-release go. Perhaps Amy had seen her arrive. She ran lightly upstairs.

Amy opened the door and, with a brief 'Hi', walked back into the flat.

At first, Bree thought that she was still angry with her but she sensed it was something more. Amy's eyes looked red. She must have been crying. It was important she handled things tactfully – no good would come of alienating Amy further.

'Lovey, you seem a bit down. I don't want to pry but you know that you can always talk to me, don't you?' Bree said.

Amy turned her back and shrugged. Tentatively Bree touched her lightly on her shoulder.

'I can see that you've been crying. Is it Jason? Has he done something to hurt you?'

Amy shrugged and flung herself into a chair. 'It's nothing. Don't make a big deal of it. We just had a row. Couples do, you know!'

'Yes, but remember you don't have to take any crap from boys.'

'What would you know about relationships, Mam? You dumped Daddy as soon as you had me. Granny said he wanted to marry you, but you wouldn't hear of it, and I haven't seen you in a serious relationship for as long as I've lived with you. So, what do you know about relationships?'

Bree stared at her. 'I know enough to know when my daughter is hurting.'

Amy flushed and dropped her gaze. 'Sorry, Mam, it's really not a big deal. If you don't mind, I'd rather not go into it now. Would you like some tea?' Amy walked towards the kettle and started to fill it.

'Don't bother, Amy. Let's get out of here and eat our blues away. I promised you a nice brunch and that's what we'll have.'

Amy hesitated. 'I do have a lot of work to catch up on. I can't take the whole day off.'

'Yeah, but you still must eat. How about we go somewhere local, and I'll have you back at your flat in a couple of hours. Deal?'

Amy smiled and nodded.

They went to a local café, and Amy had waffles and bacon, and Bree ordered a cheese omlette with toast and tea. Initially Amy was quiet but soon her natural good humour was restored and for a brief while it was like old times.

Brunch consumed, Bree asked hesitantly, 'Granny tells me that you rang her a while back. She seemed to think you were worried about me.'

'Mam, it's true I've been concerned about you. You seem really tense, *and* you never told me about the break-in at Granny's, so of course I was worried.'

'Amy, it's not your job to worry about me. I'm the mother. That's my department.'

'Yeah, well, you're always so chilled, but you really flipped the lid over Rory, and you were unfriendly to Jason. It's not like you to be so hostile.'

'I'm sorry if I came across as hostile. Perhaps I could meet with Jason again. Why don't you both come down to Dundalk and we'll have a nice meal and ask Granny along too.'

'Mam, we've only been going out a few weeks, and I don't want to scare him off with a meet-the-family routine. It would be fine if you met casually, but I think it's best to wait for a while now. To be honest, I think he's a bit scared of you now.'

Bree paid the bill, and they left the café. 'Do you fancy a walk, Amy; we could do a few rounds of the park or drive out to the pier?'

'No, Mam, sorry, I really do have a lot of work to do. And, look, Mam, I know you don't want to hear it, but Rory has been a godsend. Because he doesn't just teach me, he can help because he knows exactly what my lecturers are looking for and is steering me in the right direction. My marks have really improved and, to think that only six months ago I was considering dropping out of college if I couldn't continue with Psychology. Rory has made all the difference. You ought to be grateful to him for doing so much to help me. But instead, you are so harsh and unpleasant to him.'

Bree kept silent for a while. She didn't want to spoil things by arguing. She needed to be careful what she said. 'I'm glad Rory has been good to you. I really am, but please don't get too dependent on him. You can do this on your own.'

'Mam, I don't think you realise how much I struggled last year. I'm so glad my marks then didn't count towards my degree result because I was only scraping through, but now I'm scoring so much better in all my essays. And it's down to Rory.'

Bree opened her mouth to object again, but realised there was no point.

'Mam, I know you want me to do well because you had to drop out of college when you were pregnant with me. I want to make you proud, to do really well.'

'Amy, I gave up college because I wanted to be with you, to focus on you. I never regretted for a moment the decision I made. You were the best thing to ever happen to me. And I'm always proud of you. You don't have to do anything to prove yourself to me.'

Her eyes filled with tears and she saw that Amy looked emotional too.

'Hug?' she said, and they both embraced, giggling self-consciously.

Then Amy broke away. 'Bye, Mam, call me during the week.'

That night back in bed, Bree managed to get some sleep. She felt more hopeful.

The next morning at work, Colm was wearing his worried face.

'Bree, I've just had Ryan Carty on the phone. He's just lost out on a big land deal. He's convinced that details of his bid were leaked from this office. Do you remember when you were reorganising the filing cabinet the other day?'

Bree nodded, her palms sweating.

'Is there any chance that you could have left a file lying around and someone saw it?'

She stared at him, uncertain of what to say.

Then he flushed bright red. 'Oh God, I'm sorry, Bree, I know that you're not careless. It could just as easily have been me.' He ran his fingers distractedly through his thinning hair, causing it to stand up.

Her heart thudded as she asked, 'Is it important?'

'Well, it was confidential information to do with a sale of land in Dublin for development. Carty felt that he had the perfect bid and everything in hand, but he was pipped to the post by PJ Gowan. That man has an unerring ability to just outbid him by precisely what's needed. Carty is coming here this morning, and he's a sore man. Think about who was in the office during the week. Is there any time we left the place unattended?'

In the afternoon, Colm was closeted with a furious man whom Bree took to be Mr Carty.

As he was leaving, Carty approached her. 'Colm says you were here all week and didn't go near my papers. Is that right?'

Her cheeks reddening, she nodded.

'Hey, Ryan, leave her be,' Colm interrupted as he joined them. 'I can vouch for her. Look, Ryan, we'll get to the bottom of this but leave Bree out of it.'

Grunting, the man left, slamming the door.

'Sorry about that, Bree. I think I've lost a client there. But it's a puzzle. I suppose we'd better up our procedures for dealing with confidential documents.'

Feeling sick, Bree stumbled through her day, her heart scalded by the sympathetic looks that Colm gave her.

Back at home, she stared at the bin, thinking about the money she had hidden there. It was where it belonged.

Rory was drawing her deeper into his malevolent world and she felt powerless to stop him. Where was it going to end?

CHAPTER 18

On Tuesday Colm was out for most of the morning, and Bree had some typing to occupy herself. Later in the morning, she walked to the shops to post several business letters. It was a crisp November morning, but a high blue sky failed to lighten her mood. She had received two cards in the post yesterday, reminding her that it was her birthday today. If she could, she'd have pretended the day was just another, but she knew that her mother would expect her to call around and no doubt Amy would be ringing her tonight. Her mother still insisted on baking a birthday cake for her. It would be better to call over after work and get the celebration over with. The cards were from Mammy and Anita, nothing from Amy. But then again, she wasn't great at remembering. Usually, her granny kept her in the loop about her birthday but, since the burglary, Mary had been a bit distracted. Having her home invaded had taken more out of her than she expected. Maybe she'd have forgotten to do the cake.

On her way back from the post office, she decided to treat herself and Colm to a couple of cream buns from the bakery. There was a queue in the little bakery, but it didn't take long to disperse, and she got her pastries. She hadn't much of a sweet tooth herself, but Colm loved his cakes and buns. Hopefully, tomorrow she would be able to offload some of Mammy's cake on him too. However, he would be annoyed that he had forgotten her birthday when he saw it. Colm was like an affectionate puppy, eager to please and so damned nice.

The mood of impending doom that had assailed her since she saw Rory at Amy's bedside had momentarily dissipated, and she decided to postpone all her worries for today and just try to enjoy the morning and its simple pleasures. She walked slowly back to the office.

Colm was in his little private office where he met clients on confidential business. She could hear voices. He was with a client.

She busied herself by dealing with correspondence that had come in the afternoon post. She was humming under her breath when the door to Colm's office opened, and Ryan Carty strode out. He didn't acknowledge her as he left. *Shit!* He must still be suspicious of her, and who could blame him?

Colm was standing at the door to his office. He looked oddly unlike himself. It was as if all the soft edges were removed, and he looked harder and colder.

'Colm, what's wrong?'

He glanced at her and said that he had a lot on and that he'd talk to her later. Usually, if Colm was in bad form, she could cajole him and pester him into telling her what the problem was. But there was something so forbidding and remote about his demeanour that she decided to leave him alone. Perhaps, later, he'd want to talk. Please God I haven't caused harm to his business, she thought, and Carty hasn't been bad-mouthing him all over town.

She worked solidly up to her lunch break.

Colm still hadn't left his office. She tapped on the door and opened it. 'Do you want me to pick you up something from the deli for lunch, Colm?' she asked.

He stared at her blankly. 'No, I'm not hungry.'

Usually, at that she would have made a crack about pigs flying, but today it didn't feel appropriate.

She took her sandwich to the park. It was chilly outside but she didn't feel comfortable eating in the office. Shivering, she went into a café to have a quick cup of tea to warm herself up.

She headed back to the office and had just started typing up a letter when Colm opened his door.

'Bree, come in here, please.'

His tone was so formal that she felt alarmed. Was he ill? He was in his early forties, but he was overweight and he didn't exercise. She braced herself for the worst.

The office was the usual den of messiness. The chaos that only he could make sense of. He pointed to a chair across from him. She sat down nervously. The last time she sat in this seat was when, as a girl of twenty, she had interviewed for the job.

'Colm, is everything OK?' she asked.

He shook his head and took a seat opposite her. The desk was covered with papers. Usually, when he saw a client and wanted to make a good impression, he swept the whole lot into a box hidden under his desk. On top of the mess of papers was a slim manila envelope.

They sat in silence for what seemed centuries to a now alarmed Bree. Then, he passed the slim manila envelope across to her. Puzzled, she opened the flap. Inside were several photographs. With trembling hands, she pulled them out. The first picture showed her walking into the Whitehouse Bar carrying a bag. A large folder could be seen peeking out from it. The second photograph was of PJ Gowan walking

139

into the pub. The final shot was a blurry picture of Gowan and her sitting with a thick envelope on the table between them. She stared, stunned.

He was watching her closely. 'You know, Bree, I've sat here looking at those pictures since Carty brought them in. I couldn't believe it. I sat here all day, refusing to believe that a woman I've worked with and been a friend to for nearly twenty years could betray me. But I don't doubt it now that I've seen your face.'

'Colm, I'm so sorry . . .'

He held up his hand to silence her. 'I don't want to know you're sorry, but I do want to know why, why you betrayed my trust? *Why*, Bree?'

Her heart thudded viciously against her ribs. She stared at him, unable to speak.

'Was it money? Did you need money? But surely you must have known I would have done anything for you? What a blind stupid fool I've been!'

'No, Colm, please, I'm so sorry.' She could hardly speak, horrified by the hurt she had caused.

Colm stared at her. He had never looked at her that way before. His eyes were laced with pain and contempt. They burned her soul.

'Pack up your things. I'll send you two weeks' severance pay. But you are never to step into this office again – and, Bree, I never want to see you again. So, keep out of my way. Now, get out of my sight.'

Bree struggled to her feet. She groped her way to the door, her eyes blinded by tears. She gathered up her personal belongings, a picture of Amy and one of her mother. She didn't want the plant she had bought to brighten up the office or the mug she drank her coffee out of. She picked up her coat and scarf. Pausing, she took a last look at this place that had been her haven, her means of independence and a new beginning after she left college. Her heart broke for it all but especially for the friendship that had been destroyed and the pain she had caused to a truly lovely man.

She closed the office door quietly. Outside, the weather had changed, and it had started to drizzle. Good, it provided camouflage to the tears that coursed down her cheeks. She hurried towards her car, afraid that she would meet someone she knew and have to deal with their concern over her appearance. She had no words to give them.

When she got home, she closed the front door with relief and sank to the floor. Fierce animal sobs came from deep within her. Shame, misery, and guilt swept over her, causing so much pain that she wanted to die. For a moment, she did think about ending her life. Then the misery would end. But what about Amy? She couldn't leave Amy to the mercy of that fucking monster. No, she had to live for Amy.

This had turned into some birthday. After she had washed her face and taken off her office clothes, aware that she wouldn't need them again, she went to the shops to buy a pack of fags and a bottle of wine. While in the off-licence, she picked up a naggin of whiskey as well as a bottle of wine. She never drank spirits, but tonight she reckoned that wine alone wouldn't cut it.

The phone was ringing as she opened her front door. It stopped ringing before she could pick it up. She glanced at her watch; it was gone six. *Shit!* Mammy would expect her to call for her present and to eat her birthday cake. There was no way she could go. She couldn't pretend to her mother that everything was normal. Then again, what was her entire life but a massive pretence, a lie she no longer had the energy to sustain, at least not tonight. She dialled her mother's number. The cheery voice answered.

'*Aww*, Bree, I was only after ringing you.'

'I know, Mammy, I just missed your call. Listen, I can't make it tonight. I have a blinding headache, and I'm just going to bed.'

'Oh no, pet, that's awful. I'll call around, make you a hot drink, and look after you.'

'Mammy, I'm not a child. I can look after myself. Look, let's pretend my birthday is tomorrow, and I'll call over then, OK?'

Her mother agreed, and with relief Bree replaced the receiver.

She made some toast and washed it down with black tea – she had forgotten to get milk. What was she going to do about the shit-show her life had become? Eventually, her mother would find out that she had lost her job. Hopefully, she'd never find out why. And, God, how was she going to manage all Amy's bills? Joe, Amy's dad, paid half the college fees and half her rent, so she needed to meet half of the cost of keeping her daughter in college. She needed to get another job. But where? Colm wasn't about to give her a reference. She had no qualifications, no skills. All she could think of was working as a waitress or cleaner. Neither job paid well. Her insides knotted with panic. What the hell was she going to do? She checked the calendar: Amy's rent was due in two weeks. She had some savings, but they would dry up fast unless she got work soon. Thank God that she had her two weeks' severance pay coming. Undeserved but a lifeline and a breathing space.

She wouldn't solve anything tonight. Why not get drunk? She set about it quite purposefully, drinking the wine first. She wasn't usually much of a drinker, but tonight she'd make up for her amateur status. The bottle was finished in an hour, and then she started on the whiskey. She realised that she should have got a bottle rather than a naggin. The alcohol was barely touching her. It stung her throat and chest, but she felt depressingly sober, and it was still only ten o'clock. She thought about going for more alcohol, but the off-licences would probably be closed by now, and besides there were too many gardaí around. She didn't need a drunk driving conviction. Losing her licence would limit her job opportunities even further.

The phone rang, jarring her out of her reverie. Should she answer it? It might be Mammy checking up on her. Or it could be Rory, messing with her head. What to do? Thankfully, the ringing stopped, and she slurped a little more whiskey. This was the last drop, so she better savour it. The ringing started again. Sighing, she answered it.

'*Happy Birthday to you, Happy Birthday to you, Happy Birthday, dear Ma-am, Happy Birthday to you!*' Amy warbled the song tunelessly. 'Oh, Mam, I'm sorry I forgot all about it. But Granny rang and told me not only was it your birthday but that you were sick as well. Poor you!'

'Thank you, love, but I don't care about birthdays at my age.'

'*Aww*, come on out of that, Mam, you're not even forty yet. Of course you should celebrate. How are you feeling? Granny said you had a bad headache and told me not to disturb you in case you were sleeping. But I had to check you were OK.'

'I'm not too bad, Amy.' Conscious that she was slurring slightly, she added, 'I took some cough medicine, and it's making me very drowsy.'

Amy giggled. 'That's a relief! I did think you sounded tipsy. Look, I'll leave you in peace. Love you!'

They hung up, and Bree sat staring at the receiver. She had made such a mess of things. She had played Rory's game, and look where it left her: out of a job, betraying a friend, mixed up in dodgy dealings and receiving money in brown envelopes. Then again, at least one thousand quid would ease her financial difficulties for a while. Shaking her head in despair, she wondered was this what she had come to? Who was she? Was she seriously planning on taking that crook Gowan's money? If she did, she would be sliding deeper into the pit that Rory had dug for her. No, no way. She would give the money back. If she couldn't give it to Gowan, then she'd throw it in Rory's face. But Rory would be delighted. He'd take it and spend it, taking pleasure in her misery. Perhaps she could donate it to a charity. Then at least it would do some good in the world. Her thoughts whirled and she couldn't decide what to do. Maybe wait and think it over later when she wasn't so twisted.

Long ago, she had realised that there was something wrong with Rory. She got hold of a medical encyclopaedia when she was a teenager, eager to understand her cousin and how she had fallen under his spell for so long. She learned about antisocial personality disorders. These were psychopaths and sociopaths. Crucially, sociopaths had some slight sense of right and wrong, unlike psychopaths. She learned that psychopaths could pretend to have empathy and be interested in others, but it was a ploy to use and manipulate people. It was the reason why so many people liked Rory, and he knew how to charm and manipulate. It had puzzled her for years because no one could see through him. But now she understood. Rory figured out what people wanted or needed and then set out to give it to them. He eventually became a drug for people because he made them feel special. He had made her feel special once.

She had to find a way to stop him. Amy couldn't be allowed to fall further under his spell. She wouldn't let Rory hypnotise her daughter into disaster. She would do anything to protect her daughter. *Anything*.

CHAPTER 19

Bree lay in bed, her head throbbing, her tummy feeling queasy. She kept her head on the pillow, knowing that the real pain would start once she lifted it. How would she pretend she was working when she was sacked? If she didn't get up and leave the house at her usual time, her neighbour Trish would eventually suspect something was wrong. The last thing she needed was for her mother to find out. Christ! What the fuck was she going to do? Well, for starters, get out of bed, shower, and dress. She forced herself to get ready as if it was a normal day. A cold shower woke up her body, making her even more conscious of the pain she had inflicted on herself by drinking last night. She had never been a big drinker because she feared a tendency to get maudlin and depressed might lead to confidences she needed to keep unsaid. And now was not the time to use alcohol to deal with her life. She needed all her wits about her to prevent Rory from ruining everything and everyone she held dear. He had made a good start, but by fuck he wasn't going to finish the job.

She avoided her kitchen as the very sight of food made her stomach heave. She hurried outside.

Brian, Trish's husband, was opening his front door. 'Hey, you're late. You're usually away long before me,' he said, grinning at her.

'Aye, well, I slept in,' she muttered.

Then she got into her car and drove off. Where the hell was she going to go? She drove through town and headed out towards the Cooley Peninsula. She stopped at Gyles's quay and sat huddled in her car as she stared out towards Dundalk Bay. It was quiet, and she had the place to herself. The whole world seemed to be at work. She sat until she grew cold and started the engine. She spent the morning driving around the peninsula. She stopped for a coffee in the hotel in Carlingford. Normally she loved exploring the pretty medieval town, but today her vision was turned inwards. Her stomach still churned, so she still couldn't eat.

By two o'clock, she was tired of listlessly wandering around, afraid of bumping into people she knew. She still had four hours to put in before she could go home and, getting in her car, she drove on. This was crazy. She couldn't keep wandering the county. She needed to get a job. At Omeath village, she stopped to buy a local paper and wandered down a laneway that led to the sea. It was cold, but she couldn't bear sitting in the car for a moment longer. She sat on a low wall and read the job vacancies. Most of the jobs she would usually have looked for – secretarial or clerical – were out of her reach now. Colm would never in conscience be able to recommend her, even if he wanted to. That left cleaning jobs, waitressing, or hotel work. But, while she had no experience, the real stumbling block was the lack of references. The thought of asking Colm to give her a reference and then explaining to a prospective employer why she was making such a career change was problematic. Her life was constricted, and fear tightened its grip on her.

She circled a few possibilities in the ads section. Then she thought maybe she could get work in Newry. Getting the *Newry Reporter* might be worthwhile. It was only another few miles away. But she hadn't the heart for it. Instead, she drove home.

She pulled up at her door at four-thirty. Let Trish make what she liked of it. She was feeling better and able to face food. She heated up a tin of tomato soup and had it with a slice of bread.

Her doorbell rang its silly cheerful sound. Christ! Who could it be – not Trish surely having a nose? Should she ignore it? No, better get it over with. Trying to put on a cheerful face, she opened the door to her mother and by the look on her face she knew that she had lost her job.

Mary pushed her way past Bree and walked straight into the kitchen.

'Well?' Mary said, her lips thin as she confronted Bree.

'Mammy, I'm not feeling great. Can we talk later?'

'I can see why you're not feeling great,' Mary said, lifting the empty bottle of wine from the table. Then she spotted the naggin bottle and saw all the cigarette butts piled up on the saucer and wrinkled her nose in disgust.

Bree walked to the sink and filled the kettle with water. 'Do you want a cup of tea?' she asked.

Her mother nodded and sat at the kitchen table, drumming her fingers. Neither spoke until the tea was made and poured.

'Are you going to tell me what happened?' Mary said.

'You clearly know what happened!' Bree snapped.

'OK, then, I met Colm Dolan in town this morning. He looked like he was trying to avoid me but I called him. He looked shifty, so I asked him what was wrong. He tried to fob me off, but I insisted. Bree, I couldn't believe it. He told me you no longer worked for him. Is he telling me the truth?'

Bree didn't answer, just nodded.

'Colm wouldn't tell me anything except to say that he asked you to leave. I demanded to know what happened, but he kept repeating "Ask your daughter". My God, Bree, I thought you were great friends. From the way he was acting, it sounded as if you did something terrible. What in the name of all that's good did you do, Brenna?'

Her mother's use of her old childhood name felt like a scald and she flinched. But all she could do was stare at her helplessly.

'Are you going to answer me, Bree, or do I have to go pounding on Colm's door and demand he tells me what you did?'

For a moment, Bree imagined telling her mother everything. Pouring her heart out about Rory and Coleen, about the dark miasma Rory was shedding over Amy. But she was afraid. Afraid of how things would end. She knew that Rory was emboldened by all his past successes with manipulating and destroying people. She was terrified of what he might do next. And she was afraid her mother would think she was spiralling. That Rory turning up had sent her back to the tortured time as a youngster when she was mute and broken. She was scared that her mother wouldn't believe her. She couldn't risk it.

The moment passed, and she got to her feet. 'Mammy, I don't want to talk about it. I didn't get much sleep last night, and I want to lie down for a while. You need to go.'

Mary stared in disbelief. 'Are you throwing me out, your own mother?'

When Bree didn't answer, Mary walked to the door. As she put her hand on the latch, she turned back.

'Bree, what are you not telling me? I can't understand it. Colm has always been so good to you. Why, at one time I thought you and he might get together. Did something happen between you that made it difficult for you to continue working together? I can't believe Colm would do anything inappropriate, especially not after all this time.'

Bree laughed harshly. 'No, Mammy, he didn't try anything on. Please go. I'll talk to you in a few days.'

But Mary still wasn't ready to leave. 'How are you going to manage for money?'

Bree shrugged, and then Mary whispered, 'I have a bit put by, don't be stuck.' Then she turned on her heel and left.

Bree watched TV, put on a wash, and did some long-overdue ironing. Then, at seven, she sat in front of the TV, putting in time until she had to face the bed, where she knew she would toss and turn all night long. She couldn't recall what she watched, but somehow her thoughts were subdued, and she gazed zombie-like, at the flickering set.

CHAPTER 20

A few days later, Bree received her final pay slip from Colm with a terse note asking her to call at the office on Monday at nine. When she arrived, her reception was icy. Colm avoided her eyes. Clearly he couldn't bear to look at her.

He handed her a reference. It was more generous than she deserved.

'Thanks, Colm, I really appreciate –'

'I'm not doing it for you. It's for Amy. I realise you will need to get another job to support her in college. I strongly suggest you find work in some other sphere. I don't want a recommendation of mine to come back to bite me.'

Bree flushed at the contempt in his voice. She picked up the reference, mumbled her thanks, and left.

Since she had lost her job with Colm, she had answered ads from several cleaning companies and had received a couple of job offers. They offered work in offices all over the county. The pay wasn't great, and the hours were horrible, but then it wasn't as if she had anything to do with her evenings, and she would be glad to be busy. At least now she had a reference to show them, thanks to Colm. She was just about to take the first one she applied for when she saw a flyer on her car for a new company. She rang up, and the pay was a fair bit better than the other companies. They also offered lots of overtime. She had a brief interview, and the job was hers. There were no awkward questions about her previous employment. They seemed keen to get more staff and asked her to start immediately.

They were true to their word, and she was rostered to work the next day. Someone had failed to show up for work, so they needed her at short notice. From what she gathered, she was expected to drive to some jobs but if the work was further afield, like in Drogheda, she would be collected in a minivan. It was hard to judge at such an early stage but the work was OK. She couldn't complain. The other workers were either foreign nationals or a few older Irish women. She avoided getting too pally with anyone. She was pretty sure the older women thought her stuck-up as she avoided the casual banter they engaged in. But she didn't care. She was really lucky to have got the job so quickly. The pay was less than she earned with Colm but she could supplement it with overtime.

A week later, Amy rang to say that Sandra, a school friend of hers, was having a 21st party in Dundalk on Saturday night. The pub where they hung out as youngsters offered a free room upstairs provided it got to cater for the party. She said she'd be down on Saturday afternoon. Bree debated whether she should tell her about losing her job. Clearly, she couldn't say that she was sacked, so she'd need to think of something plausible to explain why she left.

Luckily, she wasn't working on Saturday, so she would have time to spend with Amy. Not that Amy would have much time to spare as she was only arriving at four and would be heading out at eight. She hadn't seen or spoken to her since the night she rang to wish her a happy birthday.

On Saturday afternoon, Bree was cooking a bolognese when she heard Amy's key in the door. She had a battered backpack slung over one shoulder and her thick brown hair loosely tied at the back. She looked healthy and happy.

'Hey, Mam, how's you?' she greeted, dropping a quick peck on her mother's cheek.

Bree beamed at her and gave her a hug.

Amy poured herself a glass of water from the tap and leaned back against the sink.

Bree glanced at her watch. 'You're early – I thought the bus didn't get in for another half an hour.'

Amy turned away and rinsed off the glass, setting it down on the draining board. 'Yeah, well, I got a lift.'

'Oh, who with?' Bree asked.

Amy muttered, 'You don't know them. Listen, I'm going to have a look at what I'm wearing tonight, and maybe I'll have a quick shower.'

Bree was instantly suspicious. Who had driven her home? Rory or the boyfriend?

Amy pounded up the stairs, and she could hear her walking around her bedroom, opening and closing drawers as she tried on different outfits. Should she demand to know how she got home? But she didn't want a confrontation. She needed to find out what was happening in her daughter's life, and a row would not achieve anything.

They ate the bolognese she had prepared, and Bree was pleased to see Amy eat with relish and demand seconds, laughing as she rubbed her tummy. 'I need soakage for tonight.'

Bree casually asked after Jason.

Amy shrugged. 'Well, we're still going out but, to be honest, he's being a bit difficult at the moment.' She shook her head as she saw the alarm on her mother's face. 'I don't mean anything bad. He just wants me on tap for when it suits him, and I have a life. He does everything he wants and expects me to drop everything for him. But maybe this weekend, when I'm off doing my own thing, he might appreciate me a bit more.'

They washed up after dinner, and at seven Amy went upstairs to do her make-up and get ready. At eight she appeared in low-slung jeans and a bright green top. She looked like a lovely wholesome princess, and Bree ached with pride.

She drove her into town and dropped her off at the pub.

'Don't you have a gift for her?' Bree asked.

'Of course, one of the girls has it. We teamed up and got her a nice pair of earrings with a matching necklace and a bottle of wine. OK, thanks for the lift. Not sure when or even if I'll get in tonight.'

She grinned as Bree slipped a tenner in her hand, saying, 'In case you need a taxi. Tell Sandra I wished her a happy birthday.'

Bree watched as her daughter hugged a friend she met at the entrance to the pub.

She started her engine and drove home.

The house was in darkness. She thought she had left a light on. Amy must have switched it off. She fumbled for the light switch in the living room.

Rory sat grinning at her from the battered armchair. She stared at him, her heart thumping uncomfortably.

'How did you get in? I changed the locks.'

'Well, Brenna, I have friends who have taught me many useful skills, but you made it easy by not turning the deadbolt. *Tut, tut,* don't you ever learn from experience?'

'Get out, get out of my house now.' She was pleased that her voice sounded steady but adamant.

'Brenna, don't be like that. I was looking forward to a nice chat. Amy said that you've been a bit moody recently. And she mentioned she could have sworn, when she rang you on your birthday, that you had been drinking. But then that was the night you lost your job, wasn't it? So, I think we'll have to allow you a little latitude.'

'*You bastard!* Was that your plan all along to have me sacked?

'Really, Brenna, you give me too much credit. It was your friend PJ who told me you no longer worked for nice respectable Colm. I can't think how he found out about your little bit of business with PJ.' Rory grinned. 'A little bird must have informed on you.'

'Get out of my house and stay away from Amy.'

'Now, that's a bit difficult as I'm her little helper and, I'm delighted to say, her confidant. We had such a nice chat on the drive down here today. She was so sorry she couldn't invite me in. The poor child is mortified that you are so rude to me.'

'Rory, I'm warning you, don't push me too hard!'

'Or what, cousin? What are you going to do?' Lazily he got to his feet. 'I hear that you have a little job scrubbing loos – bet it doesn't pay much. But not to worry, I'll find ways to supplement your income.'

'I did what you asked, Rory. Now will you leave me alone?'

'Yeah, well, Brenna, I'll have to think about that. After all we're having so much fun. It's like the good old days.' He winked at her and walked to the door. 'By the way, your bolognese was delicious.' Then he blew her a kiss, and she heard the door slam after him.

Amy stayed out all night. Sick with worry, Bree phoned all her friends.

Eventually, after the fourth call, Amy answered. 'Mam, what the hell, why are you ringing at this mad hour?'

'You never came home last night. I was worried sick.'

'For fuck sake, Mam, I'm nearly twenty. I'm an adult. Stop treating me like a child. I told you when you dropped me off that I mightn't make it home after the party. You know I sometimes stay with a friend if it turns out to be a late night.'

Vaguely, Bree remembered Amy saying something like that, but Rory's visit had made her catastrophise. She saw only danger everywhere.

A few hours later, Amy arrived back. Her face was cold with anger. She pushed past her mother and went upstairs. Shortly afterwards, she arrived in the kitchen with her backpack slung across her shoulder.

'Are you leaving now? Your bus isn't until the afternoon.'

'Mam, what has got into you? I've heard you rang all my friends' houses at an unearthly hour demanding to know if they had seen me. I can't believe you are still treating me like a child.'

'I wouldn't treat you like a child if you told me the truth.'

'What's that supposed to mean?'

'Rory drove you here last night, didn't he? You lied and told me I wouldn't know your driver. Well?'

'For fuck's sake, Mam, you *don't* know him – you're living back in the past. He's been so sound to me and is always on at me to be kind and patient with you. It was he who persuaded me to ring you on your birthday. I wasn't going to bother when Gran reminded me. And this is how you repay him.'

'Amy, please, You have to trust me.'

Before she could utter another word, Amy laughed harshly. 'Trust you? That's a joke. One of my friends told me that you lost your job with Colm. Her dad knows him well. She said you must have had a big falling-out because Colm wouldn't talk about what happened. So, Mam, as you're so keen on trust and honesty, how come you didn't tell me that Colm gave you the push?'

Bree backed away from Amy's angry face.

'It's complicated, love, I can't explain now but –'

'Oh really, well, that's fine then. When do I have to leave college now that you're unemployed? Dad can't afford to put me through on his own, and he's got the twins to support.'

'Amy, it's fine. I can afford it. I've got another job. It pays enough to keep everything on track, I promise you. You won't have to leave college.'

'Mam, I'm not sure what to believe anymore. Rory thinks that you may be under a lot of stress. He thinks you should get counselling.'

'Rory should mind his own fucking business, and I'm warning you to stay away from him!'

Amy glared at her mother and shook her head. 'There's no talking to you anymore, I'm off.'

Her heart aching, Bree heard her front door slam.

CHAPTER 21

Working for a cleaning service proved more tolerable than she expected. One of the managers was a creep – she had to put up with him invading her personal space and staring at her boobs – but the crew and the other managers were nice. Everyone had their story, but they just wanted to get on with the job and get paid. She didn't have time to get to know them. The schedule was tight, and she wanted to keep the job. Finances were concerning, but the severance cheque helped. There was no way she was using the money Gowan gave her. So far, she had managed, and she knew that at a pinch her mother would chip in if extra expenses cropped up.

Mary called one evening, catching her before she set out on her cleaning round. By tacit agreement, they didn't speak about her old job or her reasons for leaving. She looked tired. Mary was getting older and, of course, the burglary and worry over her only child didn't help. Bree wished she wasn't a cause for her mother's drawn look. She had half an hour before she needed to leave for work, so she invited her in, and they sat in the kitchen.

Mary refused a hot drink.

'Bree, I have something to tell you. Please don't be angry, but Rory has been to visit me.'

Bree's breath stuck in her throat. She realised she was holding it so that her chest felt rigid. She forced herself to exhale. 'Go on,' she said. Her jaw felt sore, and she tried to relax it.

'He called to see me a week ago. He is concerned about Amy. He said that she's stressing out about you. She told him that you are acting out of character.'

'*How dare he say that! He's a fucking liar!*' All semblance of control had slipped, and she realised with disgust that spittle from her mouth had landed on the table.

'Calm down, Bree, you need to hear this. He has noticed that her work is slipping again, and he feels her concern about you is making her careless and distracted. She's missed lectures too.'

'OK, and what's Rory's solution? Does he want me to disappear from my daughter's life?'

'On the contrary, he believes your dislike of him is the issue. He feels he should stop coaching Amy as it is causing a rift between you.'

What was Rory playing at? There was no way he was just going to walk away.

Her mother hesitated. 'He told me what happened when you were children.'

Bree felt the room swim, and it seemed like everything had slowed right down. She heard the clock tick and the buzz of the refrigerator.

Mary pulled her chair closer to Bree and picked up her hand.

As her mother placed it between her warm ones, it felt like it wasn't part of her anymore. Her lips parted, but no sound came.

'Bree, I'm sorry. I never realised that you and Coleen had a fight that day and that you dared her to steal apples from the orchard. He thinks that you blame yourself. It explains so much of your behaviour at that time, darling. But you mustn't blame yourself. The only person to blame is that man, Patsy Cullen. He's the one who harmed her, not you. Rory thinks that you've been carrying this load for so long and that seeing him again triggered an emotional reaction. You dealt with your guilt by blaming him – and Bree, he understands. He was affected too. He realises it may have seemed like he took Coleen from you. She wanted to play with him all the time. He felt bad for years – in fact, it's why he became a psychologist. He wanted to deal with the trauma of that terrible summer.' Mary watched Bree's face and squeezed her hand. 'Love, he says he can get someone to talk to you, help you forgive yourself and move on. He gave me the names of several people who would help. Don't you see, Bree, there's a pattern to all the things that are happening? You losing your job, fighting with Amy and all the harsh things you've been saying about Rory.'

Bree pulled her hand away. 'He's poisoned you all, hasn't he?'

'Bree, please, we all want what's best for you. Rory will tell Amy that he can't help her anymore. He'll find someone else, of course, and I'll pay for the coaching.'

What was Rory playing at? Did he really mean to disappear? No, it was part of his game.

'Mammy, I'm going to be late for work.' She got to her feet, and her mother stood up too.

'Bree, will you take on board what I've said? Please, I'm worried about you.'

Bree nodded. 'Yes, of course, thank you, but now I must go. I can't afford to lose this job.'

Her mother brushed Bree's cheek lightly with her fingers. 'OK, I'll let you get on.'

* * *

Bree drove to her office block, changed into her overalls, and started emptying wastepaper baskets and hoovering. As she worked, her mind whirred and twisted. She knew that Rory was up to something. She just didn't know what, but she would find out.

The next morning, she drove to Amy's flat. The beauty of her working hours was that she had the mornings and early afternoons free. Her shift didn't start until five and finished at midnight. She sat outside. Amy had a morning lecture on a Thursday, and then her afternoon was busy with tutorials. If she knew her daughter, she would rush out to her lecture and then come home and have a late breakfast.

At eleven, Amy arrived, and Bree gave her time to get inside before she rang the buzzer for admittance. She pressed the bell and was sad to hear the suspicion in her daughter's voice when she answered. Amy buzzed her in.

The flat was the usual student shambles. Her fellow flatmates were medical students with very full schedules, so the place was quiet.

Amy was stiff but polite and offered to make her something to eat. To ease things, Bree said that she'd love a bacon butty. As Amy prepared it, she struggled to find something to say to ease the tension.

'Amy, love, I'm so sorry about the weekend you came down. I was completely out of order. I'm sorry for embarrassing you in front of your friends.'

Amy shrugged and continued preparing the sandwiches.

'Please, Amy, can't we get past this? We have had worse arguments. Do you remember when you had a party when I was away and trashed the house? I found the couch in the garden.'

Amy looked at her and then grinned. 'OK, we're quits then.'

Instantly the air lightened, and Bree felt a wave of happiness. Everything was going to be OK.

They sat down and ate the bacon sandwiches in companionable silence until Amy asked, 'But why didn't you tell me about losing your job?'

'I didn't want to worry you, and I hoped I'd find a new job before you even noticed.'

'But I don't understand. Colm wasn't just your boss – he was your friend. What happened, Mam?'

Bree shook her head. 'I'm sorry, Amy, and I promise that someday we'll talk about it but not today. But you must know the fault lay entirely with me. Colm is a good man.'

Bree heard a mewing noise behind her. A little black-and-white cat shot out from the bathroom. Transfixed, Bree stared. It was as though Daisy had been transported through space and time into the flat – her little kitten.

'Oh, sweetie, come here. I bet you're hungry,' Amy said.

Bree stood and watched, horrified, as Amy opened a can of cat food and spooned it into a pink plastic bowl.

'Mam, I know you're not keen on cats, but you cannot help but love this little one.' She picked up the wriggling creature, 'Say hi to Daisy, Mam. Isn't she adorable?'

Bree backed away – her face white. '*Where did you get that?*'

The kitten wriggled out of Amy's arms, disturbed by the raised voice.

'God, Mam, take it easy. It's only a kitten.'

'*Where did it come from?*' Bree shouted.

'Stop shouting, Mam! If you must know, Rory found it abandoned in the street. He was going to give it to a shelter, but I said I'd take care of it. Why are you so angry?'

Conscious that Amy was looking at her as though she was deranged, she forced herself to calm down. The evil bastard. The atmosphere in the room had thickened again. Her chest tightened, and she felt lightheaded.

'Mam, I think you'd better leave. I have a coaching session in fifteen minutes with Rory, and I don't think that you should be here.'

'Amy, please, you *must* stay away from him. *He's evil. Please, I'm begging you!*' She knew her voice had risen, but she couldn't bear this any longer. Her breathing became faster, and she couldn't catch her breath anymore. She gasped.

Amy was staring at her, her eyes wide with alarm. The buzzer sounded, and she raced past her mother to let the caller in.

Bree felt as though she was going to pass out. The room began to spin. Moments later, she was breathing into a paper bag and sitting slumped in a chair.

'Come on now, Brenna, you just need to take slow, steady breaths,' came Rory's voice. 'That's it, nice and easy. Amy, get your mother a glass of water.'

Eventually, her breathing returned to normal.

She watched as Rory drew Amy aside and spoke quietly to her. She couldn't hear his words, but Amy looked distressed.

He moved over to Bree and sat down. He reached for her hand, but she recoiled.

'OK, Brenna, sorry, I mean Bree, I think it would be best if I leave. I will arrange for someone else to tutor Amy, not that she needs much help now. I can see that you don't want me around. I've explained things to your mother, and perhaps Amy needs to know too. It's up to you how much you want to tell her. But remember that I'm always here if you ever feel able to talk.' He stood up and looked at Amy. 'Don't worry, love – you'll be brilliant in your exams.'

Then he smiled at Bree, winked and then left.

'Mam, what's he talking about? What do I need to know?'

But Bree couldn't speak through her dry throat. She made a couple of attempts and then just said, 'Ask your granny.'

Then she walked out, back to her car. As she rooted in her bag for her car keys, she noticed poking out of an inner compartment a small envelope. She opened it, but the note inside was blank except for a large question mark. That scared her more than words ever could. It opened an infinite vista of ugly possibilities.

CHAPTER 22

BREE

Rory was true to his word. He stopped helping Amy with her studies. The university offered up a short list of postgrad students who would be willing to work with her, but Amy refused to consider any of them as a replacement for Rory. Amy insisted that Rory didn't just help her with her work, he made her believe in herself. Bree kept asserting that she didn't need Rory in order to believe in herself. But Amy's unspoken resentment was present in their every phone call. She blamed her and hadn't been home since the encounter in the flat.

Bree was relieved that Rory couldn't assert his influence over her daughter, but still couldn't rest easy. Convinced that Rory wasn't done with her yet. She was hyper-alert, expecting another envelope with twisted instructions to materialise anywhere. Even at work, she felt nervous, terrified she'd find something hidden in her work trolley. Her sleep was poor to non-existent. Most nights, she spent tossing and turning only to doze off at 5 a.m. for a couple of hours. Then she had the long hours of the day to put through until it was time to go to work. She offered to do more shifts later at night. She might as well be busy earning money rather than tearing her bed apart in the hopeless pursuit of sleep.

In the two months since Rory had shown up, her life had descended into a chaotic mess of anxiety and fear. She tried to remember the time before that first letter arrived, ripping her life into pieces. Her life had been one of contentment if not happiness. She had built a safe world for herself and Amy, and now it was invaded by a parasite eating them up from the inside.

Mary was coming for dinner that evening. She was on her day off, and her mother suggested calling around, so Bree planned a simple dinner. First, she cleaned the house. It had been neglected and she didn't want her mother's silent disapproving gaze. She cooked lamb chops and vegetables with boiled potatoes. Wholesome food with no frills that her mother preferred. It was the first proper meal she had cooked in a while. Food had lost its appeal for her and tasted of damp cardboard.

Her mother was a little early, and she persuaded her to sit in the living room until dinner was ready. Ten minutes later, she called her to the table.

Mary seemed to relish the meal but, after an initial burst of praise for the food, they both relapsed into silence occasionally interspersed with comments about the weather and a few attempts by Mary to talk about her neighbours and their families. Bree asked about her mother's garden and somehow they got through the meal. But their nice easy companionship had disappeared.

Mary dabbed her mouth with a napkin and placed her cutlery on her plate. 'That was lovely, pet.'

Bree lifted the plates and offered a dessert of tinned peaches and ice cream.

'Sorry it's not something nicer, I meant to buy an apple tart, but I forgot.'

'That's OK, love, I've had my fill. Those lamb chops were gorgeous, really juicy, and I ate far too many spuds. Really, I couldn't eat another thing.'

Bree offered to make tea but Mary refused and Bree had no choice but to resume her seat.

'You've got very thin, lovey,' Mary said, breaking the silence.

'Still the same on the scales,' Bree lied.

Silence resumed, and Bree feared that the evening ahead would drag endlessly.

As if reading her thoughts, Mary said, 'Perhaps I will have that tea after all.'

They carried their cups into the living room.

Her mother looked uncomfortable. Bree knew the signs. Mammy had something to say and was struggling with how to go about it.

Eventually, she said it. 'Have you heard from Amy lately? I'm worried about her.'

'Why? She was grand when I last spoke to her.' Bree's body tensed. 'Has something happened?'

'She told me what happened when you called at her flat. That you insisted that Rory stop helping her with her work.'

'She doesn't need his help. It's time she stopped depending on him. Anyway, you told me that he promised to stop working with her. Besides, I said I'd pay for any extra help she needed. She wouldn't accept anyone the college suggested.'

'You may be right about her not depending on him, but she seems to be struggling now. I know you think Rory was a bad influence on her, but she seems to have lost all her confidence. Bree, I know that seeing Rory has stirred up bad memories for you, and I wish you would get some help for yourself.' She held her hand up to stop Bree from interrupting. 'OK, you're an adult and will make your own choices, but Amy is only nineteen, and I'd hate to see her messing up her opportunities in college.'

'Mammy, I have –'

'Bree, this isn't about you,' Mary said, quelling Bree with a sharp glance. 'I'm concerned for my grandchild, and maybe you should let go of your obsession with Rory and the past and focus instead on your daughter.'

Bree took a breath. No good would come of being defensive. 'Look, I'll talk to her again and see if I can persuade her to take on one of those postgrad students. They would be perfect for her, closer in age and they will know exactly how to help her. She's being so stubborn about it. In fact, why don't you encourage her to give one of them a chance? She might listen to you. They'll give the help she needs and one thing for sure is she definitely doesn't need Rory.'

Mary shook her head but didn't pursue the argument.

They shifted to safer topics and therefore ran out of things to say quickly, and soon Mary got to her feet. She kissed Bree lightly on the cheek and left. Her perfume, the same one she had used since Bree was a child, lingered in the air.

The phone rang, and Bree nervously looked at it. Her phone had become a harbinger of doom, but she still had to answer it in case Amy needed her. She picked up the receiver, taking a deep breath.

It was Leah, Amy's flatmate. Her musical Newry accent sounded crisply in Bree's ear.

'Mrs O'Hagan, I'm sorry for disturbing you. Amy will kill me, but I'm worried about her.'

'What's wrong, Leah? Is she sick?'

Leah paused and then spoke rapidly. 'If it were anyone else except

Amy, I wouldn't be so concerned, but it's just not like her. She's not going to lectures. She's out every night and in bed all day. She's like a wasp to us all. Mrs O'Hagan, Amy was always up for fun, but now she is neglecting everything. I think she broke up with her boyfriend, maybe that's it, I don't know. But myself and her friends felt you had better know.'

'Thank you for telling me, Leah. I really appreciate it. I'm going to drive up to see her tomorrow. Don't mention that I'm coming in case she tries to avoid seeing me. And thanks again – she has good friends. I'll not mention that you rang me.'

She put down the receiver. Was this more of Rory's work? He didn't come around anymore. But that wouldn't stop him from manipulating behind the scenes. She debated driving up to Dublin now. But Amy would probably be out. No, best to wait until tomorrow.

She left home early the next morning and was sitting in her car outside the flats at nine. She saw two girls leaving as she pulled up: Leah and Susan heading off to college.

She waited a few minutes, wondering again what she would say to explain her unexpected visit. When inspiration still didn't come, she figured she would just have to wing it.

In the foyer, she pressed the bell. No answer. Amy must be asleep. She kept her finger on the bell, determined that Amy would let her in.

Eventually, through the intercom, she heard Amy's irritable voice mutter. 'Who is it, and what do you want?'

'Amy, let me in this minute,' Bree demanded.

The pause went on so long that she pressed the bell again. This time she was buzzed in, and she headed upstairs.

The door was open, and Amy stood there in a filthy sweatshirt and

168

nothing else, glaring at her. She walked back into the flat and Bree followed her.

'Why are you here?' Then a look of panic crossed her face. 'Is it Granny or Dad?' she said, her fingers at her throat.

'They're all fine, Amy. I was just worried about you, and so is your granny. She thought you were very down in yourself the last time she spoke with you.'

'I'm fine!'

'You are clearly not fine, Amy. For a start, you're stinking. It's like you haven't washed in days. I don't know how you can stick yourself. And it's a Thursday, and I know you have a morning lecture. So why aren't you in college?'

Amy flushed. 'Look, I was out late and thought I'd take a day off.'

'Stop lying to me, Amy. You haven't been to lectures for days and are staying in bed all day and getting drunk every night. What the hell is wrong with you?'

'Have those bitches I'm living with been touting on me?'

Bree bit her lip – she hadn't meant to give Leah away. 'They're not bitches, they are friends, friends who are worried about you. So, get in the shower, and I'll make some breakfast because, even if you're not hungry, I am.'

Amy glared at her as she left the room. Moments later, Bree heard the shower going. She opened the fridge. Each girl seemed to have her section. She guessed Amy's shelf as it was the one populated by a decayed carrot and some past their sell-by-date sausages.

She shouted to Amy that she was going to the shop, and picked up the set of apartment keys she found on the counter. She stocked up on fruit, vegetables, some ready meals, and the fixing for a cooked breakfast. When she arrived back, she instructed a cleaner, more subdued Amy to put the groceries away and set the table. She cooked the bacon and sausages, fried a couple of eggs, and popped two slices of bread in the toaster. Then she served the food and poured them both strong tea.

The kitten wandered around mewing for attention. Bree did her best to ignore it.

They ate without speaking. Amy wolfed her food down. She obviously hadn't eaten properly in a while. Occasionally, she fed small bits of sausage to the kitten that curled affectionately around her legs.

When they had finished, Bree said, 'OK, out with it. Why are you behaving so out of character? It's not like you to slob around and skip lectures.'

'I'm just having a bad day. I'll snap out of it. Look, you can go home now. I'm grand.'

'Forgive me for not believing you. I'm here now, so how about the truth?'

Amy said nothing. She just stared at her plate.

'Leah said that you and Jason have broken up?'

Looking fierce, Amy snarled, '*Leah should keep her nose out of my business!*'

'Come on, Amy, what happened? I'm not going to leave until I find out. You know me, I'm like a terrier. I won't stop until you tell me everything.'

Amy sighed theatrically. 'Fine. He cheated on me. First, he swarmed all over me and got cross if I spent time with anyone else. He even resented Rory coming around. Then when we do what *you* wanted, and Rory stops coming over, he ups and does the dirt on me. So, Mam, thanks to you, I lost Rory and now my boyfriend.'

Bree ignored the crack at her. 'I'm so sorry. How did you find out?'

'Thanks to Rory. He caught him sucking the mouth of some girl in the pub.'

'Rory told you this?'

'OK, Mam, hold the paranoia! It wasn't just Rory – my friends saw him too. Rory just told me to save me from finding out some other way. He was great.'

'Amy, I'm sorry that you've been hurt, but you can't let college work slip. You've been doing so well.'

'Yeah, because of Rory.'

'Come on now, pet – you're a smart girl – you can do the work. I mean, Rory wasn't writing your essays for you, was he?'

Amy bristled. 'Of course not. But, somehow, he made me believe in myself. He made me feel confident. I feel like a complete fucking loser now.'

'Why not accept help from one of those postgrad tutors the college suggested. Surely they are worth trying at least for a couple of weeks?'

'It's not that simple. Rory has been guiding me for months, he knows how I work. Look, I get it, you hate Rory. Can we please just leave it alone?'

The bell for the flat rang.

'Who the hell is this now?' Amy went and pressed the intercom. 'Well?' she snapped into it.

'Amy, it's me, Jason. Can we talk?'

Amy turned to Bree. 'Get rid of him, Mam, please – he'll ring the bell all day if you don't.'

Her chin up, Bree said, 'I'll deal with him, but I want you to get ready to go to college. I don't care if you haven't any more lectures on today. I want you to speak to your college tutor and say you need some additional support. Tell him that you are willing to work with one of the postgrads he suggested. When I return, I want you ready to leave. I'll drop you off at college.'

Downstairs, Jason was still standing with his thumb wedged on the bell.

'OK, that's enough!' Bree snapped.

He whirled around. His face blanched when he saw her. 'Mrs O'Hagan, I can explain.'

'Explain what? Why you cheated on my daughter, or why you are harassing her?'

The boy flushed. He was a handsome lad. His jet-black tousled hair and dark eyes gave him the look of a friendly pirate. He was tall, and her neck ached as she glared up at him.

'I'm not trying to harass Amy – I just wanted to explain,' he said.

'Explain why you were cheating on her?'

'But I *wasn't*!'

He looked so indignant that she almost believed him. She raised her eyebrows.

'Listen, it was a crazy misunderstanding. I was at the bar, and this girl suddenly came on to me. She starts flirting, and OK, I will admit I enjoyed it, she was a looker, but then she starts snogging me. I was so surprised that I froze for a second. That's when that bastard, Rory, saw us. He drew Leah's attention to it, and before I knew it, yer one was eating the face off me. But, I swear, I didn't instigate anything. I've never seen the girl before or since. You have to believe me!'

Bree did believe him. The minute he mentioned Rory's name, she knew that, somehow, he had orchestrated the whole thing.

'Jason . . . I'm inclined to believe you . . .'

'*You do?* Oh, thank you, Mrs O'Hagan!' Tears sprang to his eyes.

'I do – and I will try to convince Amy, but it won't be easy. But . . . I'm curious why you call Rory a bastard?'

'Because he's always around! OK, he doesn't still have a weekly tutoring session with her, but he shows up everywhere we go. And she's always quoting him, shitty psychobabble stuff. She talked to him about us all the time, and I got fed up. We have argued over him, and it's bloody ironic that now he's no longer helping her with her work, we end up breaking up.'

Bree patted his arm. She had misjudged him and she understood only too well why he was feeling as he did about Rory. He obviously liked Amy and seemed sincerely interested in making things right between them.

'Jason, I promise to put in a good word for you with Amy. Without mentioning Rory, I'll tell her what you said happened with that girl, and I'll tell her I believe you're sincere.'

'Oh, thank you, Mrs O'Hagan!'

'Alright.' Bree smiled. 'Off you go then.'

Back in the flat, she tried to pass on what Jason had told her, leaving out the part about Rory. But Amy shut her down and refused to listen to anything Jason had to say. Bree decided it would be better to leave things be, at least for the time being.

Amy put on her jacket and grabbed a backpack, and Bree drove her to the campus, having extracted a promise that she would attend lectures and call her the next day.

CHAPTER 23

She found the envelope in her coat pocket. How it had got there or when baffled her. She wore the coat to and from work and supposed that someone at work could have put it in her pocket. But who did Rory know in her workplace? Most of her fellow cleaners were casual workers, some only stayed for a few days, so in theory he could have paid someone to do it. But it seemed so bizarre that he could arrange it. And, yet, apart from visits to her mother and Amy, she never went anywhere except to work. She decided to wait until after her shift to read it. But all the while, as she hoovered and cleaned, her mind was consumed by thoughts of what it might contain.

When she knocked off just after midnight, she sat in her car, hating how her hands shook as she opened the envelope.

The note was terse. **Be ready to have a visit from the gardaí on Saturday. They will ask you to confirm an alibi. You will do so! Details to follow. Don't Fail!**

* * *

In the morning, after a sleepless night, she rang her mother to ask for Rory's phone number. Bree remembered that he had given it to her when he visited.

Mary was pleased. She obviously was hoping for a rapprochement between her daughter and her nephew.

'Bree, I'm so glad that you are trying to sort things out with him. Believe me, you can't keep avoiding the past. You need to face it head-on and come to terms with it.'

'You know what, Mammy, you're absolutely right.'

Then she hung up. She stared at the number for a moment and then dialled it.

A woman answered. 'This is Mr Straffen's secretary. How may I help you?'

'I need to speak to Ro– Mr Straffen.'

'He's busy at the moment. May I say who's calling?'

'Tell him it's his cousin and that it's an urgent matter. I'm here until four o'clock.'

Rory called an hour later. 'Well, coz, this is a lovely surprise.'

'Cut it out, Rory. I'm not getting mixed up in your latest scheme. I'm not lying to the gardaí, for God knows what scum you associate with. So, fuck off and keep away from my family, or you'll regret it.'

She heard Rory sigh gently. 'Brenna, darling, this is getting a bit monotonous. You say you won't do my little tasks, and then you invariably do. Why waste time?'

'I mean it, Rory. I'm not giving a false alibi for anyone.'

'*Mmm*, I see, Brenna. Well, thanks for letting me know.'

Then he hung up.

* * *

She kept busy for the remainder of the week and obsessively checked in with her mother and Amy. A sense of impending doom settled on her, but days passed and nothing happened. She was almost beginning to hope that he had finally got bored and would leave her alone.

Then she got in from work at two on Sunday morning and all the lights were on in the house: ceiling lights, bedside lamps, and even her torch. So much for locks! She didn't even feel afraid. If this was it, then Rory was losing his touch, playing an old trick.

She put off going to bed until nearly three. By then, she hoped that she would drift away exhausted. She turned off all the lights her intruder had left on. Then she got ready for bed and slipped between the sheets. She turned off the lamp and stretched out her tired body.

That's when she felt it. At first, she thought her hot-water bottle had leaked, but it felt soft as well as damp. She jumped out of bed. Horrified, she looked down at her feet, and they were covered in a bright sticky red substance. *Christ, was it blood?* Her heart hammered – she was terrified that she would have a heart attack. Holding her nerves together, she pulled the covers off the bed. At the end of the bed was a black-and-red furry thing. Then she recognised what it was, and her stomach heaved.

The kitten – Jesus, it was Amy's kitten – lay covered in blood and gore. The blood had soaked through to the mattress. But she could see the identity disc attached to its collar with the name Daisy engraved on it. She forced herself to touch the little creature – it was still warm. Oh, God, it had been killed only recently. Was Rory or one of his hired thugs still in the house? Her heart thumped so violently she thought her chest couldn't contain it. Then she heard the front door slam.

She sat on the floor, sobbing hysterically. Her head was exploding. Getting to her feet, she wrapped the kitten in newspaper and carried it outside to bury later. Then she returned to her bedroom and stripped the bed, piling everything in a heap. She knew she couldn't face washing them. There was no way she could ever sleep on those sheets again. She scrubbed at the mattress with soap and bleach.

Even after intense scrubbing, she could still see the outline of the blood as it had seeped under the little creature's body.

She went outside to where she had put the kitten and used her garden trowel to dig a hole, as deep as she could. She didn't want foxes or dogs to get at it. The poor creature had suffered enough. Shivering, she became aware that she was both cold and wet. There was a thin mist of rain coming down. She hurried back inside. Then showered until the water went cold, and even then she stayed beneath it until she could no longer bear it.

She went downstairs, made herself a hot drink and took it upstairs. She opened the curtains, watched as the black night gave way to grey dawn, and then got dressed.

The phone ringing drew her downstairs, and slowly she lifted the handset.

'Now, Brenna, I hope you've finally learnt your lesson. You know that things will only get worse for you, right?'

Bree couldn't speak.

Rory laughed lightly. 'Now, don't worry, I'm going to look after Amy. I'll comfort her for all the many crosses she's had to bear lately – poor grades, unfaithful boyfriend, deranged mother, and now lost kitty.'

Bree spoke slowly and distinctly. 'OK, Rory, you win. I'll do what you want. But when does this end?'

'My dear, it ends in the usual way these things end. By the way, I hope you gave dear little Daisy a good send-off. Did you like my homage to *The Godfather*? Perhaps it was a little clichéd. But I think it helped you to understand the consequences of failure better. You'll get a call on Friday furnishing the details you will give to the gardaí. Have a great day, as the Yanks say. Bye, coz!'

She stood holding the phone long after he had hung up.

CHAPTER 24

The message came by phone. The almost robotic voice told her she was to wait at her house on Friday evening and make sure that she had no callers. At around 6 p.m., her visitor would arrive and give her further instructions.

On Friday, watching from her front window, she saw a grey Volvo pull up her driveway. A stocky man with grey hair emerged, carrying a gym bag. She went to the door to let him in. Every fibre in her body was tensed.

He asked her for a drink of water and sat on her couch. He crossed his legs and asked if he could smoke. His voice sounded local.

She nodded, and he offered her a cigarette. She shook her head and instead reached for her own packet.

'You need to know my name for this little operation. I'm Sam Murphy and I believe you and I are an item.' He grinned at her and sucked on his cigarette.

'What are you planning to do?' she asked.

He looked at her sharply. 'I don't think that you need to know. Now, this is what I want you to do. I'll leave at six-thirty. You'll order a pizza at seven, and when it comes act as if I'm still here – shout out something so that the delivery man can corroborate your story. In a little while, when it gets darker, I'm going to leave by your back door. Do you or your neighbours have security lights?'

She shook her head.

'Good, now tomorrow the gardaí will come here, and all you have to do is say that I was here until eleven o'clock. That's when I'll come back and collect my car. Leave the back door open and the lights in the kitchen and any outside lights off. Do you understand?'

Again, Bree nodded.

They sat in silence until, grinding out his cigarette on her makeshift ashtray, he said, 'Turn on the TV, so we can pass the time until I leave. Do you have any questions, apart from why I need your help?'

'OK, when the gardaí come, how do I explain knowing you?'

'That's easy, we met through that cleaning service you work for. I'm one of the managers. We met and hooked up. Story over!'

'But, are you part of Clean Co?'

'Well, let's just say I've recently invested in the company as well as taking on a managerial role,' he said, smirking.

Her mind whirled. Then it was no accident that she got the job at the company. It offered the best money, and that's why she took it. She wondered if she was paid more than the other cleaners. And that explained how the envelope was slipped into her pocket. Rory had been the puppet master, and she was just a pathetic object to him to be used when required.

'How do you know Rory Straffen?'

'You know, you're a nosy woman who asks too many questions. Now I suggest we sit here quietly and watch the *News*, and then I'm going to head out. Exactly half an hour after I'm gone, ring for a pizza delivery. Ask for a pepperoni twelve-inch and two portions of chips.' He threw her some money.

At six-thirty, he got up. She stood too and followed him to the front door.

'What's in there?' she asked, gesturing to his gym bag.

He caught her by the neck and shoved her against the wall. 'You really do ask a lot of questions, Bree. Rory said you would. But you know what, I don't like women who ask too many questions. From now on, you just keep your trap shut and do as you're told. Right?'

He released her throat, and she gasped, trying not to sob.

'Oh, and by the way, I'd wear a scarf in case I left any bruises on that little neck of yours. We don't want the boys in blue to notice, do we? Do you hear me? *Do you?*'

She whispered through dry lips, 'Yes.'

'Right, make sure the back door is left unlocked and the lights are off.'

Then he turned the lights out in her kitchen and, checking everywhere outside was in darkness, he left.

Her heart pounding, Bree poured herself a glass of whiskey, glad she had replaced the one she had drunk with a larger bottle. She gulped it down. Her breathing returned to normal, and her heartbeat slowed. She walked back to her living room. Her legs felt like jelly, and she was glad to sink into the couch.

At seven, she rang for the pizza. The order arrived twenty minutes later. The man who delivered it was young. She thanked the lad, paid him, and then remembered to shout inside as though someone was there. '*Sam, the food is here!*'

She closed the door and, sighing, walked back to the living room.

She tried not to think about what the man was doing. Was he

robbing somewhere, or worse, was he hurting someone? Or, oh, God, maybe he was killing someone. On an impulse, she got on her knees and prayed that no one would be harmed by Sam Murphy that night. Slumped on the floor, she sat praying for help and forgiveness all night long. She remembered prayers she thought she had long forgotten. She had given up her faith a long time ago, much to her mother's distress, but tonight the words came back. Now she clung to a God she no longer believed in.

At eleven o'clock, she heard him coming back. He snapped on the light in the living room. He was carrying a brown paper bag. The gym bag wasn't to be seen.

'Have you been sitting in the dark all night? I told you just to leave the kitchen lights off. I wanted it to look like I was here all night.'

She pointed to the curtains. 'No light gets through. It's impossible to tell whether the light is on or off.'

'OK, now pass the pizza.' He tore a slice from the untouched pizza and ate ravenously. 'Eat. I want things to look normal, like a couple sharing a pizza with maybe a slice or two left over in the fridge.'

She forced herself to swallow a few mouthfuls and covertly watched as he pulled a can of beer from the brown bag. He offered her one, but she shook her head.

'*Drink it*,' he said, opening the can.

She drank.

He looked excited but also happy – no, more like he was pleased with himself.

He drank the beer then glanced at his watch. 'OK, let's go. You walk me to the door, and we make happy couple noises. I want you to giggle like I said something funny, get it?'

She nodded, just wanting it all to be over.

He walked her outside and pulled her close. He buried his face in her neck and whispered crude words, his breath hot against her skin. 'Laugh now, really loudly.'

Bree forced herself to make a sound that resembled a laugh.

Then he tilted her backwards and kissed her hard on the mouth. His stubble rasped roughly against her face, and the harsh smell of his cologne invaded her nostrils. Then he released her and walked to his car.

He called out, '*That was a lovely evening – call you next week!*'

He started up his very noisy engine, and she noticed a few curtains twitch across the close. She stood watching him drive off.

On Saturday evening, two gardaí called.

She did her best to look alarmed. 'Is there something wrong, is it my mother or my daughter? Are they OK?' She heard the panic in her voice which wasn't entirely faked.

She recognised one of the gardaí – he had been at her mother's house on the day of the burglary. He assured her that everything was fine with her family.

Then, clearing his throat, he said, 'As you may remember, I'm Garda O'Shaughnessy, and my colleague is Garda Collins. Your family are not why we're here – it's about an entirely different matter. Can we come inside?'

Bree nodded, and when the gardaí were seated on the couch she sat across from them on the armchair.

'Will you tell me what this is all about?' she asked.

'It's just that we want to corroborate something with you. Did a gentleman called Sam Murphy spend yesterday evening here?'

'Yes, that's correct.'

'What time did he arrive? And leave?'

'He arrived at six and left sometime after eleven.'

'May I ask how you know Mr Murphy?'

Bree took a breath and then said, 'We met through work.'

'But I thought you worked for the solicitor, Colm Dolan?'

Bree looked down at her lap. 'I did, but I left. I'm with a cleaning company now.'

'That's quite a career change, isn't it?' said O'Shaughnessy.

Bree shrugged. 'The hours suit me better. I can plan my own schedule and visit friends and family during the day.'

'I see,' said O'Shaughnessy somewhat doubtfully. 'OK. Could you run through the events of the evening for us, please?'

'Why? What's this all about?'

'Just tell us, please.'

She hesitated and then said, 'Well, we watched TV, ate pizza, drank beer . . . and he left at around eleven. That's all.'

'Is your relationship with Mr Murphy of a romantic nature?'

Although Garda Collins asked this question in a fairly neutral voice, she detected a sneer.

Goaded, she snapped, 'That's between me and Mr Murphy, isn't it?'

The men got to their feet and she followed them to the door.

'Garda O'Shaughnessy, you must tell me what this is all about? Why are you wanting to know about Sam?' The urgency in her voice was genuine. She needed desperately to know.

O'Shaughnessy signalled to his colleague to get in the car. He turned to face her.

'Bree, I've known your family for years, I know men at the station who worked with your dad. He was a fine man. What are you doing hanging around with a lowlife like Murphy?'

Bree ignored the question. 'What's he supposed to have done?'

The garda sighed. 'I shouldn't tell you this but there was a break-in at a house in Drogheda, and a man was badly beaten. Your friend was seen in the vicinity, and let's just say he has form with this kind of thing. I'd advise you to keep away from him.'

He turned to go, then stopped and came back.

'If he's forcing you to cover for him, we can protect you. Now's the time to speak.'

Bree backed away. 'He has no hold over me. We spent a pleasant evening here, and that's all there is to it.'

The garda stared at her intently and then sighed, shook his head in disbelief and joined his colleague in the patrol car.

Bree was conscious of Trish putting rubbish in her bin. She hurried back inside in case she came sniffing for information.

CHAPTER 25

For the next few days, Bree avoided the town, her neighbours and her mother. The news would have got around that she had the gardaí at her house. She didn't know what to say if she was asked. It was easier to ignore the phone and the doorbell, at least during the day.

On Wednesday when she arrived back from another late-night cleaning, she saw the brown package on her mat. She picked it up and threw it on the kitchen table. It was sealed with masking tape. She got scissors and opened it up. Inside was a thick wad of money. She counted it, five grand in used notes. This was her reward. Rory had her in a trap. The more jobs he got her to do, the further she became involved in the criminal world and the more he had to blackmail her with. But the biggest hold he had over her was his influence over Amy. What he did with Amy's defenceless kitten sent a message about what he could do to Amy. She still hadn't decided what to do with the money. Giving it to a charity seemed the best option but she felt incapable of making a decision. Sighing heavily, she rewrapped it and placed with the rest of the money under the liner of her bin.

How did Rory have so many connections with thugs and criminals? She felt the walls of her kitchen close in on her. This house had been her sanctuary, her safe place, and Rory had soiled it. She knew that locks and alarms couldn't keep his thugs out. Somehow, they had copied her keys, probably while she was at work, or Rory had taken Amy's. It would be easy to get them copied and for Amy to believe she had mislaid them as she was wont to do. She could change the locks again but, knowing Rory, he'd find a way. Tiredness and hopelessness sucked at her, leaving her empty. Again, she thought of suicide, but the thought of how Amy would then become even more vulnerable terrified her. She had to fight for her daughter.

It dawned on her that all her attempts to resist Rory ended in appeasement, and the more she appeased him, the more he embroiled her in his sick world. Should she tell her mother about how Rory was manipulating her? Mammy loved her and protected her as best she could. But she would see this as part of Bree's illness as a child. She had seen the broken child and teenager she was. She had seen how Rory's *supposed* death had rejuvenated her. Her mother would believe her fixated and paranoid. Rory had planted so many seeds in her mother's mind when he visited her. The fact that she had lost her job and alienated her boss and friend Colm would feed her belief that Bree had spiralled into paranoia and obsession. Besides, telling Mammy was too dangerous. God only knew what Rory might do in retaliation and she couldn't risk her mother or Amy's life.

What could she do? She had to fight back. There must be a way out. She didn't have the luxury of quitting. But she needed help to figure things out. She badly needed answers to the questions that swirled around her head. What happened to Rory when he returned to England after their summer together? Why did he fake his death?

What did he do for all those years after he was resurrected? Where did he go? What did he do? If she could only find those answers, then she might have some way of combating him. She needed someone to find out about him and maybe give her something to fight back with. A private detective! That's what she needed. Where did you find one? Did you look them up in the Golden Pages?

Grabbing her copy from the hallway, she flicked through it. Yes, there were listings, mainly in Dublin. But how did she know if they were any good? Anita! Anita worked in the Criminal Justice system. She was bound to have met and maybe used private detectives. It was too late to ring her now. But first thing in the morning, she would contact her.

It was after ten when the morning light streaming into the bedroom awakened Bree. She felt hopeful and purposeful now that she had a plan.

She had worked out what to say to her friend. Thankfully, Anita was unaware of her work situation and hopefully would supply the information she needed. She dialled Anita's mobile phone. She was one of the few people she knew who had one.

'Hey, stranger, how're tricks?' Anita said, her voice cheerful. 'I'm at the courts now, but we could chat later.'

'I'll be quick. Look, a friend of mine thinks her husband is playing around, and she wants to check up on him. She wants to make sure that if he's planning to leave her that he doesn't screw her over financially.'

'Feckin' men – that's why I'll never marry,' Anita said. 'So, how can I help?'

'She needs to gather evidence that he's having an affair, and I wondered if you could recommend a good private detective.'

After a pause, Anita said, 'Well, sometimes we've used this guy who's an ex-garda. I think he may have been forced to leave the Garda, but he's a good man for finding out information. He's pricey though, and based in Dublin.'

'That sounds good, Anita. My friend's husband works in Dublin, so it makes sense to find someone based there. Do you have an idea of how much he charges?'

'I reckon about two hundred a day and his expenses. He's not cheap, so hopefully your pal has deep pockets.'

Bree thought about the money hidden in her waste bin. 'Yeah, she has the money.'

'Look, Bree, my case is being called, and I have to go. I'll call you later and leave a message with his contact information on your answerphone. It'll be there when you get home this evening. Say hi to Colm for me. OK, bye!'

After she hung up, Bree retrieved the money she had hidden at the bottom of her bin. She dropped it on the table beside the other wad of cash. She had six thousand grand to spend on a private detective. Enough to keep him on Rory's trail for weeks. She would get the information she needed to rid herself of him or, at least, give her some weapons to defend herself and her small family.

Maybe having a plan of action made her feel hungry, but suddenly she was ravenous. The fridge was bare and she badly needed to replenish her supplies. Grabbing her keys, she went to the supermarket and bought herself provisions and some beef and vegetables. She planned to make herself a hearty beef stew. It was time she took care of herself. Her mother was right – she was losing weight, surviving on cigarettes and coffee. If she was going to fight Rory, she needed to keep her strength up.

When she got back from the shops, she checked the answering

machine. Anita had been true to her word, and left contact details for
the detective. Bree wrote his name, address, and phone number down.
Then she ate so much stew that her stomach ached.

She made her plans. She would ring him, make an appointment,
and go up and see him as soon as he could see her. There was no time
to wait about for Rory's next Game.

Feeling a sudden sense of urgency, she picked up the phone in the
hall and dialled. The phone rang and rang: no answer. Frustrated, she
slammed it down. Then, clenching her jaw, she proceeded to call the
number every half hour. It was on the seventh call that she got lucky.
It was answered on the first ring.

'Cassidy speaking.'

Now that she was through to him, she was suddenly tongue-tied.

When she hadn't answered, he snapped, 'Well, what do you want?'

In a rush, she said, 'Mr Cassidy, I want to speak with you. I have a
job for you but I need to see you in person.'

'Is it a domestic matter?'

'What do you mean?'

She could hear him sigh.

'Do you want me to keep tabs on your husband?'

'No, I'm not married, but I need you to find out about someone
for me. It's complicated.'

The detective laughed harshly. 'It always is – look, I can see you
tomorrow at nine?'

'Can we make it a bit later? I'm travelling from Dundalk.'

'No can do, I'm on a job all day. The next available appointment
will be on Wednesday.'

'OK, I'll make it for nine tomorrow.'

'OK, don't be late. I can give you half an hour, and then I have to
leave.'

'Fine, I'll be there,' she said, but he had already hung up.

Her body tingled when she walked back to her kitchen. She felt energetic and empowered. The man sounded unfriendly but, strangely, that pleased her. She had her fair share of sympathetic professionals dealing with her as a child, and their sympathy and compassion had made her feel unworthy, forcing her to retreat deeper into her painful shell. They hadn't helped her, but this man, who sounded indifferent and cold, filled her with hope. She didn't need kindness. She needed toughness and logic, not handholding.

Glancing at the clock, she saw that she was running late. Hurrying upstairs, she got dressed in jeans and a baggy jumper – her work clothes. On the drive to her job, she noticed that she was humming. It felt good. She tackled all her tasks at work with vigour. The night flew by quickly.

When she got home from work, she retrieved the money she had hidden and put a grand of it in her handbag. On TV shows, detectives always wanted a retainer. She put the rest of the money in a plastic bag and put it back in the bottom of her kitchen bin. It didn't make her shudder anymore. Now, it offered the possibility of freedom from Rory.

She set her alarm clock for six in the morning, not thinking she'd sleep, but amazingly she did, and the harsh ring of her clock awakened her. Time to take control of Rory's Game.

CHAPTER 26

Bree left Dundalk at six-thirty and was parked across the road from the detective's place of business by half past eight. She had missed the worst of the traffic, and Drumcondra was the right side of the city for her.

Cassidy's office was located above a butcher's shop. She had a while to kill, so she found a café, ordered tea and toast, and gathered her thoughts. How much should she tell him? He needed to know enough to make him want to take her case, but she was afraid of revealing too much. At five to nine, she crossed the busy road and walked into the side entrance of the butcher's shop. She climbed up a steep flight of stairs. The smell of blood and cold meat permeated the air as she stood outside his door. She had imagined he would have a glass half-door with his name and occupation splashed across the front, like in the Sam Spade movies she remembered from her childhood. Instead, she faced a plain brown door and a bell on the wall. Taking a breath, she pressed it.

The door was pulled open, and she stared at the man in front of her. He beckoned her in and pointed to a small hard chair. Cassidy was in his mid to late fifties, tall and stocky. He had a thin layer of stubble on his chin, which he was in the process of banishing with the aid of an electric shaver attached to a wall-socket.

She started to speak, but he held up his hand. He finished shaving, put the razor away and sat down.

'OK, Ms O'Hagan, what can I do for you?'

She stared at him, suddenly scared by the enormity of what she was about to do.

'Look, love, I can only spare you half an hour, but if you want to waste it staring at my ugly mug, go right ahead.'

His voice sounded harsh, and everything about him was crusty and edgy. He didn't inspire confidence, and yet Anita had recommended him. Finally, Bree made up her mind. She had to take the chance. It might be her only one.

'I want you to find out everything you can about this man,' she said and handed him her brief notes on Rory.

He scanned them briefly. 'Do you have a photograph?'

She rooted in her handbag and pulled out the envelope containing Rory's old memorial card.

'Is this some kind of joke?' he said, scanning the card. 'I'm not in the business of tailing dead people.'

'Sorry, he's not dead. There was a mix-up, and he was misidentified. At the time, he was estranged from his family, and it suited him to be dead, but his stepdad found him a year later.'

'But this card is dated more than twenty years ago. Haven't you anything more recent?'

'No, but he still looks much the same, just older. He still has the same streak of white hair.' Seeing that Cassidy still looked

193

unconvinced, she added, 'I can tell you where he works. He has a teaching post at UCD, and I think he has a private practice somewhere too. He's a psychologist. Please, I really need your help.'

'What exactly do you want to know about him?'

'Everything, from his childhood onwards, but especially about the time that he supposedly died. I need to know if there is anything shady about his dealings, whom he associated with in England and how he got his job here in Dublin.'

Cassidy sat back, contemplating her. 'Why do you want this information?'

'I can't say.'

'I see. Well, in that case I can't help you.' He glanced at his watch.

'Wait, he's causing trouble for my family and me. He's blackmailing me and making me do things I don't want to.'

'Sexual things?'

'God, no, we're cousins.'

''That doesn't always act as a deterrent.'

'Look, Mr Cassidy, I can't go into it with you now but, please, I'm begging you for help.'

Bree was aware of the desperation in her voice.

'I don't do anything illegal or work for criminals. I may not be a garda anymore, but I still respect the law, well, most laws.'

'I promise you I just need information.'

He stared at her intently. 'Anything else you need to tell me?'

'He goes by the name Rory Straffen now, I don't know why, as his father, my mother's brother, was Brown, and his stepdad is called Philip Morris. I need to know whatever you can discover.'

'A lot of this background is in England. I'll have to go over. It will be expensive.'

'Look, I have six grand available for this purpose. You can keep on investigating until the money runs out. I need you to get to the bottom of things so do whatever you have to.' As she spoke she wondered if it was wise to tell him how much money she had. He could string her along and do nothing.

'OK, my rate is two hundred a day plus expenses. You need to factor in the costs of travel. I'll furnish you with receipts. Leave me your name and address, and I'll send you a report in a week. I need five hundred in advance. Are you in agreement?'

Bree nodded and reached out her hand. Cassidy took it in his massive hairy hand. It reminded her of her father's farmer's hand, and she felt it was a good omen. She had faith that if there was something to find, Cassidy would find it.

On the drive home, she decided to call to see her mother. Mary was sitting in her conservatory, and from the driveway Bree could see that she was doing a crossword puzzle. Mary waved her in, and they worked on the puzzle together, just like in the old days when they lived together.

When they had completed it, Mary made them a pot of tea. They sat companionably sipping tea and watching the rain as it came slanting down, hitting the windows. Bree had always liked watching the rain, enjoying the warmth and security of home, safe from the elements. They both stared in silence out of the window into the sodden garden.

'Bree, are you OK?'

Bree's mother's voice dissipated her somnolent mood, and she became alert and cautious. 'Of course. I'm fine. Don't I look fine?'

Mary looked her up and down. 'You're very thin, and there're dark circles under your eyes, but you do seem in much better form today.'

'Mammy, I'm eating well. In fact, I made a stew the other day.' Bree neglected to mention that she had frozen most of it.

'Good, I'm glad to hear that. How's work going?'

Bree was conscious of the disapproval in her mother's voice. 'It's a job, Mammy, something to tide me over until I get a better one. At the moment, it suits me fine.'

'Why did the gardaí call to your place the other day?'

Mary's abrupt change of subject startled Bree.

'How the hell did you hear about that? Of course. Trish Riordan. You play golf with her mother. Ya can't sneeze in this place without people commenting.'

'Well, why did they call?'

'It was nothing, just a query about the whereabouts of a friend.'

'The friend you were kissing at your front door,' said Mary.

'Oh, for heaven's sake, can I have no privacy? Has Trish nothing else to do with her time than yap about me to her mother?'

'Bree, who is he, and why are the gardaí asking you questions about him?'

'Mammy, will you give it a rest? He's just someone I know. As for the gardaí, it was no big deal.'

'I'm just worried about you, love – you're behaving so strangely, it reminds me of . . .'

'Of what? Of when you had me locked up when I was a kid?'

'That's not fair, Bree. Your dad and I were worried sick about you. You didn't speak for nearly a year, and then you had such horrible dreams. We thought it was for the best. To get you the help you needed.'

'Well, it didn't help – only one thing helped: Rory, dying.'

'That's a terrible thing to say. I know you associate that terrible summer with Rory, but he cared about you. He wrote to us for months after he went back to England. Julie and he even came to visit when you were in the hospital.'

'What, Rory was here all those years ago? I thought he went back to England and didn't come back here until a few years ago.' Bree's fingers clenched the arms of her chair.

'I didn't want you to know that he came over after you were admitted to the hospital the first time. I was afraid it would upset you. Poor Rory was devastated that you were still so traumatised by what happened that summer in Sligo. He felt guilty about how he had taken Coleen from you. He was only a gossoon himself when he came over, about sixteen. He was desperate to see you, but we were afraid it would make you even worse. In fact, the doctors said you got hysterical every time his name was mentioned.'

Bree sat back, sickened at the thought of Rory enjoying the horror he had created and relishing his heroic role. He must have loved having her parents lap up his lies and fake remorse.

'Your Aunt Julie was very concerned about him. She felt he was taking too much responsibility on himself for your well-being. Bree, can't you see you need help coming to terms with your childhood? It's not too late. I still have the numbers Rory gave me. In fact, I called one of them. The lady was so lovely. I know that she can help you. Won't you let me make an appointment?'

'No, I don't want any more interference in my life, and I don't want any of Rory's help either.'

Bree got to her feet and walked out of the conservatory.

'If you won't get help for your own sake, do it for Amy – she needs you.'

Bree stopped in her tracks and stared at her mother.

'I'm Amy's mother and I know what's best for her and you know that I always have her best interests at heart.'

'I know that you believe that Rory is some kind of evil villain, but he really cares about Amy. He told me about her wee kitten going missing. He blames himself for giving the creature to her in the first place.'

Bree started to laugh – a hard, angry sound. 'Does he indeed!'

'Bree, you must see that you're not rational where Rory is concerned.'

'Mammy, it's fine, I called to see Amy last week, and she promised me that she'd get back on the straight and narrow.'

'Well, she hasn't.'

'What do you want me to do?'

'Let Rory come back to help her catch up on her work.'

'*No!*' Bree walked out and slammed the door behind her.

CHAPTER 27

Cassidy's report landed on her mat exactly a week from the day she had visited him. It was inside a large manila envelope with a London postage stamp. She tore it open eagerly. It was two typewritten pages. She sat down to read them, her hands clammy.

Please let it be useful, she prayed.

REPORT ON RORY BROWN, AKA RORY STRAFFEN

RB was the only child of Daniel and Julie Brown. He was born nine months after their wedding. His father worked in the shoe industry in Northampton, and his mother was a housewife. He attended Penford PS in Northampton. After his father died, his mother married Philip Morris. They moved to London, where he attended St Mark's High School. He left after he completed his O-Levels. He then went to King's Holt to do his A Levels. He achieved three A levels.

In 1966, at the age of eighteen, it appears he got involved with a gang. He was cautioned several times for anti-social behaviour. It is also believed that he was involved in using and selling cocaine. He had been offered a place in college but didn't take it up. A few months later, his body was identified in the wreck of a burnt-out stolen car. Although the body was badly damaged in the fire, his stepfather recognised a watch he was wearing. It had been stolen from him by Rory a few weeks earlier.

In 1967, Rory resurfaced. He claims that he had run away and hadn't realised his friend's body had been misidentified as his. He was arrested for possession of cocaine, and his stepfather was contacted. Rory eventually returned to the family home, but the reunion was not happy. His mother became ill and was hospitalised for severe depression shortly afterwards. Around this time, Rory changed his name by deed poll to Straffen. I have no information as to why he chose that particular name at this time.

In 1968, he was offered a place at King's College London to study psychology. His stepfather supported his college education. He went on to attain a Master's Degree and a PhD in Psychology.

In 1976, he worked in a variety of areas. He was a researcher at Cambridge, and then he worked in several psychiatric hospitals throughout England and Wales.

From 1981–1984, he worked at Mulderfield Psychiatric Hospital.

From 1984–1987, he started a successful private practice on Harley Street.

In 1987, he moved to Ireland and was headhunted for a job at St Philomena's Mental Hospital. He worked there from 1987–1989.

In 1989, he accepted a position as a lecturer in psychology at University College Dublin. He still holds this position but also has a private practice in Rathmines.

INTERVIEWS

That is the bare bones of his history. There is probably little that you don't already know. But there are a few interesting leads I want to follow up on.

The next pages are interviews with former colleagues giving their impressions of RS as a colleague and a practitioner. It wasn't easy to get access to the names of his clients, but many of the patients he treated are still in Mulderfield. The staff there would only speak if I didn't use their names. But I have passed on their insights.

Source A

Worked with RS for two years. He spoke warmly of RS. He described him as warm and empathic in his dealings with patients and staff. He facilitated many changes in the working environment that positively impacted both staff and residents. RS took a great interest in some of the most damaged patients, often going above and beyond to support them.

Source B

Worked for a year with RS. She found him to be a professional co-worker. [I sensed something behind the formal way she spoke about him and pressed her.] She admitted that although initially she had liked RS, she became concerned by some of his actions with patients. She felt that, at times, he instigated changes that occasionally resulted in conflict. Many of the patients vied for his attention, and she was concerned that he was creating an environment where favouritism flourished. She was also disturbed by what she termed a 'secret code' that existed between his patients, as though they were a special elite group. She brought her concerns to her manager but was accused of professional jealousy.

Source C

He no longer works at the facility but Source B gave me his

contact details. He was initially nervous about talking to me as he feared it might impact him professionally. I reassured him of confidentiality, and he agreed to speak to me in a local pub. He insisted I didn't record him. He is in his late forties. He worked with RS from 1985–1987. Initially, they had a cordial relationship. RS was new to the hospital, anxious to learn the ropes, and keen to learn from his colleagues. He was open to taking advice and direction and was a refreshing change from many new employees who felt they knew everything. RS was keen to establish a good relationship with him. Flattered, he was quite open with his new colleague, thinking he could act as his mentor and advisor. RS had the ability to inspire affection and loyalty in his colleagues.

But gradually he noticed that RS undermined his authority in private whilst appearing to take his side publicly. Patients with whom he had a good rapport suddenly started making accusations about him or refused to attend his therapy sessions. Over time he felt he lost the confidence of his colleagues and had a strong feeling that RS had created this atmosphere of distrust. C stressed that he had no evidence to prove this, but he sought another position for his professional and emotional well-being. Towards the end of our chat, he became tense and said that he believed RS was a disrupter. He was glad to hear that he no longer worked in Mulderfield.

He mentioned two patients RS treated and expressed concern about the impact of their treatment. Because of confidentiality issues, he referred to them by aliases.

SOL DANE (patient in his early forties, committed to Mulderfield for the murder of a family member when he was 15 years of age. He has been diagnosed with a Personality Disorder)

Sol had spent five years in the hospital when RS started treating him. Prior to treatment, Sol appeared depressed but calm. He had no interest in engaging with psychological services, but on meeting RS he decided to accept treatment. Within weeks he appeared to improve and was engaging in social activity with other patients. He played cards and table tennis. The staff were very impressed that he had come out of his shell. Then one day, he attacked a nurse, biting and kicking him. He claimed that his master had told him to stage this attack. He refused to explain who his master was. When he was denied the privileges he had previously enjoyed, such as the use of the rec room and the games room, he became violently disruptive and had to be sedated. All the while, he demanded he receive his 'reward'.

The hospital administrators felt that he had developed an unhealthy fixation on RS, and therefore their appointments were terminated. On meeting his new therapist, he was initially cooperative but then, as the session was ending, he punched him violently about the head. During the attack, he smiled constantly.

The next day it was discovered that he had obtained photographs of his surviving family, which was strictly against the terms of his incarceration. He claimed that seeing his family offered him 'solace'. He begged to have his appointments with RS continue. It was felt that it would be unwise to have these sessions continue. His medication was reviewed and increased at the suggestion of RS. A male orderly was suspected of obtaining the photographs for Sol and was sacked. The orderly denied having anything to do with it, but more photographs of Sol's family were found in his locker, which sealed his fate. Sol's relatives claimed they were stolen from their home during a recent break-in. (My source claimed that the orderly had been involved in a dispute with RS. In his opinion, the orderly had neither the knowledge nor the ability to access these photographs.)

NEIL COTTON aged 18 years. Committed by reason of insanity. He set fire to the family home, killing his two brothers when he was thirteen.

Neil was a highly agitated patient. Diagnosing his case was challenging, and the psychiatric team struggled to label his condition. He became a patient of RS and initially showed amazing progress. He became calmer and less talkative. He had requested that a toy that he once had as a child be returned to him. But his family had destroyed all his belongings, including this toy, and moved to another country. RS arranged for him to participate in a supervised craft class where he was allowed to choose fabric and fashion a little substitute. He chose the fabric and material for stuffing it, and the craft teacher sewed it up for him. He was allowed to keep it. It appeared to give him a great deal of comfort. His demeanour was calm and controlled for weeks after this until one day he became distraught, saying RS had stolen his pet. He became highly agitated and begged to see RS. When he had his usual appointment, he appeared calm, but that night he repeatedly banged his head against the wall of his room. He was discovered covered in blood and unconscious. He sustained severe brain damage and died six months later.

The source claimed that RS had a negative influence on this patient. He believed RS encouraged an unhealthy dependence on him, but when C spoke to his supervisor and he voiced his concerns. He was told that he was threatened by the work of a more successful therapist and was making complaints out of professional envy.

Ms O'Hagan, I plan to investigate the time RS spent after he 'died in the car crash' up to his re-entry into his family's world. I will send the report of my discoveries shortly, and we can meet to discuss my findings.

Bree read and reread the report. She knew about many of the details outlined in it, but she was interested in the comments of Colleague C. It appeared Rory had been busy manipulating people for quite some time and had got better at it. Was that why he studied psychology, to better control and manipulate? It seemed like he got some perverse kick out of acting as a puppet master.

CHAPTER 28

AMY

Amy lay on her back smoking a joint. She was tired. Everyone was on her case. It was so fucking unfair. Her last essay was a scrape-through. Without Rory's help, she lost focus. Yes, she wrote the bloody essays, he didn't write them for her, but somehow he made her feel she could do anything. He made her feel stronger, cleverer, and even prettier. Bloody Mam and her neurotic hang-ups. Sure, she had a bad experience while a kid, but really, all this transference crap, putting all her stuff on poor Rory, was so unfair. Even Granny agreed. And what was with her, losing her job with Colm? It had been a cushy number. But now she was a cleaner, for Christ's sake. OK, it was snobbish, but it was cringe to say your mother cleaned offices for a living.

They used to be so close. Back when she was at school, her mates were jealous of her relationship with her mam. She never felt ashamed of coming from a one-parent family. I mean, it was the 90's, and it wasn't so unusual anymore. In fact, she felt proud of her mother. But now it felt that Mam wanted to spoil everything for her. It was completely unreasonable to force Rory to stop helping her. It seemed like when Rory went off the scene, everything went south, Jason did the dirt on her, Mam went full nut-job, and poor little Daisy disappeared. She sighed as she pictured her sweet little face. Daisy was probably dead somewhere, knocked down by a car. She just wished that she could be sure she wasn't lost and terrified or that some evil bastards weren't tormenting him.

The buzzer in her flat went. She got up and hit the intercom. 'Come on up,' she said without bothering to find out who it was.

When she pulled her door open, Jason stood there. It was a pity he was so fucking hot. All her friends went on and on about what a ride he was. Well, he was riding someone else now.

She glared at him. 'What do you want?'

'Amy, can't we just talk calmly for a minute?'

'I told you to stop coming around.'

'I will if you just give me a fair hearing.'

'OK, fine, but answer me this – did the girls and Rory spot you snogging that girl in Goggin's? Yes, or no?'

'Amy, please, it's not that simple. Give me a chance to explain.'

'I said yes or no.'

'OK, yes, but *she* was kissing me. She came on to me.'

'Oh, poor irresistible you! Was it your aftershave that drove her wild with passion?'

Jason ran his fingers through his mop of hair. It wasn't its usual shiny perfection today. She was glad to see it looked lank and greasy like he hadn't washed it in a while. For a moment, she almost believed him. Should she give him a hearing?

Her buzzer went again. 'God, it's like a fucking railway station here!' She stomped over to the intercom. 'Yes!' she snapped.

Rory's voice floated from below. 'Can I come up?'

She pressed the button.

'What's *he* doing here? I thought you weren't working with him anymore!' Jason said.

'*What's it to you?*' she snarled.

Rory arrived and smiled at them both. 'Oh, I'm glad. It's forgive-and-forget time, is it? Should I go?'

Jason shouted, '*Yes!*' and, at the same moment, Amy said, 'No, stay.'

Rory looked questioningly at Amy. 'I'll do whatever you like, pet.'

'She's not your bloody pet!' Jason said, walking towards Rory with fists clenched.

Rory held his ground. 'Easy, man, I'm just looking out for Amy. Maybe you should back off.'

'No, maybe you should piss off. You're always here perving on Amy. Isn't she some sort of cousin?'

Amy grabbed Jason roughly by his arm. 'Right, get out now. Know what – I'm glad you cheated on me. At least now I don't have to put up with your jealousy and stalking. Go on, get the fuck out!'

Jason stared at her. 'Is this what you really want?'

She spoke slowly and clearly. 'Yes.'

He left, slamming the door, and she burst into tears.

Rory took her in his arms, and she sobbed noisily on his shoulder. He let her cry for a few minutes and then held her face and looked at her with those steady blue eyes. Eyes that held her mesmerised.

'OK?' he asked, taking out a handkerchief and giving it to her. 'Don't mind about a ladylike sniff – give it a good blow and mop up those tears.'

She slumped onto the saggy couch, and he fetched her a glass of water and then sat on a stool opposite her.

'Are you ready to talk now?' he asked quietly.

She sniffed and smiled through watery eyes. 'You won't want this hanky back, I'm thinking. I'll wash it for you.'

He grinned. 'Keep it.' He reached into his jacket pocket and pulled out a bar of chocolate. 'Come on. No girl can resist some nice milk chocolate. Now, how about you make us a nice cuppa, and we can chat properly.'

Amy laughed and went to put the kettle on.

When they were seated on the sofa again, balancing mugs of tea on their knees, she asked, 'How come you're here, Rory? Not that I'm not happy to see you, but I thought that Mam had banned you.'

'Hey, don't be hard on your mother. She means well. As I explained before, my return to her life has triggered bad memories, and I wanted to spare her any more grief and stress. But your grandmother contacted me, and she's very worried about both of you.'

'Why, what's wrong? Is Mam OK?'

'Your gran said that she's been behaving strangely since she left her job.'

'What, more strangely than usual?' Amy said, raising her eyebrows.

'Hey, come on, don't be like that. She can't help it. We all need to support her.'

'Fair enough, but why's Gran worried about me?'

'She heard from your mother that you're neglecting your work at college, skipping lectures and generally malingering.'

'Hey, that's not fair!' she said indignantly, then she saw Rory was laughing at her.

'OK, she didn't say you were malingering, but she is worried, and frankly so am I. Come on, love, you need to buck up and really get down to work. You and I both know what you are capable of. Your last essay barely arrived on time and wasn't up to your usual standard.'

'Well, you haven't been around to help,' Amy said, glaring at him.

'Now that's rubbish. You know that you are more than capable of doing the work. In fact, even if your mother hadn't been upset, I would probably have stopped coaching you anyway. You, my pet, are ready to fly solo. You are just using me as an excuse for avoiding work. Now how's that for a bit of reality?'

'But —'

'No buts. Now, tell me, what's really going on?'

Amy looked away. 'It just seems that everything is going wrong. Mam's gone weird, the kitten disappeared, Jason cheated on me, and then you stopped coming over.'

'Well, I'm here now, and we can talk as we have always done.'

'Yeah, and that helps so much. You made me see that Jason was controlling me with his jealousy. I would have continued to run after him like a needy baby, if you hadn't helped me see how he was putting me down, and putting himself first always. The cheating was the last straw. You know what? If you hadn't shown up when you did just now, I might even have been dumb enough to have given him a second chance.'

'Amy, he's not a bad guy, just a bit immature. Maybe he deserves a second chance, but you must ask yourself "What do I deserve? What does Amy need?" How would you answer that?'

Amy impulsively leaned in and kissed Rory. He pulled back.

'Oh, God, I'm sorry,' she whispered. 'I didn't mean to do that. Please, please don't be angry, Rory.'

He looked at her, startled. 'I think I'd better go now. Maybe your mother is right, and I should keep away from you.'

Amy gulped and hung her head. She felt like a scolded child as she waited for him to leave. She heard him walk to the door and shut it after him. The silence in the flat was dense.

But, amazingly, the door opened again. Rory had come back. He stood looking at her and then opened his arms. She ran into them.

He rained kisses on her cheeks, hair, and eyes, and, finally, he kissed her softly on her lips. As he looked at her, it seemed to Amy that everything in the world had faded, and all she could see were his beautiful eyes.

He groaned. 'You are so very lovely, Amy, but this is wrong. I shouldn't have come back.'

'I'm so glad you did,' Amy whispered.

Abruptly, he released her, and then he did leave.

She heard the door shut and the sound of footsteps running down the stairs. And her heart sang. She realised now that she kept arguing with Jason because he saw what she was blind to – the attraction between her and Rory. Oh God, did she just kiss her cousin? What sort of cousins were they? Not first, maybe second or maybe her first cousin once removed? Oh God, it was practically incest. But her entire body tingled, and she felt elated as though she was encased in a bubble of joy. Rory wanted her – he fancied her. It didn't matter if he was her cousin. She couldn't care less. And Rory, he had kept coming to see her even though she was needing his support as a tutor less and less. He obviously felt something too.

That evening, Amy surprised her flatmates by having cleaned the whole flat from top to bottom. She had even prepared a chicken curry for them. Her happiness was too much to contain. She wanted to share her joy, but she couldn't tell them. They wouldn't understand. They'd judge them both. But she felt bulletproof. *He wants me, Rory wants me*, she breathed. What did she ever see in Jason? He was just a boy. Rory was a man. She liked the sound of that. It made her feel powerful and womanly. Tomorrow she would have to deal with all the obstacles, their age difference, that he was her cousin and, of course, her mother. But for today, she let her heart sing.

CHAPTER 29

MARY

Mary's life felt as though it was divided into two parts. The happy early years of building a home with Patrick, and later, the time of darkness. Her mind drew her back to the idyllic time in Sligo with Patrick and Brenna on the farm, their own Garden of Eden. A time of quiet contentment interspersed with their regular heart-breaking losses through miscarriage or stillbirths. But when Brenna was born, it seemed as though their cup had overflowed with happiness. When she thought back to those days, it seemed like they were enveloped in a golden haze. Patrick loved his job in the local Garda barracks, but working on the little farm was his real joy.

Even the farm hands who helped Patrick were part of that warm, happy time – kind elderly men, glad to work to supplement their old-age pensions by helping on the farm. But a snake had ripped apart their Eden – a snake they had taken into their hearts. Even after the poor child's death, Patrick still struggled to believe his neighbour and friend capable of such evil. This was the man he visited to listen to matches on the radio on a Sunday afternoon, a man he met in his local pub on a Saturday evening. It was a blessing for Patrick that Patsy Cullen had died before he could face justice. It would have ripped out Patrick's heart.

And Brenna, it had destroyed her. She had been having such a lovely summer with her cousin Rory too. But she had changed over that summer, even before poor Coleen died. She had become moody, dishonest even, telling lies, and once she even discovered her stealing money from her purse. Rory had stood up for her, but the child looked as guilty as sin. Patrick thought that perhaps she was jealous of Rory and feared he would usurp her place. Rory was kindness himself to Brenna. He arranged lovely games for them to play and had even persuaded her, against her better judgement, to get that little kitten for Brenna.

Brenna had become a sulky, jealous child. She was mean to everyone, especially poor Coleen. Halfway through that summer, she fell out with her. Rory had admitted reluctantly that she called Coleen names and wouldn't let her play with them. He said he felt guilty, so he tried to stand up for Coleen, and that was when Brenna started to fall out with him too. If she wasn't so young, Mary might have blamed it on her hormones, not that people spoke of hormones then. But perhaps it was the beginning of the dark depression that overtook her after Coleen died. Guilt is a terrible thing. For Brenna to have fallen out so badly and said such cruel things to Coleen and then for her friend to die must have tortured her. Mary had forced Rory to tell her what had happened. The boy was reluctant, but he eventually told them. He said that Brenna had goaded Coleen into breaking into that man's orchard. Mary couldn't bring herself to even think of his name. It soiled her mind.

The poor child had a complete mental collapse after the evil man died. Mary's Christian nature struggled as she fought her wish that he rot in hell. He stole not just Coleen's life but Brenna's too. She was never the same girl again, sobbing hysterically whenever she saw Rory, so they had to pack the poor child home to his mother in England. But she knew that Julie was worried about her son staying in a place where a murder was committed and was glad to have him home safe with her. Rory couldn't have been sweeter. He didn't hold it against Brenna, even when she refused to enter a room he was in. After he left, they hoped that she would improve with lots of love. She tried to talk to her about Coleen, but the child seemed to have fallen into a dark hole of despair. The priest tried his best to console her but to no avail. For a year, she was silent. They went to doctors and psychiatrists. They concluded that she had transferred some of her guilt onto Rory and blamed him for Coleen's death. They wanted her to stay in the hospital, but the thought of a mental hospital for her child disturbed them both. Brenna would never get over the stigma of being in what the locals called the 'looney bin'.

Then, in answer to a prayer, Patrick got a transfer to Dundalk. He was heartbroken to leave the family farm, but she was relieved to get away from the looming presence of the Cullen house. Locals had set it alight, but the rotting husk was a stark reminder of everything she had lost. Poor Mrs Foley was like a shadow. She walked the roads at night because she couldn't sleep, and her husband never left their farmhouse. The once prosperous little farm had run down. The cows were sold off as poor Tom Foley hadn't the energy to milk them. He just sat in his kitchen looking out of the window. His older boys had long left, and Callum, who was to take the farm, emigrated to America. Soon it was just the two of them. Tom died ten years ago, but poor Alice Foley was still alive. She had moved to the county home when she started showing signs of doting. Her family were good to her, visiting whenever they could, but the Alice she knew was long gone. She left the day her daughter's body was brought out of that orchard. Dementia just ended her torment.

She remembered her visit to Alice when she went to Sligo in September. The poor woman sat vacantly knitting with invisible needles and wool. Then she would grow animated and speak about her family as though they were just out in the fields. It was like she had drifted back to the time when they would call to visit each other and swap women's magazines and share knitting patterns. It was a blessing for Alice, but it saddened Mary to see the woman she knew so lost in the past, even if it was peaceful. But then, thank God for it. At least the woman's fierce grief had eased.

The move to Dundalk was tough. She remembered the upheaval, the feeling of being misplaced. Patrick found it difficult. The work so close to the border was more challenging, too, and sometimes he came home exhausted with a haunted look in his eyes. He no longer had his farm, but she encouraged him to grow things in their garden. He planted carrots and potatoes and grew lettuces under frames in the spring. But for all the time he spent out there, she knew it was a poor substitute for what he had left behind in Sligo.

She loved her little house. A bungalow was much easier to manage, and she made friends through the church and sang in the choir. She still had the same group of friends from those early days. They had supported her through the difficult times with Brenna, and God knows they were difficult times. Primary school was hard for Brenna. The other children didn't know what to make of the silent child. They weren't cruel – they just avoided her. It was impossible to have a relationship with her classmates when she wouldn't speak to them. She only spoke to her parents and other adults and that was an effort. But when she started secondary school, it was truly a time of anguish.

Every morning, Mary's heart ached as Brenna begged to stay home with her. It was heart-breaking to have to force her out the door. She refused to take the bus and, as the school was five miles away, Mary had to learn to drive. Patrick couldn't take her to school with his irregular hours of work. Every morning when she dropped her off, she watched as Brenna dragged her feet slowly towards the school entrance. She could see that the child was avoiding the moment as long as possible. But she waited until her girl was safely inside. Safe – that was a sick joke because Brenna wasn't safe. She was called names, pushed around, and excluded. The teachers tried, but no one knew how to help. The counsellor in the school tried to get her to open up to her, with no success. Mary had asked her to see if she could get her to talk, but the poor woman soon gave up.

In the end, they were forced to send Brenna back to the hospital when she refused to get out of bed. She barely ate or slept. She stayed in the mental hospital for two months. It was in Dublin, and they visited as often as they could, but Brenna seemed to get sicker. At times she was dopey with medication, and when more lucid she pleaded to be taken home. She begged to die. Many nights, Patrick and Mary lay staring at the ceiling, each alone in silent despair.

Salvation came one weekend when Brenna was allowed home for a visit. She was her usual silent ghostly presence. They did their best to make things nice for her. Patrick planned outings, and Mary cooked tasty meals, but there was no lifting the apathy that enveloped her girl.

Then, on Sunday, just as they were getting ready for the return journey to the hospital, the phone rang. It was Julie, hysterical, sobbing that Rory had been killed in a car accident. But miraculously, out of that tragic event, the seeds of Brenna's recovery were sown. It didn't happen overnight, but within six weeks she was home, insisting they call her Bree and send her to a new school. The doctors told them to go with it and do whatever it took to give her a fresh start. And it worked. Bree rose from the ashes of Brenna. Her new school was a success. She didn't make many friends, but enough for her. Her best friend was Anita, and they still were friends to this day. It didn't feel as though they had got Brenna back, that little girl was lost forever, but they had Bree, and she was enough, more than enough.

The doctors said that Rory's death must have somehow freed her. They warned of relapse and wanted to continue therapy, but Bree point-blank refused, and they were fearful of forcing the issue. Finally, the little family were restored to a semblance of happiness, even though fear of relapse stalked them. Mary had dreaded the day Bree would leave for college, but she was delighted for her too. Now she would fly. But her flight was short. Barely a year later, she was home pregnant, a college drop-out. It was hard in the seventies to be a single mother, but Mary was determined to support her daughter and help her raise her child. A few friends made their disapproval known and suggested Bree go to a Mother and Baby home and have the child adopted. Mary ruthlessly cut those friends out. But most people were kind and offered practical help, even money on occasion, but they managed. Patrick's wages helped, and she had a part-time job in a local shop. Amy fell on her feet when she got to work with Colm Dolan. He took her back two months after baby Amy was born. The baby's father helped too, or at least his family did. They held their noses a bit at first, but they soon fell in love with Amy.

When Patrick got ill, she feared Bree would fall apart, but she didn't. In fact, she was amazing, loving to Patrick and supportive of her. She focused on their suffering and not her own. After he died, they grew even closer. They were both consoled by the knowledge that Patrick had got to know and love his little grandchild. Mary was glad she had taken so many photographs of Patrick and Amy. They sat on her bedside table, and she greeted him every morning when she woke up and asked him to look out for Bree and Amy.

The last nineteen years had been challenging, but very happy for them all. Her only wish was that Bree would meet someone. She deserved something for herself. She wanted her daughter to experience the joy of love and companionship she had with Patrick. But Bree had no interest in men – her only focus was on Amy. Over the years, she had tentatively hinted that Bree get some counselling to work through her past trauma. But Bree was short with her, and she decided it wise to let it go. She wished that she hadn't now. In her experience, what you avoid in life doesn't go away, it lies in wait to hijack you. This was what was happening to Bree, but she couldn't be told.

Rory appearing out of the blue, alive and well and so much part of Amy's life, opened a wound that had never healed for Bree. At first, she hoped it might force Bree to confront the past or rather make peace with it. But instead, she had become withdrawn and paranoid. She was acting out of character, alienating her friends, losing her job, and associating with peculiar people. Once again, Bree focused all her anger on poor Rory. When Mary learnt that Rory had become a psychologist, partly because of his concern for his cousin, she was touched. If only Bree could see that he was the solution to her suffering. If she could only let go of the past. But instead, she was removing Rory's support from Amy. Her grandchild had been thriving in college thanks to the added support Rory was giving her academically, but now she was slipping again.

It seemed like a horrible re-enactment of the past, with Rory once again cast as the scapegoat. But she couldn't let Amy suffer because Bree refused to get help. Bree wasn't a child anymore. She couldn't be allowed to continue to wreak havoc. The trouble was – how could she stop her?

CHAPTER 30

BREE

Bree took every bit of overtime that she could. She would need the money to support Amy but also to pay Cassidy. She hated using the 'dirty money', as she called the wads of cash she had hidden in her house. But work held its own terrors. One evening she saw Sam. He was talking to her supervisor outside the office block where she was working. He didn't appear to have noticed her. She hurried inside and kept her head down. Thankfully he didn't come into the building. One of the other cleaners, who also did a lot of extra work, asked her did she sleep at all, because she was always at work. The truth was that sleep was sporadic and filled with nightmares. She debated getting something from her doctor. But the idea of being in a drugged sleep and vulnerable, if someone broke into her home again, terrified her. She had a peephole and a chain lock fitted to her front door and a bolt to her backdoor. They at least would warn her that her home was being invaded.

Amy had sounded happy when she spoke to her last night. Maybe she was back with her boyfriend. She hoped so, and she hoped that he would fill up her time and help her to see that she didn't need Rory's help anymore. Jason had been the one person she had met who saw Rory as a threat. Why was everyone so fucking in love with him? Then again, when he first came to stay with her family, she had acted like a puppy around him, following him everywhere, taking her lead from him. It had taken the Game for her to understand what an evil psychopathic bastard he was. But, to everyone else, he was an angel. How were they so blind, so stupid?

It was the same in England, and apart from two exceptions, his colleagues all thought the world of him. It was interesting to see how Rory had honed his manipulation skills. She wondered whether he played a version of the Game with his patients. One of them, Sol, spoke of wanting his 'reward'. Had Rory rewarded him for attacking the nurse by gifting him with the photograph? How had he even got those photographs? Did Rory arrange the theft? But how? It made no sense, but then all the things that happened to her were insane. How did Rory have connections with criminals and hoods? Did he reward them? Was that how he got them to do his bidding? Bree shook her head. Was he some kind of modern-day Professor Moriarty? She knew they'd have her committed if she tried to tell anyone about this. Even Anita would suggest that she get help. In truth, she couldn't blame anyone for disbelieving her. The whole thing was like a dark fairy tale tangled up with a gangster movie.

Again, the sensation of being trapped started to overwhelm her. But she had Cassidy, her secret weapon. His next report was due soon, and she hoped it would have something she could use against Rory. Blackmail to counter his.

Her shift ended, and she arrived back in her dark house. She immediately went around the whole house, looking under beds, in the bed, and behind doors until she was sure she was alone. Then she put the lock on her front door and bolted the back door.

'Hi, Bree!'

Sam Murphy lay stretched out on her sofa.

Heart thumping, she backed away. But her body felt passive, like she was moving slowly through thick mud.

'Get out of my house now!' Her voice was surprisingly calm.

'Now, Bree, that's not very friendly, and we are friends. I have very fond memories of that kiss we shared the other night.'

He stood up and approached her, grinning. He stroked her cheek and she slapped his hand away.

'Get out now, or I'll scream the place down. My neighbours will call the gardaí.'

'Bree, I'm hurt. I was hoping we could develop our relationship.' He licked his lips as his eyes roved over her body. 'What do you say? I could even make it worth your while.'

He pulled her towards him, and she felt sick as he forced her lips apart and thrust his tongue into her mouth, filling it with his saliva. He squeezed her breast with his fingers until she gasped with pain.

Terrified, she broke away from him, grabbed the reading lamp and threw it at him. Her aim was good, and the edge of the lamp collided with his forehead, drawing blood.

'*Get out!*' she screamed.

But he took her words as an invitation and moved towards her threateningly. She backed into the kitchen and scrabbled for the bolts on her door. He grabbed her by her hair and pulled her back. She stamped on his foot and elbowed him as hard as she could in his neck. Choking, he released her. She unlocked the door, ran into the garden and threw herself over the fence into her neighbour's garden. She banged as hard as she could on their door, screaming all the while. In the distance, she heard Sam's footsteps on the front path running away.

Then she heard her neighbour Trish shout for her husband Brian, and soon their door was pulled open by him, and Bree fell into his arms. She clung to him, afraid to let go.

'My God, are you OK, Bree?' he said as he looked out into the darkness.

Bree clutched him, sobbing hysterically. Then Trish appeared, full of kindness and comfort. Bree gasped that someone had broken into her house. They called the gardaí.

Like bad pennies, O'Shaughnessy and Collins, the same two gardaí who had visited her the day she provided the false alibi, turned up. She began to wonder if anyone else worked at Dundalk Garda Station. They accompanied her back to her place, where they checked out the house.

Trish sat beside her on the couch, her arm placed protectively around her shoulders. She had refused to budge even though Bree had begged her to go home. 'I'm not leaving you, pet – never fear, and you must stay with us tonight.' Bree was too tired to argue and, in truth, was thankful to surrender herself to her neighbour's charge.

O'Shaughnessy sat down to take her statement.

'Bree, I can see that you've been through a very frightening experience. But can you run through what happened tonight?'

Bree had managed to calm down and was thinking furiously. If she identified Sam as her attacker, then her false alibi would be exposed, and she would be faced with lying to the gardaí and being an accessory to whatever crime Sam had committed.

She nodded and began. 'I came in from work, and there was a man in the living room. I shouted at him to leave, but instead he grabbed me.'

Her voice left her momentarily, and Trish squeezed her hand.

'Take it easy, Bree,' O'Shaughnessy said. 'I can wait until you're ready to speak. But it's always better to get details when they are fresh in your mind.'

'Yes, I know, but it all seems so surreal, as though it happened to someone else.' She took a deep breath. 'When I saw the man, I froze, and then he grabbed me, and we struggled, but I managed to grab the lamp and throw it at him and ran into the kitchen.'

'What happened then?'

'I ran for the door to unbolt it, and he caught my hair. I struggled and broke free. I made it into the garden and got help from Trish and her husband. The man ran off.'

'He didn't interfere with you, Bree? He didn't do anything to you?' Trish asked.

Bree shuddered. 'No, apart from grabbing me and scaring the life out of me.'

'Now, Bree, I want you to think very carefully. Did you recognise this man?'

Bree forced herself to look the garda straight in the eye. 'I never saw him before in my life.'

'Can you describe him?' he asked.

'He was tall, and his hair was dark. Honestly, I was so busy running and fighting that I never really looked at him.'

'I'd like you to come down to the station tomorrow morning if you are feeling up to it, and read over your statement and sign it. We'll have a few pictures for you to look at. Men who have form with this kind of thing. Are you up to doing that?'

Bree nodded.

Then Collins came into the room. 'Well, there's no obvious sign of a break-in, sir. Windows and doors are secure.' He turned to Bree. 'Is there any possibility that the intruder may have accessed your keys, Ms O'Hagan?'

Bree thought quickly. 'You know what, I think I may have left my front door open. When I got home, I ran into the kitchen – I was afraid I'd forgotten to turn off the oven when I left for work. I may not have closed the front door behind me.'

'And was it?' Collins asked.

'Sorry, was what?' she asked.

'The oven, had you left it on?'

'No, I hadn't, it was stone cold,' she said, her voice low and flat.

Trish came to her aid. 'I think she's had enough for tonight, gentlemen. Now, no arguments, Bree, you are spending the night in our spare room.'

Helpless to resist, Bree was ferried next door, supplied with pyjamas and a clean toothbrush and ushered into a room with a single bed. A hot-water bottle was thrust at her feet, and a cup of hot chocolate was handed to her. Bree lay propped up by pillows and, for a few blissful moments, she was conjured back to that lovely old farmhouse in Sligo, to a time before Rory, before everything was poisoned.

When she awoke the next morning, she could hear Trish and her husband Brian chatting over their breakfast. She dressed rapidly, anxious to get away as quickly as possible. It was just after eight. But getting away from Trish was easier said than done. In the end, it was easier to sit down and eat some toast and sip tea rather than resist her. Eventually, when Trish walked her husband to the door, she sprang after them. She thanked them both profusely for all their help, but said that she had to make tracks. She even managed to extract a promise from Trish not to tell anyone about the break-in until she had a chance to tell her mother. Finally, she broke free and called into her house to pick up her car keys and change her clothes.

At nine, Bree drove to the Garda Station. She was asked to read through her statement and sign it. Garda Collins made her look through a series of pictures of men he thought might have attacked her. She scanned the pictures and pretended to be examining them closely.

After five minutes, she looked up and shook her head. 'I'm sorry, but none of these look like him.'

'Are you sure? Take your time.'

Bree forced herself to look again. 'Sorry, I wish I could help you find this man.'

After leaving the station, Bree drove home. She felt nervous as she walked inside, but then her fear was replaced by fury. How dare Rory do this? Even for him, setting that man on her was beyond the pale.

She picked up her phone and dialled. The high-pitched voice of the receptionist answered. She asked to speak to Rory urgently.

'He's quite busy this morning. Can it wait until this afternoon?'

'*No, it couldn't bloody wait!*' Bree snapped.

She gave her name, and the woman said she would see if she could locate Mr Straffen. She listened to the clip-clop of the woman's heels heading down a corridor. Then, a minute later, the secretary returned.

'Mr Straffen is just finishing up with a patient and will call you shortly.'

Without responding, Bree replaced the receiver.

As she waited, she could feel a rage build up in her. Then the phone rang.

'Bree, how lovely to hear from you!' Rory's voice, warm and friendly, sounded in her ear.

She shouted, '*You bastard, you've gone too far now! Sending that animal to attack me. Was he supposed to rape and kill me, or was rape the sole purpose?*'

'Calm down. I have no idea what you are talking about. Who attacked you and when?'

'Don't pretend you don't know! Is this some other aspect of your sick game? I did what you asked, so why set him on me?'

'Set who?'

'You know who! Sam Murphy!'

There was a pause, then Rory said, 'OK, Bree, am I to understand Sam Murphy attacked you last night? Are you OK? Did he hurt you?'

'What do you care? Stop pretending you don't know about it.'

'Bree, I'm telling you this is not part of the Game. Now, answer me, did he harm you?'

'I'm OK, but the gardaí have been here, and I had to sign a statement pretending I didn't know who attacked me.'

'Listen, I'm sorry this has happened. It wasn't any part of my plan. It's crass. I'll take care of it. You won't be bothered by him again.'

Rory hung up before she could ask him what he meant.

CHAPTER 31

The manila envelope sat on the carpet in her hallway. She dumped the few groceries she had bought on the kitchen table and then carried the envelope into the living room. She sat on the sofa, holding it. *Please let this contain something I can use to make him disappear from my life forever.* Taking a deep breath, she ripped the envelope open and pulled out the slim report from Cassidy.

Dear Ms O'Hagan,

I have followed up on several leads, and I hope you will find my attached report informative and helpful. The subject I am investigating has proved to be more interesting and complex than expected. I have some additional leads to follow, and when I return to Ireland tomorrow, we should meet to discuss my findings. If it suits you, let's meet at my office on Thursday at 9 a.m. If it doesn't, please leave a message on my answering machine, and we can reschedule.

Yours,

P Cassidy

SUBJECT RORY STRAFFEN

I attempted to discover the following about the subject.

1. What occurred on the night of the car accident when the subject was first thought to have perished?
2. Where did he go during the period he disappeared?
3. Why did he change his name from Brown to Straffen?
4. Does he have any connections to the criminal underworld? (this query relates to stolen photographs that were passed on to the patient in the hospital where he worked.)
5. Why did he return to Ireland in 1987?
6. Has he established any links with criminals in Ireland?

1. On the 14th of May 1966, a car was stolen from a housing estate close to the subject's home in London. The car drove at speed down a motorway and crashed into a guardrail. Three of the boys were dead at the scene. The fourth, the driver, survived for a week. The subject was identified by a watch that belonged to his stepfather. The surviving boy regained consciousness for a short period. He told his parents and a police constable that he and his friends were high on drugs. He claimed that the subject supplied them with the said drugs. He stated that a row ensued over the payment of said drugs, and the subject left the car. They then went on to pick up another young man, a friend of one of the other passengers. The survivor didn't know his name. The toxicology report on the boys suggested that they had ingested adulterated LSD. The boy died shortly after giving his statement. After the subject was identified by his stepfather, it was assumed that the boy in the hospital was confused and made a mistake. As no one appeared to have reported another missing teenager, his evidence was discounted.

2. When the subject was picked up in London by the police for possession of cocaine, he claimed to be the boy who had supposedly died in the car wreck. His stepfather was called to the station and identified him as his stepson. The subject claimed that he ran away after his friends were killed. He felt that his family was fed up with him, so he decided to go and have what he called a fresh start. He believed his mother and stepfather would be glad to see the back of him. Considering the circumstances, it was decided not to pursue any charges against him, and he returned to his family. On making enquiries with the arresting officer, a retired police sergeant, he was of the view that the subject worked for a local drug dealer and may have run afoul of him. The arrest of the boy was too easy for a seasoned operator. He practically asked to be caught. The policeman believed the boy had run out of rope and badly needed to lie low. It had suited him to be reunited with his family. The dealer was a nasty piece of work, and he believed the boy had stolen a large quantity of product and money from him.

3. Rory Brown became Rory Straffen six months after he returned home. I spoke to a friend of the family as Julie Brown/Morris was residing in a mental institution. She had a severe mental breakdown shortly after the subject returned home. The neighbour, Mrs Willis, was a close friend of Julie Morris. She described the relationship between Mrs Morris and her son as badly strained. Rory had been running with a bad crowd before the car crash, and his mother was very concerned about him. When he returned home, she was delighted to see him, but immediately it became apparent that something was wrong. The subject appeared to be blackmailing his mother. She was very

fragile at this time, but she admitted that Rory knew something that upset her: a secret he held over her. Mrs Willis didn't want to press her as she felt it wasn't her business.

Philip Morris was initially reluctant to speak to me, but eventually we made contact. I explained that I was working for someone in Ireland who was under threat from his stepson. The following is a verbatim account of my conversation with Philip Morris.

TRANSCRIPT OF PHILIP MORRIS INFORMATION

From the moment I met and married Julie, I knew that the line in the wedding vows, for better or worse, would become a reality. I just didn't know how much worse it would be. Julie was a young widow. Her husband, Daniel, had died when Rory was ten. He had a traffic accident, but when taken to the hospital, the doctors discovered that he was riddled with cancer. He didn't survive for more than six months. I met Julie when Rory was thirteen. Even at that age, he was running rings around his mother. She couldn't manage him at all. Julie is a lovely woman, but she isn't strong, and I suppose it was easy for Rory to dominate her. He certainly treated her with great disrespect. When I challenged him, he reacted by doing spiteful things, cancelling appointments I made, hiding important documents I needed for business and stealing from me. Whenever I challenged him on his behaviour, he ran away, and this unnerved Julie and made her panic so I always backed down.

At the time of his 'death', he had been in trouble with the police for vandalism and petty theft. Julie and I knew that he was both taking and selling drugs. We feared it was only a matter of time before he was sent to jail. In all honesty, I hoped he would be, as then he'd be out of our lives for a while. But on the 14ᵗʰ of May, when

I went to the morgue and had to identify that poor destroyed body, I was ashamed that I had failed him. He was only eighteen. Julie was heartbroken. Her first husband's Irish family came to the funeral. I was stunned to discover they had such warm memories of the boy. Once again, I felt that I had failed him. When I got the call from the London police, I thought I was given a second chance. This time I wouldn't let him down.

Initially, all was great. Rory and his mother were reunited, and Rory seemed eager to make a fresh start. He decided to attend college and study psychology at Kings College in London. We were delighted. Despite his wayward youth, Rory excelled at school and had good A-level results. He enrolled, and I was happy to help support him. He also was very kind to his mother, bringing her gifts and taking her out for afternoon tea. I didn't know how he could afford it, but I was just so delighted that he was making his mother happy. It was too good to last.

I came home one afternoon to discover Julie in floods of tears. She wouldn't tell me what was wrong. But I guessed it had something to do with Rory. Two weeks later, he returned from college to spend the weekend with us. All the time he was there, Julie looked positively haunted. Then, casually smiling straight at his mother, he told her that he was changing his name to Straffen by deed poll. I was baffled by this decision, and when I asked him why he just giggled and said I should ask his lovely mother. At this, Julie fled from the table, sobbing.

I insisted he tell me why his mother was so upset. He laughed and said that it wasn't his job to tell me. Then he went out to meet his friends. He didn't return that night. I found Julie in our bedroom, in floods of tears and incoherent. Eventually, I got the story from her.

Before she met her first husband, Daniel Brown, she had been in love with a married man who had children. It soon became clear that he was never going to leave his wife for her. She decided to end her involvement with him, and when she met Daniel she realised he was a much better man than her married lover. When Daniel asked her to marry him, she agreed, genuinely believing they would have a good life together and that she would make him happy. A month before the wedding, Daniel returned to Ireland to visit his family. While he was away, she met up with this Straffen chap. He got her drunk and, well, she got pregnant. She didn't realise until after she was married that she was pregnant. Daniel never knew. As far as she was concerned, nobody knew. She never told a soul. She was deeply ashamed.

The first time she realised that Rory was suspicious was a few months after he returned home. He took to looking at old photographs of Daniel and saying how strange it was that he didn't take after either of his parents. Maybe he was a cuckoo in the nest. He was just trolling but Julie was unnerved, and it apparently awakened his suspicions. He asked her why his eyes were blue and his dad's and her eyes were brown. Wasn't that strange? If Julie had held her nerve or knew a bit of science, such as about recessive genes, she could have laughed it off, but she looked so guilty that it was easy for him to worm everything out of her. Julie is a deeply religious woman. Before her marriage to Daniel she converted to Catholicism. Like many converts, she became very devout. She believed that what she had done was a mortal sin and a betrayal of a good man. Her sense of shame was so great that she was terrified of my finding out, thinking I would despise her. It transpired that Rory was taking money off her to keep his silence. When he told her about the name change, she was terrified that everyone would find out – me, her church group and even Daniel's family. Rory had threatened to stand up at Mass on Sunday and denounce her as an adulterer. To add menace to his threat, he started attending church services. Poor Julie was out of her mind with fear.

Once I had discovered how Rory was terrorising Julie, I forbade him from going near his mother again. I would continue to fund his education on condition that he leave her alone and never return to our home. Rory agreed to the conditions, but I also had to settle a debt he had to a local drug dealer for two thousand pounds. I did so, glad to be rid of him. But Rory still found ways to torment his mother. Every year he sent her birthday and Christmas cards signing them 'Your loving son, Rory Straffen'. Julie had a severe mental breakdown and spent much of the following years in and out of mental institutions. A year after Rory graduated from college, my business burnt to the ground just as my insurance policy expired. I can't prove it, but I think that Rory had arranged it. The night before the fire, I received a sympathy card.

[Philip Morris asked me to pass on his best wishes to my client. He said he wouldn't wish Rory on his worst enemies.]

4. I have no hard evidence that my subject had connections with criminal elements, but I managed to meet his secretary in the private psychology clinic he ran in London. It seems he had an eclectic client list, including B-list celebrities, minor royalty, several wealthy Irish property developers, and some very shady characters she suspected might be gangsters. When she asked her boss (whom she adored) why he saw men like these, he explained that even criminals needed help and that possibly he could affect a transformation in their behaviour. It is very possible, that the subject could have used information he gained in a clinical setting, to induce criminals to do favours for him, or he may even have sold on information gleaned from famous clients.

5. The subject left a lucrative private practice behind him in England. He also had his consultancy work in psychiatric institutions. Why did he give all that up? I was put in touch with a journalist for one of the tabloid papers, and he gave me a clue. It seems one of his wealthy patients developed a fixation on him, and she was giving him not just presents but tips on the stock market. She was married to a very important businessman. He was being investigated for insider trading, and it seemed his wife was leaking information to her therapist, who in turn was leaking to his friends in the criminal fraternity. The wife of the businessman subsequently committed suicide. Before everything came tumbling down, our man took cover and took up a job offer in Dublin. London may have become too hot for him to handle.

6. This final part of the puzzle will have to wait until I return to Ireland to complete my investigations.

CHAPTER 32

Bree read and reread the report. Did it help her to know about Rory's early life? Well, she could see that he continued messing with people's heads. Was there a suggestion that he had supplied his friends with dodgy drugs? Why didn't he get in the car with them? More unanswered questions. Poor Aunt Julie! Bree's memories of her were tenuous. She once visited them with Uncle Daniel when Bree was a small child. All she remembered was marvelling at how nice Julie smelled, like freesias. Her poor aunt being tortured with blackmail threats by her son was cruel. But, if Julie got pregnant by this Straffen man, it meant he wasn't Daniel's son. Therefore, they weren't related biologically. That comforted her. The idea of sharing genes with Rory had always disturbed her. It felt like a stain she couldn't erase. He kept his secret well. It was why he let her believe that he took his stepfather's name? Did her mother know? After all, she had spoken to Philip Morris. She must have asked about Rory's name-change. Why had she never mentioned it?

She scanned the document again. Rory knew lots of people, important people. Had he upset them, blackmailing them with the information he gained from therapy? Or did he sell information about his clients? What about the businessman's wife – had she been manipulated by Rory into killing herself after she was no longer of use to him and could be a liability? She wouldn't put anything past Rory. It was interesting – the insider trading thing. So, that was why he had to leave such a lucrative set-up in London. He was afraid of getting implicated in serious fraud. And he had criminal connections, and it followed that he knew criminals in Dublin too. She wondered if perhaps Gowan was one of his Irish property-developer clients. That would explain how her house was so easily broken into and the lowlifes he had put her way. She shuddered as she thought about Sam Murphy.

Did she believe Rory when he said he had nothing to do with the attack on her? Every word that came out of his mouth was a distortion of the truth or a lie. But she heard one thing in his voice that she had never heard before: surprise. He sounded like the attack wasn't part of whatever sick plan he had cooked up. God, that reminded her, she better talk to her mother about the attack, before Trish burst a gut from holding in the news. She had better visit her mother now, this minute. She also needed to be sure that her mother was turning on her alarm every night. She didn't want her to have any more intruders.

She pulled up outside her mother's bungalow. From her car, she could see Mary sitting in the conservatory, enjoying the winter sun, whilst reading a book. She hesitated, reluctant to bring darkness into that quiet domestic scene.

Her mother saw her and waved. She waved back and, by the time she got to the door, her mother was holding it open. She gave Bree a warm hug.

'What a lovely surprise, Bree! I wasn't expecting to see you today.'

Bree followed her mother into the conservatory.

'Would you like some coffee, Bree?'

'No thanks, Mammy.'

They sat down on sturdy wicker chairs.

'Mammy – look, I have something to tell you – but, please, don't get upset. Everything is fine now.'

Mary's face tensed, and she leaned forward. 'What's happened, Bree? Is it Amy?'

'No, Mammy, it's nothing to do with her. Look, last night, a man followed me into the. house when I got home from work.

Mary's hand flew to her mouth.

'I'm OK, Mammy, really. I managed to get out the back door and over to Trish and Brian's house. They let me in and called the gardaí.'

'Did they catch the man?' Mary asked anxiously.

'Not so far, but they're looking hard.'

'Right, well, you're not staying in the estate anymore – you're staying with me.' Mary's eyes were big with concern.

'Don't be daft, I'm perfectly safe. I very foolishly left my front door open while I went to check something in the kitchen, and that's how he got in. Look, I have a deadbolt, a security chain, and bolts on the back door. Even the gardaí were impressed with my security. Besides, a break-in can happen anywhere. Look how you were burgled, and you are still in your home. You haven't been scared away. By the way, I hope that you're putting your alarm on every night. There are too many crazies about and I need to know that you are safe here.'

Mary whispered, 'Yes, I put it on every night.'

Bree was startled to see tears slide down her mother's face. She hurried to her, knelt beside her and held her hand.

'Mammy, please, don't worry. I'm grand, honestly.'

'Oh love, it just seems that everything is going wrong lately. Break-ins, you losing your good job, Amy struggling at college. We all used to be so happy and contented. It feels like we are drifting apart.'

Bree paused and then burst out, 'Everything started going wrong when Rory showed up!'

Mary shook her head angrily. 'No! Don't start that again, Bree! You have made Rory a scapegoat since you were a child. I wish you'd grow up and take some responsibility. Rory didn't lose you the job with Colm, and he didn't break into your house. You must stop this crazy talk!'

Bree stared at her mother. 'Is that what you think – that I'm crazy?'

'Of course not, but I'm sick of telling you that you need some help for yourself. You need to talk to someone. This obsession you have with Rory is pulling us all apart.'

Mary had got to her feet and Bree stood up slowly.

'Mammy, I promise I'll never mention his name again, but I need to know something. Will you answer me honestly?'

Mary bridled. 'I've always been honest with you. I don't know what you're implying.'

'OK, calm down. Let's sit down and have a civilised conversation.'

They both retook their seats, but each sat bolt upright.

'Well, what do you want to know?' said Mary.

'Do you know why Rory doesn't call himself Rory Brown anymore?'

Mary flushed. 'Well, I'm not sure if I really should be telling you about this, because I want to respect the confidences of the people involved. But I can see keeping confidences could seem like I'm keeping secrets. But I didn't believe it was my secret to share and I wanted to protect Julie.'

Bree looked at her mother intently. 'Go on,' she said.

'I asked Rory why he no longer used the surname Brown. I knew his stepfather was called Morris and I was puzzled at this change of name. Anyway, he told me that he discovered Daniel wasn't his biological father. It seemed that Julie had an affair or a fling just before she got married. Thank God, Daniel never found out. He believed Rory was his son and loved him to bits, but when Rory found out that Daniel wasn't his natural dad, he confronted his mother about it. He admits that he wasn't tactful or kind, but he wasn't expecting Julie to be so angry. He said that she denied everything and said cruel things to him. He set about finding out the truth, and Julie went to pieces. He changed his name to his biological father's. The poor boy felt he didn't deserve to keep Daniel's name. And that's all there is to it. The lad was terribly upset to realise the father he adored wasn't his natural one. He admits he handled it badly. But, Bree, can you imagine if you found out your dad wasn't your dad? It was horrible for him.'

'I see. I just wondered if you knew.'

'Oh – I suppose Rory told you too. But now, Bree can't you accept that Rory isn't this source of all evil? Like the rest of us, he's trying to make his way through life. He dedicated his life to helping others. Right now, he could do with the love and support of family.'

'But he's not family, is he?'

'That's cruel. Julie did wrong by Daniel and Rory, but she's paid a terrible price by not facing up to the truth. Rory thinks her deep depression is because of her guilt and repression. He's very worried about you. He thinks that you could end up like Julie.'

'Locked away, you mean.'

Mary sighed. 'Bree, I just want you to look after yourself.'

'Mammy, are you still in contact with Rory? Do you still speak to him?'

Mary looked uncomfortable. 'We do keep a little contact. He's been kindness himself to me, especially after my burglary. And he keeps an eye on Amy.'

'What do you mean? He's stopped coaching her, hasn't he?'

Mary looked angry. 'Bree, we have all gone along with your unjust behaviour towards Rory and, yes, he no longer helps her with her college work, but I still think of him as my nephew, and he genuinely cares for Amy. If he chooses to meet with her occasionally, that surely is their business.'

Bree got to her feet. 'I see.'

Then she walked straight out of the house.

Mary stood at the door, watching her drive away.

Bree drove on autopilot. She was furious that her mother was still in contact with Rory and was so completely taken in by him. There was no way she could make her understand what Rory was capable of. He was so plausible, and had thought of everything. He had convinced her mother that he was the victim, the poor abandoned son, and the family scapegoat. Her mother believed that she wasn't rational where he was concerned. There was nothing she could say to persuade her. There was no point in even trying. The constant feeling of being hemmed in and trapped intensified. Thank God she had Cassidy working for her. He would find something that would give her a way of fighting back. And the dirty payoff money she had been given was put to good use.

So, Amy was still in contact with Rory. Why was she not surprised? He was a virus infecting every aspect of her life. She must find a way to cut herself free. She *would* find a way.

To distract herself from thoughts of Rory, she switched on the radio, and its cheerful music proved more of an irritant than a distraction. She turned to the RTÉ News at One. She let the words wash over her until she heard the newsreader intone: *A man's body has been discovered close to the border. Police believe it to be Sam Murphy, a businessman from County Louth. He is believed to have links to criminal gangs on both sides of the border.'*

She pulled off the road, her heart hammering. Rory had said he would deal with Sam. Was this what he meant? She had no sympathy for the man who had coerced and attacked her, but the fact that Rory could organise his murder terrified her. What else was he capable of? All she knew was that she must stop him by any means necessary. Her meeting with Cassidy couldn't come soon enough.

CHAPTER 33

Traffic in Drumcondra was bumper to bumper, and she was glad she had left Dundalk early. She was able to find parking down a side street about a quarter of a mile from Cassidy's office. The butcher shop below had a couple of customers, and she decided to pick up some chops for dinner after she finished her meeting. She ran upstairs and rang the doorbell. Cassidy shouted to come in. He was on the phone, and she took the time to look at him. He wasn't as old as she first thought, maybe early fifties. His hair was well sprinkled with grey, and when he looked up at her, she saw that his eyes were a hard pebble grey. He grunted and pointed to a chair across from his desk. She sat down and waited. He looked at her with his cool eyes and took so long to speak that she felt unnerved.

'Can I call you Bree?' was his unexpected question.

She nodded. 'What do I call you?

'Cassidy's fine. Even my ex calls me that, and possibly a few less polite things.'

'Have you any more information for me?'

'Maybe, but first I want to know exactly what your involvement with Straffen is?'

'I don't pay you to ask me questions,' she snapped, irked by his tone.

'Fine, well, you can just settle my bill and be on your way then.'

'Please, Cassidy, you can't stop now. I need you to keep on digging. It's a matter of life and death. You must keep on, please!' Her voice was shaking.

'Bree, you seem like a nice lady, but you might not be. I don't know and, frankly, when I first started this investigation I really didn't care. But now I need to know exactly what I'm involved in.'

'OK! What do you want to know?'

'Well, Bree, I did a little looking into your background. Keep the look of indignation to yourself. I make it my business to know who and what I'm dealing with. So, I'll tell you what I've discovered about you in a few sentences. Originally from Sligo, you moved with your parents to Dundalk after your dad, a cop, got a transfer. I know that you had a lot of mental health issues in your childhood and teenage years. You're a single parent to a daughter, Amy. You never married and have worked for Colm Dolan Solicitors for twenty years. Recently you left your job and started to work for a cleaning company partly owned by criminals. Speculation is that you were sacked from your job and according to my Garda sources, you were involved with a hood called Sam Murphy, whom you alibied. The same gentleman was recently murdered. Both your and your mother's homes have been broken into recently and you were the victim of an assault. Have I left anything out?'

Bree stared at him, two bright spots on her cheeks. It was galling to hear her life ground down to a handful of statements. 'No, I think you have all the salient points.'

'The thing is, Bree, it leaves me with more questions than answers.'

'Such as?'

'Why did you get sacked from your job? Why did your house and your mother's get broken into, and why were you assaulted? Why did you supply an alibi for a lowlife like Sam Murphy? And, most importantly of all, why are you having Rory Straffen investigated? Now before I supply any more information to you, I want the truth.' He looked at her sharply. '*All* the truth. I have a nose for a lie. So don't bother fobbing me off with half-truths. I want it all. If you can't do that, settle your bill and clear off.'

Bree sat in silence, her mind whirring. What should she do? He looked like he meant it about closing the case. What should she tell him? The strain of keeping silent for over thirty years weighed on her forcefully. The relief to be gained by telling this man everything was a terrifying but also tempting prospect. Could she trust him? But then, what choice did she have? There was no point in telling him half the story. This man was smart and would see prevarication, which would be the end of their partnership. It was an enticing prospect to have a partner in her fight against Rory. But if he didn't believe her, she wasn't sure she could cope.

Cassidy waited patiently. For that, she was grateful. Then she sat back in her chair and sighed. She made up her mind that she would trust him.

Slowly, painfully, she recited her story, starting with that summer in 1960 and the death of Coleen. She struggled to make him understand how Rory had terrorised her into agreeing to the deception. The burden of keeping the secret and the guilt she felt towards Patsy Cullen poured out. Unable to continue, she was horrified by the loud sobs and incoherent words issuing from her mouth like a burst dam. Cassidy fetched her a glass of water. She continued her story, interspersed with questions from Cassidy. As she spoke, she realised how insane and farfetched her words were. How could she make him understand how alone she had been, how Rory had twisted things so that he looked like the victim? But once started, she couldn't contain her words. She told him about Gowan and the documents she gave him, of how she was found out and sacked, about Clean Co and how Rory had coerced her into providing the alibi and how Sam had attempted to rape her. Rory had had him murdered not because he cared about her but because Sam had broken the rules.

When she finished, she scanned Cassidy's face. Did he believe her? And, more importantly, would he continue with the investigation? She sat in anxious silence while he digested her words. She watched him tap a pencil on a jotter. She was terrified. She had never exposed herself like this. In the hospital, they spoke of her unburdening herself so that she might experience a breakthrough. Now she realised how vulnerable the truth had made her. After all, she had just admitted to committing serious crimes.

Finally, unable to bear the silence anymore, she whispered, 'Do you believe me?'

Cassidy looked at her through narrowed eyes. 'I believe you.'

At those words, the room started to spin, and then she was lying on the floor, her head supported by the rough wool of a man's jacket.

Cassidy loomed over her. 'Are you fit to get up?' he asked in a quiet voice.

She nodded as he helped her to her feet and led her to a chair. He handed her the glass of water. She drank thirstily.

'What are you going to do?' she said. Her voice sounded calm, detached.

'I don't know,' Cassidy said.

'Will you help me stop him?'

He looked at her. 'I will.'

Those two words gave her an injection of what she realised was hope.

'Are you ready to find out what I have discovered about Rory since he moved to Ireland?'

She nodded eagerly.

'OK. Well, he got a job offer as a lecturer at UCD. It's a part-time job, and he also has a lucrative private practice in Rathmines. He rents a small office space above a dental surgery and employs a secretary five mornings a week. She works from nine to twelve noon and is usually gone by lunchtime. She is a perfectly respectable young woman with a fiancée and still lives with her parents. Rory generally appears at the office at ten or thereabouts and the first client usually arrive at eleven.'

'Did you recognise any of his clients?'

'I watched his office for a few days, and he seems to have a diverse selection of clients, all ages, men and women. But I've recognised one or two politicians. And that man you mentioned, PJ Gowan, also goes to see him, but outside of his normal business hours, so I don't think the visits are therapeutic. I haven't seen any known criminals associate with him, but I think after his experiences in London, he's wary of messing up.'

'What about the man who attacked me, Sam Murphy? Did he visit?'

'Well, he may have. How about you look through my photos and see who you recognise?"

'You took photos?' She was surprised.

'That's part of the service, madam,' he said, smiling, and suddenly he looked softer, less intimidating.

He went to his filing cabinet and pulled out a folder. Inside were dozens of photographs. He must have a great camera because, despite the apparent distance, she could clearly make out faces. She immediately recognised Gowan and thought she recognised a few others, but they were probably the politicians he spoke about. She may have seen them on television.

'Does anybody look familiar?'

She started to shake her head but then picked up a picture of a woman wearing a light-coloured coat, her tied-back hair allowing a clear view of her face.

'She looks like one of the women who work alongside me at Clean Co. I suppose that explains how he slipped his envelope into my coat pocket and how he may have got copies of my keys. Now that I look back, I think she showed up to every shift I had, before something shitty happened – like a break-in or when Roy was forcing me to do things I didn't want to. It's like a horrible web that Rory has entangled me in. Everything that has happened is all his grand fucking design.'

'Yes, I think so, and in fact I think he arranged for you to lose your job. Gowan's rival for the land bid had possibly been screwed over more than once, and it made sense that he would have been putting a watch on Gowan. But I think Rory set the whole thing up and arranged for the photographs to be taken and sent to Ryan Carty. He wanted you sacked and working for the cleaning company.'

'But why? I don't understand.'

'I think he wanted to make you insecure and vulnerable, away from the safety and routine of your job. By destroying your friendship with your boss, he made you more isolated and easier to control. He seems to have a thing about you, Bree. I don't mean sexual – I think you were the first person he successfully manipulated, and I think it gave him a thrill that he's been recapturing ever since. Now he's back in Ireland, he wants to continue to make you dance to his tune. He knows the best way to control you is through your daughter.'

'What can I do to protect her?' Bree watched Cassidy intently.

'I really don't know, but I think we need to get Amy out of harm's away as soon as possible. And remember, the more he gets you involved in criminality and alienated from your family, the more satisfaction he gets. You need to be careful, Bree, you have already broken several laws.'

'Cassidy, I really appreciate you taking my side. You could so easily have turned me in.'

'I think in some ways you'd be safer in jail.' Seeing the look of horror on her face, he added, 'But I think we'll find a better way. But, Bree, you have to promise me that if Rory asks you to do anything dodgy again, you must contact me. Do you promise?'

'Yes, of course, Cassidy. You have no idea what a relief it is to be able to talk about this whole insane business to someone who actually believes me.'

Cassidy grunted and then grinned at her. 'I suppose you've been paying me with the money you got from Gowan and Murphy?'

'I had no choice. I haven't much of my own money left over after bills and supporting Amy.'

Cassidy returned to his desk. She watched as he wrote on a yellow legal pad. After finishing his notes, he folded his arms and contemplated her for a minute.

'OK, where do we go from here?' he said then. 'We know that Rory associates with underhand property developers, that he's a blackmailer, possibly involved in insider trading, and we suspect he had Murphy killed. But we have no real evidence.'

'Can you break into his office and find out if he has anything incriminating we can use against him?'

'Bree, sorry, but I work by the book or as close to it as possible. Breaking and entering is classified as illegal.' Seeing the disappointment on her face, he grinned. 'But I might know someone who has a less evolved moral compass, and he might help, for the right incentive.'

'Thank God for that!' She sighed in relief. 'But, Cassidy, I'm worried about Amy. I thought he had decided to leave her alone. But according to my mother, he's been in touch with her. Will you watch over her? Keep her safe. She won't listen to anything I say. Like my mother she thinks I'm hysterical and paranoid about Rory.'

'I'll try to keep a watch on her, but I can't be everywhere. I'll have to hire some help. We'll be needing that money that you've stashed away.'

'What do you think I should do now?'

'Well, there's one thing you can do. Take your mother up on her offer and stay with her. You need to stop giving Rory opportunities to force you into illegality.' Seeing the mutinous look on her face, he added, 'Bree, if he can't contact you, then he can't use Amy against you. Go stay with your mother, call in sick to work. But you must make your mother promise not to tell anyone where you are. Let me get on with things. Give me your mother's number, and I'll phone you every day.'

Reluctantly Bree agreed. What he suggested made sense. She reached into her bag and placed a wad of notes on the table. 'There's a thousand there. I know it's dodgy money but one does have to live.' She smiled. 'I'm expecting results from your morally light friend.' She reached over and shook Cassidy's hand. It felt warm and strong. Once again, she was reminded of her father's hands.

Then she left.

On the drive home, she realised for the first time in ages that her jaw wasn't clenched. Telling Cassidy everything was cathartic. She felt lighter. Rory was still a malign force, but for the first time she felt she might rid herself of his pestilent presence.

She was halfway home when she had a thought. Rory would know where she was if she stayed with her mother. She would be just as exposed in her mother's house. But she could ask Anita if she could stay in her Dublin flat. Anita was always asking her to visit. Now she would take up her invitation.

She drove home, rang Anita, and arranged to go to stay with her the next day. She called Cassidy and left a message on his machine, telling him of the change of plan and leaving Anita's phone number and address. Then she rang her mother to say that she was taking a few days off work and planned to meet up with friends from her college days, and Anita had offered her a place to stay. She gave her mother the phone number for Anita's flat. Her mother sounded relieved that she was taking some time off.

Bree ended the call as quickly as she could. She was certain her mother didn't know where the flat was and had no way of finding out. Giving her the phone number was a necessary risk, but it had to be done.

Then she packed a bag with enough clothes to do her for a week. When she was finished, she rang work and, faking a hoarse voice, said that she had come down with the flu and wouldn't be in for a few days. The manager sounded pissed off, but that didn't bother Bree. Finally, she checked the house carefully, ensuring all the doors were locked and bolted. She rigged up a booby trap of pans and dishes to alert her to intruders. Then she slept.

CHAPTER 34

CASSIDY

The morning of his first appointment with Bree O'Hagan, Cassidy was feeling hungover and cranky. He was always that way after a meeting with his ex, Imelda. They were finalising their separation and working out finances and, most importantly, access to their daughter Nora. Imelda was being cooperative, and they had come to a solution that gave each of them most of what they wanted. But he blew it by trying to push the boundaries. He still hoped that there might be a future for the three of them, that Imelda would forgive his actions two years ago, even if his colleagues didn't. Imelda was very clear. He would always be Nora's dad, and she would do everything she could to facilitate their relationship, but there was no way they would ever live together. She told him she was moving on and dating. The rage he felt and showed scared Imelda, and he could see that all that they had just agreed was at stake, so he swallowed his pain and took himself to Byrnes, where he pickled himself in whiskey and had to be put to bed in the publican's spare room. When he peeled his eyes open the next morning and looked at his watch, he realised he needed to get to the office to meet his new client. He cursed making the arrangement.

Bree O'Hagan looked nervous when she appeared at his door, but so did most of his clients. Hiring a private investigator wasn't something most ordinary folk expected to be doing. Come to that, he didn't expect to end up as a PI, either. Yeah, well, life was surprising. But the O'Hagan woman was interesting. She was dressed as though she didn't want to be noticed – her clothes, jeans and jumper were of a nondescript colour, and she wore her brown hair tied back in a ponytail, not a flattering look once a woman was past the age of twelve, he thought. But it suited her. She wore no make-up, which he found unusual. Most women he encountered tried to enhance their appearance when calling at his door. Not because they wanted to impress him, but rather to bolster their confidence. He knew from Imelda that many women used make-up as a form of armour. But not this woman. It all added to the effect of someone who wanted to disappear into the woodwork. She should have looked drab, but she had something. Maybe it was her eyes, which were a soft hazel and glowed, adding life to a curiously immobile face, but it was more the air of restless watchful energy she generated. Her face wasn't beautiful or even pretty, but it was arresting. If he had to describe it, he would say it was an intelligent face, but those hazel eyes looked fearful and watchful.

The task she presented him was intriguing. He felt that there was a lot she wasn't telling him. Normally he didn't like going into a case without having all the facts, but he realised that if he pushed too hard she'd back away, and he found himself reluctant to let that happen. He thought he'd take a punt on her. He didn't like the secretive vibe he got from her but he reckoned that he'd get to the bottom of what she was hiding over time. He always liked a challenge, and he had the feeling that whatever had brought her to his door seeking help would be intriguing.

Despite her cautious demeanour, she managed to let slip that she had six grand to spend on hiring him. He could see she regretted the slip. He looked her over again. Her accent was Dundalk. His mam came from there, so he recognised it. Her clothes looked cheap, and he doubted she spent much money on the little luxuries women seemed to enjoy. She didn't look like a woman with much spare cash. Six grand was a lot of money for a cleaner with a youngster to have put by. She said her daughter was in college, so she would be pricy to maintain. He scanned her hand and noticed the absence of rings or the tell-tale imprint of one recently removed. Where did she get the money to hire him? But then, that wasn't his business, and it was good to know she had the means to employ him.

The information she gave him was intriguing. This Straffen guy seemed to have a hold over her, and she wanted to find a way to even the playing field. But what was she being blackmailed over? She looked respectable, almost schoolteacherish. Was she involved in something illegal? Maybe it was as well not to ask too many questions in case he needed plausible deniability.

He booked flights to England to start making the inquiries she requested, and his week there had proved informative. But the more he uncovered about Straffen, the more intrigued he became. The guy, on the face of it, seemed like a solid citizen, a well-respected professional. But the more he investigated his life, the shadier he appeared. It was like the face he presented to the world hid something darker. He was particularly interested in Straffen's work in Mulderfield. His colleagues' conflicting views of him as both a hero and villain, showed him to be a complex character, and the reluctance and even fear some of his colleagues expressed about him was intriguing. OK, he could understand the danger of slandering a colleague, but he had seen the whites of their eyes, and was convinced that it was more than professional caution and the fear of being sued, that gave them the anxious squirrely look. He looked into the case of the orderly who had supposedly supplied pictures to the patient Sol Dane. He ended up in jail, but everyone he spoke to, his wife, and fellow colleagues were all convinced that he had been set up. The poor bastard was released two years ago, and from what he gathered, he was unable to get back on his feet. His wife couldn't live with him because of his drinking, and currently he was dossing in homeless hostels.

But it was after he discovered more about Straffen's business dealings and his association with some unsavoury characters from the criminal world that he became concerned. The guy had a lucrative practice in London, he was minting it, and his client list was stellar except for the handful of hoods he was seeing. It was interesting to notice that he was also meeting with Irish businessmen, and he knew from his days on the force that some of these guys were on the outskirts of shady deals and criminality. The business dealings he had in London looked shifty. Straffan was even mentioned obliquely in a newspaper report on insider trading. It was hinted that the wife of a prominent businessman had passed on information to him that he used to line the pockets of his criminal friends. The same woman took an overdose and died shortly afterwards. The papers were careful not to make direct accusations or name him explicitly, but the dots were there to be joined. What was a nice respectable woman like Bree O'Hagan doing mixed up with Rory Straffen? He decided to have it out with her. He liked to know just what he was mixed up in, and there was no way he was willing to work blind.

His latest meeting with Bree O'Hagan was a revelation. The story she told stretched plausibility, and yet she convinced him. It explained her air of haunted vulnerability. When she looked at him with tears streaming down her face, he didn't feel he was being played. She looked like a woman who was finally telling her story, and it rang with the truth. She also took a risk coming clean with him. She was guilty of committing an impressive selection of crimes. What the hell was he to do about it? Something about her made him feel protective, and he couldn't allow that. The last time he got emotionally involved in a case, he ended up losing his job and Majella. There was no way he would make that mistake again. But, damn it, she looked terrified. She didn't have anywhere to turn, and no one believed her. Despite himself, he had to hand it to Straffen, he knew how to manipulate people, to play on their weaknesses and get them to do exactly what he wanted – the sick bastard.

Well, he was interested. He realised that he wanted to get to the bottom of the mystery of Rory Straffen and try to help Bree O'Hagan escape from the Machiavellian trap Straffen had placed her in. But there was no way he was risking his investigator licence, so he'd have to handle things delicately. At least he still had some contacts from the old days, so he might be able to unearth something that might be useful. But, for now, he managed to persuade her that she needed to lie low and wait. He just hoped she did as he asked. At times she had a reckless look in her eyes, and he knew that fear over her daughter's welfare might make her do something foolish.

CHAPTER 35

BREE

Anita's flat was at the top of Dorset Street. It was a ground-floor two-bed apartment with a kitchen-cum-living-room. One corner of it was set up as a home office. Being a barrister meant Anita often had to work late nights. Bree was surprised to discover she even had a word processor, just like the one she used when working for Colm. The thought of Colm made her squirm, so she turned her attention to Anita. Her friend wasn't wearing her usual smart, professional attire, but she looked chic even in jeans and a pullover. If she didn't love Anita so much, she could seriously resent her ability to look sophisticated even when slumming around at home.

They ordered a Chinese meal, and ate as they watched a video. After they cleared away the meal, Anita opened the bottle of wine that Bree had brought, and they sat side by side on the couch. The film played on but it was just for background noise because they paid it scant attention. Anita regaled Bree with hilarious stories from her days in court. Anita always had a way with words. She could make even the dullest encounters seem amusing. She had the capacity to pull enjoyment from everything. It's what made her such interesting company.

Eventually Anita asked, 'How did your friend get on with Cassidy?'

For a moment Bree was confused, then she remembered how she had got Cassidy's number from Anita. 'I think she's happy with him, but after I passed on his number I left her to it.'

'Well, he's a good guy and usually gets the goods. I hope your friend gets what she needs to deal with her husband.'

Bree nodded and drifted away, lost in thought.

'Bree, are you all right?' Anita's tone was concerned. 'It's just that I met your mam the other day. She was so worried about you. She told me about you leaving Colm's firm and that you're working as a cleaner, and she said that a man had broken into your house and attacked you. So, again, are you OK?'

'I'm fine, Anita. Yes, the break-in was scary – to be honest, that's why I'm here. I decided to get away from the house and take some time off to recuperate.'

'God, it must have been so frightening. Did you get a look at the guy?'

'No, I was too busy trying to get away from him. The gardaí showed me some pictures to see if I recognised anyone, but I didn't.'

'Your mam said he was in the house when you arrived.'

'No, I left the front door open, and he followed me. Look, Anita, do ya mind if we don't talk about it? To be honest, I want to stop thinking about it.'

'Of course. I'm sorry, Bree.'

They sat on, drinking wine and talking about old school friends, until Bree felt she should let Anita get to bed.

She was about to make her excuses and head to the spare bedroom when Anita asked, 'Why did you leave Colm's? You and he got on great. I bumped into him a few days ago, and when I mentioned you and asked what happened, he got very squirrely. Eventually, he said to ask you.' Anita looked at her expectantly.

Bree shrugged.

'Oh my God, Bree, stop being so mysterious! Was that it?'

Bree snapped, 'I wish everyone would mind their own business! I just wanted a change, no big deal, OK!'

Anita looked offended. 'OK, that's me told then.'

'Oh, Anita! Sorry for snapping – but I'd just like to forget about all the shitty things that have been happening lately and have a few days of fun.'

Anita looked contrite. 'Sorry, love, I'm a nosy cow. It's none of my business, but you know that I'm here if you ever need to talk, don't you?'

For a moment, Bree was tempted to offload her entire mess onto Anita. It had helped when she talked to Cassidy. But what if Anita refused to believe her? Anita knew that she had her difficulties in the past. And what about all the illegal stuff she had been involved in? Telling Anita would put her in a very difficult position. No, she couldn't tell her – after all, she had Cassidy at her back, and that would have to be enough.

She grinned at her friend. 'You're a good mate, Anita, and someday I promise we'll have a proper chat, but for now I just want a bit of craic. If you want to help, how about taking me out on the town?'

'It's a deal. Tomorrow night will be party night, my friend.'

Impulsively, Bree hugged her warmly before heading off to her bed.

Next morning Bree slept until noon. She couldn't recall when she had last slept so long or so late in the day. She stretched out in the bed, luxuriated in the soft sheets, and snuggled under the warm duvet. It was wonderful that no one, apart from her mother, knew where she was. Even if her mother let her whereabouts slip to Amy, no one knew where Anita's flat was located. The important thing was that Rory couldn't contact her. For the first time since Rory had come back into her world, she felt safe, untouchable. It wouldn't last, but while it did she planned to revel in it. For the next few days, or at least until she heard from Cassidy, she would take a holiday from the anxiety that stalked her day and night.

In the afternoon, she strolled into town, glad she had packed her runners. The hard city pavements were cruel on her feet, and today she didn't need any flagellation, self-inflicted or otherwise. It was a dull December day, but the city sent out vibes of Christmas to come. In most streets, the decorations were up, and the shops filled with determined shoppers clutching shopping bags. She wandered into O'Connell Street and stopped to admire the Anna Livia Plurabella, or the Floozy in the Jacuzzi, as it was irreverently called. She had always loved the lovely bronze of a woman sitting on a slope as water poured over her and liked the idea of people having a place to sit and chat with friends after a hard day shopping. Then she wandered into Cleary's department store and availed herself of squirts from the sample bottles of perfume. Smelling delicious, she headed towards Grafton Street, stopped in a café and ordered coffee. She wished she had brought a book to read. She still loved to read, but she could no longer lose herself in books as she did as a child when she was such a passionate reader. Being vigilant reduced her capacity to let go of herself and totally immerse herself in a story. Rory had robbed her of that pleasure. She then wandered around Stephen's Green, feeding the ducks with the remains of a sandwich she bought from a deli. As she sat on a bench there, it occurred to her that it would be nice to cook something for Anita's dinner. She decided on a simple chilli.

She bought everything she needed for the meal and went back to the flat. Anita wouldn't be home until well after seven. She cooked the meal and left it on the hob, ready to heat up when Anita arrived. Impulsively she turned on the radio and, finding a music station, sang and danced as she washed up the mess she had made and set the table. The simple domestic tasks were smoothing out any residual tension and fear.

When everything was ready she picked a book at random from Anita's bookcase. It was a John Grisham, and she sat down to read. She had barely turned a page when the phone rang.

She picked it up and Cassidy spoke, his voice loud and harsh in her ear.

'Bree?' he asked.

Her body tensed. 'Yes, have you any news? Is everything all right with Amy?'

'Yes, she's OK. I've been tailing Rory, and I discovered he has an apartment in Howth. It's pretty swish, but he doesn't own it. PJ Gowan owns that apartment and three others in the complex. As far as I can gather, he's been living there since he arrived in Dublin three years ago. Gowan also owns the office he has in Rathmines. I did a bit of research into Gowan, and he's a slippery character. He has a reputation for ruthlessness and, according to my sources, he's happy to pass well-stuffed brown envelopes to councillors or politicians if he thinks it will help his property deals. There is also a suggestion that he has friends in the Neary crime family. My informant is a Garda detective, and he's been trying to bring down that shower for a while. He's convinced that some of Gowan's money comes from his dealings with the Nearys. But he's as slippery as an eel.'

He paused, and she knew there was more coming.

'Go on,' she said.

'The thing is . . . I think Amy is seeing Rory. I mean in a going-out-together way.'

'*Shit!*' Bree's knees wobbled, and she sat on the floor, holding the receiver tight to her ear.

'Are you still there?' he asked.

'Yes, go on. Are you sure about them being together?' Her voice shook with the horror of it. The idea of Rory touching Amy made her flesh crawl.

'The thing is, I saw her at his flat.'

'Maybe he's helping her with her work again.'

'I don't think so, Bree. Last night she called to his place at nine, and she only left this morning at around eight. He drove her to college and then went to his Rathmines office.'

As she sat on the floor, she was aware of the carpet rough under her hand and bare feet. She explored the swirly pattern with her fingertips.

'Bree, are you still there?' Cassidy's voice was sharp.

'Yes, I'm still here. Cassidy – time is running out. He's going to use Amy and then discard her. I know what he's capable of.' Her voice rose, and even her ears could detect the panic it held.

'It's going to be OK – we can find something to incriminate him.'

'Don't you get it? This is Rory, the master manipulator. He'll always find a way for someone else to take the blame. He started with me as a child and has honed his skill since then.'

'Bree, don't give up. I'm certainly not finished with him. I'm sure we'll find a way to stop him.'

'Cassidy, thank you for all your help, but I think it's up to me to stop Rory.'

'What the hell does that mean, Bree?'

Bree didn't answer and replaced the receiver. She ignored the phone when it rang again.

She saw everything clearly now. The Game had come to a head. Rory had to be stopped. She couldn't allow Amy to be collateral damage in whatever scheme he had lined up. There was no way he was going to destroy her daughter. She was going to end this the only way possible. She just needed a plan, and it didn't have to be perfect. It just had to be effective.

When Anita arrived, they ate, and Bree drank more than she usually did. The girls headed out for a night on the town. Anita was obviously happy to see her friend in such good form, laughing, even flirting. For Bree, it was as if a weight had been lifted, and now she was finally floating free. Now she knew what she must do.

CHAPTER 36

Bree spent the next day working on her plan. The solution was obvious. Rory had to be got rid of. He had to die, and she knew she had to kill him. The easy part was making the decision. That surprisingly caused her no moral qualms. The execution was the difficult part. She smiled grimly at her pun. How to kill him was the problem to be solved. She ran through her options. She could try to poison him, but where could she get poison and how could she get close enough to administer it, and ensure no one else ingested it?

Alternatively, she could buy a sharp knife and stab him. That had attractions for her. She liked the immediacy of plunging a knife into Rory's chest and watching while the light faded from his eyes. Yes, that would be satisfying. But Rory wasn't likely to let her next or near him with a carving knife and, even if she did get close, he was a strong man and would easily overpower her. She could hire someone else to do it. But again, she didn't know how to locate a hit man, how much they charged, and she didn't trust one not to betray her either to the gardaí or to Rory.

Her brain whirred. She found it deeply pleasurable to contemplate ways of ending Rory. But plotting to kill him wasn't going to be an academic exercise. She was determined to make it a reality. Now that she had made the decision, she felt clarity and peace.

There were other practicalities to be considered. She needed to find out where Rory lived, and unfortunately she hadn't thought to get the address from Cassidy. She'd have to follow him from his office in Rathmines. At least she knew from Cassidy's description where that was. If she was to succeed, she needed to gather as much information as she could. It felt good to be taking the first steps to achieve her objective. Failure wasn't an option.

The following morning, she parked her car a safe distance from the surgery. She was terrified of Rory recognising her car, terrified that he would see her. At least it was a damp, mizzly day so hopefully she'd pass unrecognised amongst the miserable-looking pedestrians. She wandered up and down until at nine she saw a pretty young woman arrive, open the surgery's side door, and go inside. Bree bought herself a coffee and a sandwich in a nearby coffee shop. Cassidy had mentioned that Rory didn't arrive until later in the morning, so she had a bit of time to kill. She was too distracted to read but she glanced at a paper someone else had left befind. At around ten she got up and walked to a small park she had noticed across from Rory's building. She could make out who was coming or going and it was unlikely that she would be noticed. She was getting very damp when she saw Rory arrive. Even though it was a wet wintery December morning, she immediately recognised him by the bright streak of white hair brushed across his forehead. He went inside, and she waited. He had parked his car in the parking area just behind his office. Keeping her head down she darted over to check it out. It was a BMW and looked solid and muscular. It wasn't a 'look at me' car, but it drew attention by its very subtlety. A perfect car for Rory. And that's what gave her the idea. She just needed to mull things over.

By lunchtime, she was getting extremely wet and bored. She supposed this was what Cassidy had to do when he was following people. God, but it was boring as hell! She headed back to her car and decided to risk moving it closer to the building, so at least she got some shelter. Over the course of the day, several people entered the side door, stayed about an hour, and then left. Rory's clients. She bought a sandwich, coffee, and a newspaper to help pass the time. At five, he got in his car, and she followed him. It was a risk tailing him. He might recognise her car, but it was a risk she had to take. She was able to keep well back until they neared Howth. She was lucky that he was heading back there, and not off on other business. She concentrated on keeping at least one car between hers and Rory's BMW. Her nerves jangled but, even if he saw her, it wasn't the end of the world. After all, he didn't know what she was planning for him. She smiled grimly at the thought. For once in their cat-and-mouse game, the mouse was going to be the pursuer. She saw his car turn into a small block of apartments. She drove past the turn-off, giving him enough time to get inside, then she doubled back and parked as far away from his car and the building entrance as she could get.

She was thinking about heading home when a taxi pulled up, and Amy got out. Bree was lucky that the insistent rain and Amy's keenness to get inside the building stopped her from noticing her car. Bree's heart thumped uncomfortably as she watched her pay the driver and run inside.

The last faint hope she had that Cassidy was mistaken drifted away. The thought of Rory and her daughter together sickened her. He was a vile human being, but he wore an attractive mask that only she could see through. He had to be put down like a rabid dog. She just needed the cunning and the nerve to do it. She longed to go up to his flat, hammer on the door and drag Amy to safety. But she knew that would only make things worse, and feed into the scenario that she was deranged. Perhaps she was deranged. Well, fuck it, she'd go full 'bunny boiler' and make his life a living hell. She had always thought of the Glenn Close character from *Fatal Attraction* as an evil psycho, but now she experienced sympathy for her, a sense of kinship. Neither of them was going to accept being played by a man. But it hadn't turned out well for the vengeful woman in *Fatal Attraction*. She needed to think things through if her plan was going to work.

She drove off and plotted her next move. At eight, she returned to Rory's apartment. Hopefully Amy would have left though she thought it unlikely. But she needed to get into his apartment whether or not Amy was there. As she didn't know which apartment was Rory's, she buzzed a few flats until finally he answered.

'*Let me in!*' she shouted.

'Brenna, this is a surprise, but now isn't a good time. I'm entertaining.'

'Let me in, Rory, or I'll let every one of your fucking tyres down and key your precious car. Your choice!'

He buzzed her in. She took the lift. He was waiting for her at his open door. He grinned at her and ushered her inside and through to the kitchen.

Amy was sitting on a high stool at the kitchen counter. She was wearing a little slip dress in dusty pink and a grey bomber jacket was draped around her shoulders. Her long legs dangled from the high stool. She looked lovely and a little decadent. This dressing up was for Rory – normally Amy wore jeans and shirts. She was playing at sophistication. Bree's heart ached for her.

Amy glared at her mother. '*Why are you here?*' she demanded, her voice shrill.

'I might ask you the same thing, Amy. Surely it can't be college work, can it?'

Amy flushed. 'It's none of your business. I'm an adult. I can do as I please.'

'So, Rory, you're corrupting children still, I see.'

'Brenna – sorry, I keep forgetting you prefer to be called Bree – I'm sorry, Amy and I meant to tell you about our relationship, but we were waiting for the right time.'

'Mam, it's OK. Rory isn't even related to us. He explained to me about Daniel not being his dad.'

Bree ignored Amy and stared at Rory. 'Daniel was a father to you until he died. He'd be horrified at what he nourished and called a son.'

'Brenna, Bree, I'll always appreciate that he did his best, but I need you to understand he wasn't the saint you and your mother believed. He suspected my mother of being unfaithful, and, well, I was witness to many arguments.'

'*You're a liar, Rory.*' Turning to Amy, Bree snapped, 'Every word that comes from his mouth is either a lie or a twisted truth. Get your belongings and get out now.'

'No! You can't just order me around like a little child. Rory and I love each other!' Amy slid from the stool and ran into Rory's arms.

Rory held her protectively and gently stroked her hair.

Bree walked over to a shelf, lifted a pretty glass sculpture of a deer and dropped it. The glass shattered. To Bree, it was the sound of beautiful discordant music. She reached into a cupboard where there were dozens of Waterford crystal glass tumblers. She took one in her hand and dropped it, and then another crashed to the floor.

Amy stood staring, her mouth agape.

Rory went very still and then said, 'Amy, my love, I know this is hard for you, but perhaps you'd better leave. I'll see if I can talk some sense into your mother. She's obviously not going to stop until I can calm her down.'

'But, Rory, I don't want to leave.'

'*Get out, Amy, or I'll smash everything in this fucking place! Clear out!*' Bree screamed.

Her eyes brimming with tears, Amy glared at her mother. 'I'll never forgive you for this. You have completely lost the plot.'

'*Go! Now!*' Bree shrieked.

Picking up Amy's backpack, Rory led her out of the room.

From the kitchen Bree saw him hand Amy some money, telling her to call a taxi. She watched, nauseated, as Amy clung to him and he kissed her on the lips.

Closing the apartment door, Rory walked back into the kitchen, clapping his hands slowly.

'Bravo, Brenna, well played! But I think you rather made my case for me. Everyone's going to be convinced that you're in the throes of a complete mental breakdown or a psychotic episode.'

'I don't care anymore, Rory. I'm done with your games. Leave Amy out of it.'

'Or what, Brenna? What are you going to do?'

He smirked then, and she threw the half-drunk bottle of wine sitting on the countertop at him. She missed and the red liquid splattered everywhere, and she wished it was his blood.

Rory lunged forward. His hand lashed out and he caught her by the throat, almost lifting her off her feet. He dragged her from the kitchen and threw her on a couch.

'Brenna, you made a big mistake coming here. I think that you'll find that there are consequences when you mess with my Game.'

'I don't care what you do to me, Rory,' she said, rubbing her neck.

'*Aww*, but what about your lovely mother and the delicious Amy who dotes on me? I might have tired of her sooner if you hadn't interfered but, now, I think I'll just have to get creative.'

Bree stumbled to her feet and hurried to the door. She said nothing as she left. She took the stairs rather than the lift.

As she drove out of the car park, she clipped her car door on the side of the gateway at the exit. It would cost a bit to fix, but needs must. Then she drove out to the waste ground she had noticed on one of her regular getting-lost visits to Dublin. It had a few burnt-out cars and cannibalised machines scattered around but, thankfully, it wasn't overlooked. She drove a mile past it and parked her car. Hopefully, it would be safe there, for a while at least. She checked her watch. It was after ten.

She changed into her runners and took her coat, hat, and woolly scarf from the back seat. Then she walked briskly back towards town. She was tired out by the time she reached a busy area. It was now after eleven. She decided to get herself a coffee at a burger place. It was too soon to put her plan into action. She felt excitement bubble inside, but she damped it down. She needed to keep her focus and stay alert.

At midnight, she hailed a taxi and asked to be dropped off at an apartment complex next to Rory's. She paid the driver. Then she hurried towards Rory's block. The place wasn't in complete darkness. A security light threw a beam across the space. She kept to the edges of the carpark and soon stood beside Rory's fancy jalopy. She reached into her pocket for the keys she had stolen when he walked Amy to the door.

She smiled as she thought about Rory having to clean up the mess she had created. When would he miss the keys? She got into his car.

It felt luxurious, a world removed from her little Ford Fiesta. It took her a while to get used to the feel of it. But it started easily and she headed out onto the main road. She drove to Rathmines and parked in the car park at the back of his office space, where he saw his patients and his hoods. It was quite big as it supplied car parking for all the businesses nearby, and for the residents of the nearby flats. The carpark wasn't overlooked by the road and there were no pubs or clubs nearby so with luck no one would see what she got up to. She took what she needed from the boot and scratched a message on the passenger door with her nail scissors. There was no CCTV in the carpark, but she kept her woollen hat pulled low over her eyes, and wrapped her scarf tightly around her neck.

She walked to the phone box at the corner of the street. Hopefully, it would be operational, or she would have to keep searching for one that worked. It seemed as though the gods were with her. The phone booth was in perfect working order, apart from the stench of urine which scorched her nostrils.

She called Rory's number. It took a while, but eventually he answered.

'Are you missing something?' she whispered.

'Brenna, this is getting to be tiresome. I would advise you to stop what you're doing before I get really annoyed.'

'Take a look out of your window.'

He put the phone down, and she waited until he returned.

'Where is my car, Brenna?' His voice was sharp with irritation.

'I left it in a safe place, Rory. Why don't you check for a little clue? I know how you like games.'

She flinched as he slammed the phone down. Good, he sounded rattled, music to her ears. He'd find the clue she left in his jacket pocket. She slipped it in when he grabbed her. She felt proud of herself. Rory needed to know what it felt like to be manipulated and to have no idea what was coming.

In less than half an hour, Rory arrived at the car park. He sent his taxi away. It hadn't taken him long to find and figure out her clue. He hurried over to his car and moaned when he saw what she had scrawled all over the passenger door.

The tyre iron hit him square on the back of his head. The sound reminded her of Daddy sharply tapping his boiled egg, before slicing the top off. Rory lay slumped alongside the car. She stepped over him and ran to the driver's side, quickly reversing the entire length of the car park. She waited. Rory was stunned, but she could see him rising from the ground, staggering like a drunk. She turned on the full beam and he covered his eyes, struggling to get his bearings and see what was happening. She too, wanted him to see what was coming as she ground her foot on the accelerator and drove straight at him. His body went flying, and it seemed an age before it hit the tarmac with a loud, satisfying smack. Was he dead? Or should she reverse over him again? She hesitated. She watched in the rear-view mirror. Unbelievably, she could see his hand rise. She slipped the car in reverse and gunned her engine. Feeling sick, she drove over his prone body. This felt more visceral than hitting him full-on had been. Thankfully, now, his body was still. But she felt compelled to check. To make sure.

Slowly she walked over to the still figure lying on the ground. She shone her torch over him. He was lying splayed out. She ran the torch over his body slowly. When she saw his face, she knew. His eyes were open, and he stared sightlessly up at her. He wasn't smiling his crooked smile now. She reached into his jacket and retrieved her clue. It was a gamble to give it to him and a relief that he had brought it with him. Satisfied, she switched off her torch and hurried back to the car.

She drove away until she came to the disused piece of ground. She got out and carefully wiped everything she had touched, the steering wheel, the gear stick, the rear-view mirror, and the tyre iron. She had worn gloves, but she wasn't taking any chances. Finally, she left the keys in the engine. By morning it would be long gone.

Then she ran the short distance towards her waiting car.

She drove back to Anita's flat. That night she slept like she hadn't slept since she was a small child, safe in her little bed in Sligo. In the peaceful time before Rory.

CHAPTER 37

Bree awoke to a world that felt lighter, a world without Rory. A malevolent force was gone. Come what may, she had no regrets. She turned on the radio and waited for news of Rory's death to break. She guessed that the earliest his body would be found was around seven-thirty. It was nearly eight now, and she hoped that whoever did discover his body wouldn't be too traumatised.

She felt edgy, unable to sit still, until the early morning news described how the body of a middle-aged man was found dead in the Rathmines area and she could breathe easily. The news report said that the police had the area cordoned off and were keen to find out if there were any witnesses to the incident. It took her hearing the news of a man's body being found to finally believe that she was free of Rory forever.

Did Amy know? Whom would Rory list as his next of kin? She wondered what to do next. Anita's telephone rang. It was her mother, sounding anxious.

'Bree, are you OK?'

'Of course I am. I told you I was spending a few days relaxing at Anita's and that's just what I've been doing. Why? Is something the matter? You sound worried.'

'The gardaí are at my house. They want to know where you are.'

Bree's heart thudded against her ribs. 'Why? What do they want me for?'

'They wouldn't give me any information, except to say it's nothing to do with Amy when I asked them. They just wanted to know where to locate you. You have to give me Anita's address for them. They want to pass it on to the crowd in Dublin. They said they needed to speak with you as soon as possible. What's going on, Bree?'

'I have no idea, Mammy. Gosh, I wonder what they want. Did they say anything at all?'

'Not a word. Here give me the address and, look, ring me as soon as you find out what this is all about. I'll be here.'

Bree called out the address and got off the phone. Why did the gardaí want her? OK, she would have been seen at the apartment, but surely she couldn't be connected with his death? At least not this soon. She made herself a strong coffee and waited. It was impossible to plan what to say when she didn't know what they wanted her for.

At nine, the front door buzzed, and she let two gardaí in. A man and a woman, both in uniform. Her heart hammered as she stared at them.

'Ms Bree O'Hagan?'

'Yes, what's wrong?' she asked, licking dry lips.

'May we come in, please?'

They introduced themselves, but Bree couldn't hear over the blood pounding in her ears. She led them into Anita's little living room and invited them to sit down.

The two gardaí looked uncomfortable and glanced at each other uneasily.

Then the male garda blurted out, 'I'm sorry to have to tell you that your cousin Rory Straffen has been found dead early this morning.'

Bree sat back. The lousy bastard had named her as his next of kin. Why not Philip or Julie or even her mother? Even after death, he was mocking her. She composed her face to look how she imagined a concerned relative would.

'Oh my God! What happened?' she gasped. 'A heart attack?'

'No – I'm afraid he was assaulted during the night. Near his office in Rathmines. A shift worker coming back from the hospital found him.'

'You mean it was a mugging? A robbery?' Her voice sounded sufficiently shocked.

'We're making enquiries at the moment. This is an active murder investigation.'

'Murder?'

'Yes, Ms O'Hagan. He was hit on the head with a blunt object but then run over by a car and there is evidence that was deliberate.'

'How horrible! Poor Rory!' Bree closed her eyes and covered her mouth with her hand. Then she took a deep breath and said, 'May I ask why you have informed me and not his family?'

'You are listed as his next of kin and ICE contact.'

'I didn't know that. But his mother and stepfather will need to be informed. They live in London.'

'If you give us their address, we can send an officer from London to let them know in person.'

'I'll have to ask my mother. I don't have their address. I'll let you know as soon as I have it.'

'When was the last time you saw your cousin?'

'Actually, I saw him last night. I went to his flat and stayed a short time. I left around nine-thirty.'

'How was he when you saw him?'

'He seemed fine. Look, this is a lot to take in, and I really need to contact my mother and daughter.'

'That's perfectly understandable, but we may need to speak to you again. Once again, we are very sorry to have to bring you this awful news.'

Bree saw them out.

She needed to ring her mother and Amy. Her mother first. The phone only rang once.

'Well, Bree, is everything all right?'

Her mother sounded tense.

'I'm afraid not, Mammy. It's Rory. He's dead.'

The word hung in the air, and her mother gasped.

'He was killed, Mammy. Attacked.'

'A mugging?'

'No – they said he was hit with a blunt object and then by a car and there's evidence that it was deliberate. He was found early this morning near his office in Rathmines – by a shift worker coming back from the hospital.'

'Oh my God, poor Julie! This will finish her off. Should I call Philip?'

'No, Mammy. The gardaí want Julie and Philip's address. They'll pass it on to the police in England. You can call later.'

Mary gave her Julie's London address, and Bree rang the Garda station and gave them the contact details.

Then she got in her car and drove to Amy's flat. No one was home. It was just after ten, so Amy would probably be at college.

She drove to UCD and walked to the block which housed the

psychology lecture halls. She waited until the morning lecture ended and dozens of young people streamed out, talking and laughing.

She spotted Amy, her arms loaded with file blocks.

She stopped short when she saw her mother, blanked her, and walked away.

'*Amy!*' Bree called loudly, forcing her to acknowledge her presence.

'Go away. Haven't you done enough? I don't want to see you.' Amy glared at her with naked hostility.

'Amy, I must talk to you. I have some bad news.'

Amy stopped and stared at her. 'Is it Granny? Is she sick?'

'No, Amy, Granny is fine. I'm afraid it's Rory.'

'Rory! What's happened to him?'

'I'm so sorry, love, but I'm afraid that he was killed last night. The gardaí think it was deliberate.'

As Amy's legs buckled, Bree caught her and led her to a bench.

'Deliberate? Amy gasped. 'What happened?'

'Amy, love, I'm sorry – he was hit on the head and then run over by a car – it looks like it was done deliberately.'

'A car? Where?' Amy looked at her mother, eyes wide with disbelief.

'It seems he went back to his office in Rathmines in the middle of the night. That's where the gardaí say he was discovered. A shift worker coming back from the hospital found him.'

'But why did he leave the apartment?' Amy turned fierce puzzled eyes on her mother. 'What did you say to him? Did you say something to drive him away last night? If you hadn't come, he'd probably still be alive.'

Bree said nothing. Her eyes dropped at seeing her daughter in so much pain.

'You must be glad. You hated him, didn't you?'

'Amy, it's complicated, but, yes, it's true I didn't like Rory.'

'Well, I *loved* him, and despite everything you did to poison our relationship, he loved me back. If you hadn't called that night, I'd have stayed over with him. It's all your fault. If it weren't for you, he'd still be alive. *I hate you! Get away from me!*

Sobbing, she raced off.

Sick to her stomach, Bree watched her go, powerless to stop her.

Over the next few days, Bree followed every news report. Rory's car was discovered burnt out on an industrial estate. The gardí contacted her after it was found, and asked her to come to the station.

Bree had been preparing herself for this moment and felt strangely calm. Since Rory died, her anxiety levels had dropped, replaced by a calm acceptance of whatever would be. The Garda station was in the city centre, and she decided to walk there. It wasn't too far from Anita's place.

She was invited into a small interview room and offered tea or coffee, which she declined. The men who ushered her in introduced themselves as Detective O'Connor and Garda Hall. They sat opposite her. The detective, a burly chap with greying hair, cauliflower ears and a boxer's nose, asked the questions while the younger man, with hair already starting to thin on top, took notes.

'Can you think of any reason why your cousin would take a taxi from his apartment to his office? It seems the car that ran over him was his own car.'

'But that doesn't make sense. Unless he left his car in his office carpark and needed something from it.'

'The thing is, his neighbours say he arrived home in his car. They also mentioned a woman calling to see him.'

'I told you that I called to see him,' said Bree.

'Yes, but the residents say he was also visited by a young woman, possibly in her early twenties. When you called at the apartment, did you see her?'

Bree hesitated. 'Yes, I did – it was my daughter Amy.'

'The residents say that you buzzed several flats looking for your cousin.'

'Yes, that's true. I forgot which one was his. It had been a while since I last visted him.'

'The residents also said they heard raised voices coming from the flat and the sound of broken glass.'

'I may have dropped a glass.'

'Or three, we found quite an amount of broken glass in Mr Straffen's bin.'

'OK. Look, he was seeing my daughter, and I was angry about it. He was a relative – my first cousin – and a great deal older than her. I sent Amy home, and I left shortly afterwards. He was perfectly well when I left.'

'But you seem to have been the last person to see Rory Straffen alive.'

'Except for his killer. And I can assure you I was long gone by the time he was killed.'

'What time did you leave the apartment?'

'I'd guess that I left around nine-thirty.'

'One of the residents in the apartment block says that you damaged your car when you were exiting the building.'

'Yes, well, I was still angry with Rory. But, for God's sake, not angry enough to harm him! Come on! You can't seriously think I had anything to do with his death. Anyway, doesn't this prove that I left the apartment when I said I did?'

'Your daughter has been in touch with us. She's was extremely upset and, well, she made some serious allegations about you. She claims that you hated your cousin and had a vendetta against him. She claims that you went . . . let me see how she put it.' He glanced down at some papers in front of him. 'Yes, her exact words were "she went fucking psycho on Rory and started smashing the place up". Would that be an accurate account of what happened, Ms O'Hagan?'

Bree took a deep breath. She had been expecting this. Amy was angry, heartbroken. She would want to lash out – to hurt her. She forced herself to smile at the garda.

'My daughter is inclined to be emotional. She fancied herself in love with Rory. It's true, I didn't approve of the relationship. I didn't like him but I know my daughter and eventually she would have seen through him and things would have fizzled out. It was foolish of me to get so agitated. But it was a mother's overreaction. After she left I calmed down. I told Rory that I would report him to the college authorities about his involvement with a young student. It probably wouldn't have done any good as he's not one of her lecturers, but he still wouldn't like it being reported. He's ambitious and he wouldn't like any hint of scandal or impropriety to sully his reputation. I think he'd have realised a fling with a girl half his age who was a student would have made him look bad, and Rory never liked looking bad.'

'How did he respond to the threat of being reported?'

'He acted as though he wasn't particularly bothered, but I knew he wasn't happy about it either. Anyway, I felt better for saying my piece and, although it was far from an amicable end to the evening, it was civilised. Then I left.'

'Where did you go when you left the building?'

'I went back to my friend Anita's flat.'

'I see, and did your friend Anita hear you come in?'

'No, she was away. She had some business in the courts in Dundalk. She's a barrister and planned on spending the night with her family.'

'So you went straight home from Mr Straffen's apartment?'

'Yes – wait, no, I did stop to buy cigarettes – and I lost my way.

But eventually I made it back to the flat and went straight to bed. Why are you asking me all these questions? I thought Rory was killed long after I visited him?'

'We are exploring several different avenues in our investigation. Can anyone corroborate the time you returned to your friend's flat? Perhaps someone in a neighbouring flat heard you return.'

'I really can't say. I don't think I made much noise, so it's unlikely anyone heard me. You'll have ask them.'

'We intend to.'

'Look, can I go home now? My mother and daughter are really upset and I'd like to spend time with them, and I need to get back to my job in Dundalk too.'

'You're free to go, Ms O'Hagan, but please leave your contact details with the front desk when you leave. We may need to get in touch.'

Bree walked back to the flat. Anita was busy in court all day, so she would have time to herself. She didn't need Anita's concern. All she needed was peace and quiet.

She turned the key in the lock.

'Well, hello, stranger!'

The voice seemed to come from nowhere, but when she whirled around she saw Cassidy standing behind her. *Shit!* She didn't need him right now. Cassidy knew too much, and she couldn't put him off easily. Besides, he probably suspected her. But that's all he could have: suspicions, no evidence, no facts.

'Hi, Cassidy, what are you doing here?'

He smiled, and it brightened up his face.

She realised that she had never seen him smile before. It worried her. Why was he smiling now? He pointed at her door.

'Let me in, Bree, we need to talk.'

Realising there was no way she could get rid of him, she shrugged, opened the door, and led the way into the flat.

He made himself comfortable on the sofa while she made coffee.

'Sorry, I'm out of milk,' she said, handing him a mug.

'No matter, come and sit.'

Bree perched on the edge of her armchair, all her senses alert. She feared Cassidy more than the cops. 'OK, Cassidy, what brings you here?'

Cassidy laughed. Again, something she had never heard him do before.

'I've come to congratulate you, Bree. Your troubles are over. I saw the news reports about Straffen. I'd have come sooner, but I had a little business to attend to.'

'Yeah, well, there was no need for you to come. But I won't pretend that I'm sorry Rory is dead. You know how I felt about him.'

'Bree, last time you spoke to me, you said it was up to you to stop Rory. What did you mean by that?'

'I was planning to confront him about Amy and then tell her everything and hope she'd believe me. So that's what I did. I visited the flat, Amy was there, and I persuaded her to leave. She wasn't pleased to see me, but I planned to have a proper talk with her when she calmed down and make her understand what kind of monster Rory really was. After she left, I threatened Rory with going to the college authorities but I could see it was pointless staying and I left shortly after Amy. '

'It was very convenient that he died so soon after your visit.'

'Cassidy, what are you suggesting? Are you accusing me of having something to do with his death?'

'I don't think you're a killer, Bree.'

Bree felt her shoulders relax as she waited for him to continue.

'But I do think that you've been put under enormous strain, and I think your instincts as a mother, wanting to protect her young, could have overridden any moral qualms you had.'

He held up his hand to make Bree hold back her words.

'If he had been found stabbed in his flat, I would certainly be convinced it was you acting in rage, but luring him to a secluded car park and hitting him with a tyre iron, running over him and then reversing to make sure he was dead, is too dark, too cold for you.'

'I see, then you see me as more of an impulsive homicidal maniac, not a cold-blooded, deliberate, smart one.'

Again, Cassidy laughed. She liked the sound.

'Well put, Bree! Have the gardaí spoken with you?'

'They had a few questions – but where did you get all your information?'

'Maybe I arranged it for you, Bree.'

Bree stared at him. 'What's that supposed to mean?'

'Maybe I got a friend of a friend to get rid of your little problem.'

'*What?*' Bree's throat muscles constricted, and she gasped, 'That's impossible!'

Cassidy caught her arm. His fingers felt like iron bars as he pulled her to her feet.

'Why is it impossible, Bree?' He pushed her back against the wall, forcing her to look into his pebble eyes, terrifying her. 'Tell me why it's impossible, Bree?'

'I don't know, I can't believe you would do something like that. You're a retired garda.'

Cassidy laughed again. 'Your friend Anita never told you why I left the force, did she?'

Bree shook her head.

'I beat a man to within an inch of his life. He's still in the hospital and will never leave, move, or speak again. And you know what, Bree, I enjoyed every minute of putting him there. He was a mean bastard, a bit like your Rory but without his finesse or subtlety.'

He released her and sat down.

She stared at him with sick dread. 'Why are you telling me this?'

'Because I knew that you were going to do something as soon as you put the phone down on me. I just didn't know what. I followed you over the last few days and tailed you the night you left your car at the waste ground. I managed to follow you to Rory's apartment and saw you drive off in Rory's car. But my car acted up on me, so I didn't see where you were heading to. That was clever, stealing his keys. Clever to get him away from the apartment and lure him to his place of execution. How did you get him to come?'

'I left him a note with a clue.'

'Brilliant! You enticed him with his love of games. What was the clue?'

'It was silly. I typed a note on Anita's word processor. It said: "**Come to work to avoid an accident. Don't be long, or the car gets it!**"'

Bree's arm hurt. She could still feel the pain from the pressure of his fingers. She sat down opposite him. 'How did you get away with it, beating that man?'

'He was a piece of shit. I have no regrets. I'd do the same again. My fellow cops suspected me, and they could probably prove it if they wanted. Instead, I was encouraged to take early retirement. They were desperate to avoid a scandal, and, well, the "victim" couldn't testify.'

'I see.' Bree sat in silence. Then she sighed, 'OK, what are you going to do?'

Cassidy shrugged. 'Nothing.'

She stared at him. 'You know what I did. It was premeditated, cold-blooded. I hit him, ran over him, and then reversed over him. Doesn't that make me a monster too?'

'What you did was wrong. What I did was wrong. Would you do the same thing again?'

Bree nodded. 'I would.'

'Do you think that you will ever do anything like that again?'

'God, no!' she said and then, biting her lip, asked, 'Am I a suspect?'

'I talked to a few lads I know on the investigation. They've found out a lot of what I discovered about Rory's links with criminals and his adventures in England. I think they believe that a lot of people had scores to settle with Rory, and you are way down the pecking order of suspects.'

'But I don't want someone blamed for it, an innocent person. I wrote a confession, just the facts, admitting what I've done.'

Cassidy smiled. 'I hope you've put it in a safe place.'

Bree walked into her bedroom. She opend her bedside locker and retrieved a sheet of paper she had hidden there. She returned to the living room and handed it to Cassidy.

He scanned it and then ripped it into pieces. 'Let's wait and see what happens, shall we?' Then he got to his feet.

Bree walked him to the door. 'How do you live with it?' she asked. 'With knowing what you did to that man?'

He looked at her, raising his eyebrows. 'I live with it just fine. But you, I'm not sure. I have a feeling that you'll find a way to torture yourself to the end of your days.'

'Can we talk sometimes, Cassidy, when it gets hard?'

'Why not?'

Then he left, and she watched as he strode away until he was out of sight.

CHAPTER 38

The weeks slipped by. Mammy had come around. Philip had been more open about Rory's treatment of his mother, and she began to ask Bree about the time in Sligo when Rory visited.

Bree at last told her about the Game they had played and how Rory had manipulated her and made her family believe the worst of her. It broke her mother's heart to realise how she had been duped and made to believe the worst of Bree. She cried as she remembered the time she had punished her for stealing. She berated herself for taking Rory's word over her own daughter's. Bree comforted her and explained that Rory manipulated everyone he encountered, it was his gift. But that was as far as Bree was willing to say about her time with Rory as a child. No good would come of telling what had happened to Coleen. That was a burden she would continue to carry. But she promised herself that some day she would find a way to vindicate the memory of poor Patsy. For now, she decided to keep the past in the past. Besides, Rory was now part of the weight she always carried. It puzzled her how the murder of Rory seemed to balance the guilt about Coleen and Patsy Cullen, so she never felt totally overwhelmed. A nice balance of guilt was achieved.

Nevertheless, sometimes at night she had dreams of driving straight at Rory, and the horror she felt wasn't on those nights when she killed him but for the nightmare moments when he struggled to his feet, smiling no matter how often she ran over him. Then she awoke drenched in sweat as the memory of his crooked smile lingered.

Amy still refused to meet with her, despite Mammy's efforts to bring about a reconciliation. According to Mammy, she was still devastated about Rory. However, news had trickled down about Rory's links with criminals, and perhaps over time she would come to see him, if not for the monster he was, but at least as a deeply flawed man. It hurt to not have contact with Amy, but at least Bree knew that she was safe from Rory and for the time being that would have to be enough. Mammy told her that Jason was being a good friend to Amy and, who knew, perhaps over time she might get back with him. According to her mother, he was being really mature and patient. He was 'Jason the Good' after all.

At least Amy wasn't still accusing her of murder. Mammy had been hugely supportive in this regard. When she heard that Amy had gone to the gardaí to accuse Bree of attacking and possibly killing Rory, she had rounded on her in anger and somehow convinced her to accept that Rory had been murdered by someone else. So, perhaps with time and her granny's healing love, Amy might come back to her. But, if not, then that was the price she had to pay for stepping outside the Pale. She was no longer like the rest of humanity – she had deliberately and cold-bloodily taken a life. That was something she would have to live with. An open wound that would never heal but hopefully wouldn't fester.

She spoke with Cassidy a few times on the phone. It helped that he knew everything. Sometimes she longed to ask him to meet her. She found she had fantasies about him. Since Amy was born, she had never slept with a man. All her emotions were tied up in her fierce love for Amy, and she needed nothing more. But now she found herself daydreaming about Cassidy, and once she dreamed that he was kissing her. Perhaps like two Cains, they could wander the earth together, no longer alone, sharing their secrets and needing nothing else. Once or twice, she was tempted to ask him to come down to see her. But she felt she didn't deserve even a sliver of happiness. But maybe one day . . .

She gave up her job at Clean Co and found a job working in an old people's home. She trained in the care of the elderly and hoped she could work as a home help.

One day she met Colm in the shopping centre. He turned away, and she ran after him. She apologised for her actions when she worked for him. She made no explanations or excuses, just apologised and walked away. He called her back, thanked her for her apology and wished her well. Later, Mammy told her that he was engaged to a nice girl who worked in the bank. She was glad. He deserved happiness.

It was now two months since Rory died, and she wondered when she would stop measuring time by his death. Every day in the Home was tiring and physically tough. Lifting old bodies to sit up in bed and washing and caring for them took a toll, but she enjoyed their company and the stories they told.

She removed her plastic apron in the sluice room and pulled a coat over her work uniform. She longed for a shower and hot tea. On the way home, she stopped at the corner shop and bought cigarettes and milk. She didn't feel like cooking, so she picked up a frozen pizza.

When she opened the front door, she saw it. A large brown padded envelope. It was postmarked in London. All letters, small, large, white, or brown, still had the ability to cause her stomach to contract. But she stepped over it and went upstairs, where she had a long hot shower. Afterwards, she put on her pyjamas and the woollen dressing gown her mother had bought her several Christmases ago.

When she went downstairs, she picked up the package and dumped it on the coffee table. She poured herself a glass of wine and opened her cigarette packet. She lit up and inhaled deep into her lungs until she felt dizzy.

She tore open the package. Inside was a typewritten sheet of paper, two other envelopes, and a small jiffy bag. She picked up the typewritten sheet. It was written on headed paper. The letterhead was for a firm of solicitors. **Waters, Waters & Grimes.**

Dear Ms O'Hagan,

Rory Straffen was our client when he resided in London. Unfortunately, we have not had any business dealings with Mr Straffen since his move to Ireland. In fact, we only recently heard of his sad passing from a former colleague now residing in Ireland; hence our contacting you now.

On behalf of the firm of Waters, Waters and Grimes, I'd like to pass on our sincere condolences to you and his family. It was a tragic end for such a talented and much-admired man. We were deeply shocked at the news.

Several years ago, Mr Straffen instructed me to write to you In the event of his death. As you are no doubt aware, he suffered from Huntington's Disease, and his condition was set to worsen over time. When last we met, he spoke with great fondness of his Irish cousin

and the enchanting summer he spent with your family as a child. He asked me to express his gratitude to you for all your kindnesses to him since early childhood, but especially for the last service you performed for him. He has bequeathed the items in the envelope enclosed.

As you are no doubt reeling from the shock of his sudden and untimely death, I would again like to express my condolences.

Yours,

Patrick J Grimes

Bree stared at the letter. What was this illness the letter mentioned? She stared at the padded envelope and the second letter. Her heart beating rapidly, she opened the envelope. Inside was a letter addressed to Mr R Straffen. It too, was written on headed paper.

St Thomas's Hospital, London

Dear Mr Straffen,

I am sorry to inform you that your test results have been confirmed. You do indeed have Huntington's Disease. Please contact my secretary to arrange an appointment to discuss your prognosis.

I have attached a leaflet which will give you some information which may be helpful to you in managing the condition. The support of the medical team at St Thomas's will be available to you as your condition progresses.

Yours,

Mr H Hendrix

(Consultant)

There was an accompanying leaflet which documented the prognosis of the disease and the support available.

She tore open the next envelope. It was addressed to Brenna O'Hagan. The letter was written in a flowing hand.

Dearest Brenna,

It's such a joy when a plan comes together. And I enjoyed playing our Game. You were my first and favourite contestant. You never failed to entertain.

Over the last thirty years, I have amused myself and, at times, enriched myself with my little diversions. But, unfortunately, several misfortunes befell me in rapid succession – a business opportunity turned sour and some of my associates got a little angry with me, but all that paled beside the news I received from my doctor. I had been concerned by a few symptoms, and when I received the bad news I confess I was a little angry. The illness was bequeathed to me by my dear old dad. Well, not so old. He died in his forties of this illness. But every cloud has a lining of silver, and that, my dear, was you. I realised that you were the one person who would allow me to enjoy a final Game. It was so delightful watching you struggle with that oh-so-strong little conscience of yours. But I realised that your rather sweet altruism would lead you to walk along the dark side with me.

Sometimes I doubted you, fearing you would falter at the last hurdle. But, as you read this, I can rest happy in knowing you completed the Game for me. I love the symmetry of our association. The Game began with you, and today it has reached its conclusion. So, my dear sweet cousin, I have always thought of you as my cousin despite Mummy's little dalliance. The end has finally come.

It only leaves me to say, with, I'm afraid, a degree of gloating . . . Game Over, I Win!

Rory Straffen

PS: I hope you like my final gift and your reward for a game well played.

Bree tore open the jiffy bag and out tumbled dozens of black-bordered little envelopes with their embossed forget-me-nots in the corner. Her hands shaking, she opened one of the envelopes. It was a memorial card. A twin to the one she had of Rory as a young man, but this picture didn't show an adolescent Rory but Rory as a man in his forties. In the picture, he smiled his crooked smile.

Bree sat paralysed for a minute, and then she started to laugh until the tears ran down her cheeks. She laughed so hard that her sides hurt. She wondered if she would die of laughter.

The End

Now that you're hooked, why not try

LET
THEM
LIE

FLORENCE GILLAN

Here's a sneak preview of the
prologue, chapter 1 and 2

PROLOGUE

The box sat on his lap, and he stroked each item nestled within. He held them one by one to his face, inhaling the memories and images they evoked. Soon they worked their familiar magic, soothing him. He held the ring the longest, enjoying how it glinted in his dirt-engraved palm. It was small and delicate, too tiny for adult fingers and yet it had slipped off easily. He slid it on his little finger; it stopped fast at his knuckle, looking incongruous. He felt close to his little one, closer than anyone else could ever be, remembering how he drew her breath deep inside, renewing and making him whole.

'Ye belong to your father, the devil, and ye want to carry out your father's desires. He was a murderer from the beginning, not holding to the truth, for there is no truth in him. When he lies, he speaks his native language, for he is a liar and the father of lies.' **John 8:44**

CHAPTER 1

April 2015

Racing from the school at full tilt, trying to dodge the fat raindrops dribbling from the sky, Aoife prayed her boss wouldn't see her. He'd want to discuss the latest suspension and she just didn't have the time. She slid the car out of the car park and joined the snarl-up of traffic converging from all corners of Dublin. God, what a week! If only she could stay home curled up next to Connor, watching a movie and eating takeaway! Instead, she was heading home to Sligo for her dad's anniversary. If it didn't mean so much to her mam, she'd have made excuses. But to Mam, the loss of Dad still ached like a yanked-out tooth.

Despite the passage of twenty years, the day he died was etched like scar tissue on Aoife's consciousness. When he didn't turn up at supper time, her mother had grown alarmed. Dad was a creature of habit, rising early every morning to milk the cows and in bed by ten thirty, worn out from his day. He was never late for a meal, always ravenous from working outdoors. Mam rounded up everyone in the locality to look for him. Aoife recalled the commotion all this drama created – it didn't occur to her that something bad had happened; she was convinced he would return with an exciting tale to tell. Soon the yard had filled with neighbours holding flashlights and blankets, with women talking in hushed voices in the kitchen. He was found in the early hours of the morning. The memory of his still body being carried upstairs still caused her chest to tighten.

Overhearing the whispered words of neighbours, as she sat huddled in the kitchen, she learned he had cracked his head on a stone wall in the top field. Perhaps he might have survived if they had found him earlier. He was last seen at lunchtime, so they thought the accident probably happened in the afternoon. It hurt to think of Dad lying out in the fields, alone in the cold and dark. Between concussion and exposure, he had no chance. The child Aoife had shivered with terror. She had never seen a dead body but it was the behaviour of the adults, rather than the stiffening body upstairs, that upset her most. Mam, always so comforting, sat frozen, staring blankly. When Aoife ran into her arms seeking consolation, she was met with a stony stare. Later, as an adult, when watching the movie *Invasion of the Body Snatchers*, it reminded her of her mam that awful night. Of course, by that time she'd realised her mother was in a state of shock. The child Aoife, frightened and confused, sought her sister and brother, but Sam and Kate, each locked in silent misery, had no time for a bewildered ten-year-old.

Her memories of her dad were few but treasured. He was always busy with the farm but took time to play with her, chasing her and throwing her high in the air, setting her heart racing with excitement mingled with terror. As she grew older, he lost interest in horseplay, concerned perhaps that he would hurt her. But he took her on long nature rambles, encouraging her to look up the common and Latin names for the flowers, plants and trees they observed. When she succeeded in these naming games, he would wink at her and slip her a bar of chocolate, warning her not to let her mam know or he'd be a dead man. To this day she still could name most wildflowers and identify trees by their leaves. One day after she fell into a cluster of nettles and her leg stung hard enough to make her cry, he rubbed the stings away with dock leaves and explained about the plants he called nature's medicine, so she learned about willow bark, feverfew, and meadowsweet. But she was enthralled when he dwelt on nature's deathly side and warned of the perils of *Digitalis purpurea* (foxglove) and *Atropa belladonna* (deadly nightshade). She much preferred the Latin names as they conjured up an intoxicating mash-up of wonder intertwined with fear, much as his horseplay had done when she was a small child.

After he died, her memories of him dwindled until all that remained was a recollection of a benign presence, shrouded in a thick cloud of cigarette smoke, hovering on the outskirts of her childhood. Sam took on the vacated role of father and protector. With Kate and her mother burdened by grief, she turned to Sam in those early days and his fierce protective kindness sheltered her.

A blaring horn jerked her back to the present. God, how she wished she could have got out of this family get-together. She'd have brought Connor, but practicality demanded that he stay in Dublin to get his thesis finished. Marking the anniversary meant everything to Mam. She loved having the family together and, in anticipation, spent hours baking and preparing the house for visitors. It was lovely to see how her quiet, almost timid mother blossomed. Making this pilgrimage was a small price to pay when it made Mam happy.

The lights of the oncoming cars scorched her eyes. Night driving was not her thing. Connor didn't seem to mind; he usually took it on, knowing how she hated it. Instantly she felt comforted, thinking about Connor. They had met three years ago at her birthday party, which

Connor had crashed. Aoife smiled at the memory. Passing her door and hearing music and laughter, he just rocked up, acting as if he belonged. By the time she realised no one knew him, he had charmed her. Odd, because he wasn't her type, the opposite of the sporty guys she usually dated. But, tipsy as he was, he impressed her with his subversive humour and easy-going vibe. He asked her to a concert, and she agreed. After all, she liked the band and had nothing to lose by attending.

Six months later they moved in together and she felt an instant sense of belonging. Connor was the opposite of her practical self. He loosened her up, shook the seriousness out of her, and encouraged her to try new things. They had travelled, done parachute jumps and treks in the jungle, all at his instigation. He pushed her outside her comfort zone and opened her up to the joy of spontaneous adventure. After three years of cohabitation, they were now ready to take the next step and get married. Strange that the moment Connor became her fiancée their relationship entered its rockiest phase. The attitude of Connor as a boyfriend, which inspired and widened her horizons, now frustrated her. Did every engaged couple go through this period of adjustment? Getting married was a serious business and her practical side came to the fore, whereas Connor acted as though getting married was just a chance to party and celebrate. No doubt they would have a meeting of minds before too long. Hopefully, tonight Connor would take her absence as an opportunity to begin completing his thesis. Hopefully! Then they would be free to plan the wedding.

It was in this lighter mood that she drew up outside her mother's house. The soft light glowing from the porch illuminated the old two-storied farmhouse. Her mother must have heard the crunch of the car on the driveway for she stood in a pool of light in the doorway, waving eagerly.

As Aoife got out of the car, she was pulled into a warm embrace.

'You've got thin!' Agnes accused her, squeezing Aoife's arms as if to check for wasting.

'Thanks, Mam, that's what I'm aiming to be.' Smiling, she hugged her mother back.

'But, Aoife, I think that you're getting a bit too thin. I'm sure Connor doesn't want to marry a stick because as sure as anything that's what you're becoming. At least I'll have a chance to fatten you up this weekend.'

Aoife groaned. 'Mam, please don't start! Where's Sam?'

'He's locking up the sheds – the Caseys had loads of stuff taken from their outhouses recently, so he locks up all the time now. It's sad to see how much things have changed. In your father's time, a person never had to bother with locks at all.'

'What about Kate, has she come, and did she bring the kids?' Aoife asked, her eyes bright with anticipation.

'She rang to say she won't get here until tomorrow but you'll be glad to hear she's bringing Sandy and Colm with her.'

'That's great!'

The two women walked into the house, Aoife weighed down with her case and a bag containing wine and cake.

In the kitchen, she handed the bag to her mother.

'You're not a visitor, Aoife – you don't have to be bringing stuff!'

Aoife looked around at the old familiar things. Impulsively, she hugged her mother.

'It's good to be home, Mam!'

Her mother beamed back at her. 'I'm cooking a dinner – I know you city people have dinner in the evening so I expect you're starving.' Agnes, like most farmers' wives, cooked the main meal in the middle of the day. Farming was hungry work, and the cold weather encouraged the desire for a hot meal. 'Sit down there and we'll eat as soon as Sam comes in.'

'I hope you didn't wait to eat with me! I told you I'd be late leaving Dublin and to go ahead without me.'

'I know, pet, but Sam said he'd rather wait for you, so we could all eat together.' Agnes smiled at her daughter and, whipping an apron around her expansive waist, set about producing the meal.

Aoife, luxuriating in the atmosphere that drew her back into childhood, carried her case upstairs.

The bedroom door was open, and a swathe of moonlight flooded the room. It gave a beautiful, austere feel to what was a very homely space. As soon as she hit the light switch the elusive beauty vanished. It had changed little since her childhood. Originally, she had shared it with Kate, but her memories of that time were dim. She was only thirteen when Kate went off to train for nursing in London. At first, the belongings of her elder sister had dominated the room but, as Kate removed more and more of her things, it became Aoife's kingdom. As sisters, the age difference of four years created a gulf, but Kate was a benevolent sister who patronised her in a kindly fashion.

Although the teenage Aoife had lived in this room, she had never fully displaced Aoife the child. Long-neglected teddy bears and small cuddly toys sat on the shelves, forgotten. The ageing wallpaper still acted as a busy canvas for the tattered remains of Nelly, Eminem and NSYNC posters. Every time she came home, she had meant to rip those dated posters down, but a nostalgic part of her refused to break the link with the girl she had been. So, she resisted attempts to redecorate and hung on to her time capsule. The bed was covered by the same brightly patterned quilt that she had wrapped around herself when studying for exams. Aoife felt glad that at least in this small corner of her life things remained the same.

Downstairs she could hear the clatter of dishes, the lovely domestic sounds of home. She threw her bag on the bed and swiftly unpacked, hanging her clothes in the small wardrobe and putting socks and underwear in a drawer. Remembering it was Sam's birthday, she took the card she had brought from her bag and slipped it into her back pocket.

Taking the stairs two at a time, she burst through the kitchen door just in time to hear Sam ask, 'Well! Is she here?'

Racing over to him, she was immediately engulfed in a fierce bear hug. As a child, she had worshipped Sam, devoted to him in a dumb, dog-like way. To her, he was a hero. How did you look at a hero? Certainly not in the eye, so she had always hung her head and peeped adoringly up at him. Of course, over time she outgrew some of the awe, but never completely. It was through rose-tinted glasses she saw him even now. But she took the time to look him over more objectively. Sam was a big man, easily over six foot three, no longer the gangly youth he had been. His shoulders had expanded to match his length until he was a tank of muscle and sinew. His hair, once a scalded red, was now subdued with more than a scattering of grey. But his eyes were still as blue and clear as ever. Aoife had always considered her brother to be handsome, and at thirty-seven those looks remained. They stared delightedly at each other.

Shyly, she pushed the card into his hand. 'Happy Birthday, bro – sorry I forgot to post this.'

He tore it open, scanned the brief message and grinned. 'Hey, go on with you! I'm too old for birthdays. I told Mam I'd leave the house if she dared make me a cake, so she knitted me a jumper instead.'

'Oh God, what's it like?' Aoife asked, knowing her mother had weird notions about colour combinations.

He lowered his voice so Agnes couldn't overhear. 'Yellow and brown. I looked like an angry wasp. But I wore it yesterday, so she'll be OK with me abandoning it for a while, I hope.'

'I'm going to ask her to get you to model it for me tonight,' Aoife threatened, laughing as he raised his fist in mock anger.

'OK, you two, dinner is ready so get eating!' Agnes came and pushed her son and daughter towards the table.

Sam winked at his sister as he sat down. 'I could eat a bit, I suppose,' he said, heaping his plate full of stew from the bowl on the table.

His mother smiled fondly at him as she sat beside Aoife. She doted on her son, although she fiercely denied that was the case when teased by her daughters.

'How's work going?' Sam asked. 'Are those kids still driving you to distraction?'

'Well, they keep me busy. I'm enjoying my first-year class. They're a mad bunch but great craic too. I've promised to take them on a trip to Tayto Park if they behave themselves for the remainder of the term. But I'm not holding my breath that they'll manage to keep out of mischief.'

Aoife loved her job as a secondary-school teacher – well, most of the time anyway. But there were days when the work of shovelling information down the throats of reluctant pupils took its toll. She enjoyed the kids; she just wished the system didn't require her to bulldoze them into cramming for exams. There wasn't enough time to stop and think and explore with them. She regaled Sam and her mother with tales of school life as they ate and made them laugh as she told them of some of the antics of her students.

It was with great difficulty that she prevented her mother from piling second helpings on her plate. Sated, she sat back in her chair and sighed contentedly.

Agnes immediately jumped to her feet and arrived back at the table with a freshly baked apple tart and a jug of piping hot custard. Aoife, her stomach bursting, agreed to take a small slice. She knew only too well that resistance wasn't an option as her mother had baked it in honour of her homecoming. Sam showed no such reluctance and she watched as he practically inhaled an enormous slice.

Eventually, Sam finished eating and wiped his mouth with a paper napkin, crumpled it into a ball, and turned to his mother. 'I'd love a cup of tea, Mam.'

Aoife frowned as her mother got to her feet. Why couldn't he get it himself instead of ordering her mother around? She felt traitorous for thinking critically of her brother, but her mam seemed to have missed the feminist movement of her generation and lived to serve others, especially the men in her family. All her life Agnes O'Driscoll had cared for her husband and children. It was second nature for her to put their needs first. Wryly, Aoife realised it was also second nature for her children to expect her to.

'I'll put the kettle on, Mam,' she said. 'Why don't you sit down for a bit?'

At first Agnes protested but relented and sat back down beside Sam.

While Aoife scalded the teapot and boiled the kettle, she listened to the soft murmur of her mother's voice enquiring about the progress of work on the farm. She took out the china teacups and carried them to the table; her mother hated mugs. As she waited for the tea to brew, she shook some biscuits onto a plate. Agnes had a weakness for Fig Rolls. She joined her mother and brother and the three of them sipped appreciatively. The tea tasted so much nicer in her mother's house. Perhaps because, when she was here, she took time to make it properly, to use loose tea leaves, and to give it time to brew – the resultant tea was always more refreshing, and comforting. Or maybe it was just the lovely feeling of home that added flavour.

'How is Connor?'

Sam's deep voice shook her from her reverie.

'He's fine. He's working hard to finish his thesis in time for the wedding.'

She knew the next question before her mam uttered it.

'When's he going to get a job, love?'

Aoife sighed, irritated. 'As soon as he finishes his Master's he is going to take a job with his brother. He isn't interested in being an estate agent long-term, but it will give him time to explore his options.'

Sam raised his eyebrows.

'What's the problem with that, Sam? Not everyone knows what they want to do with their life straight off.'

'No offence, but most people have some inkling of what they want to do by the time they're in their thirties. Your Connor is a perpetual student. How many times did he jump ship from one college course to another?'

'OK! I admit it has taken him a while to find what he wants to do, but this time he will finish what he started. He is going to hand in his thesis in the next few weeks.'

'But what exactly is he qualified to do? He has an arts degree, and he's doing a thesis on some obscure poet. What is his long-term plan?'

Aoife lifted her cup and saucer, and walked stiffly to the sink. She had no answer for her brother. Connor was drifting along, and she was growing impatient herself. In a few months, they would be married and, if they wanted to buy a house, it would depend on her earnings.

She kept hoping that Connor would find his niche, accepting that writing poetry wasn't an occupation but a creative outlet. But she couldn't fault him for his commitment to his craft. He got up before six and spent a couple of hours writing before heading into college or his part-time job in the local shop and then, in the evening, he sat in their bedroom working for another couple of hours. Some nights she woke to find him still at work polishing up a poem or piece of prose.

It was a pity that being a writer didn't reward all this dedication. She knew it was impossible to make a living from writing poetry unless you were Seamus Heaney.

The job offer from his brother was a godsend. The brothers didn't get on, but Connor's parents had applied pressure and he was starting work in September. If only he would find it tolerable enough to stick at it for a year or two, at least until they could get some savings together.

Sam must have registered her downhearted expression when she returned to the table because he changed the subject. Shortly after, at Agnes's prompting, they went into the living room where they spent the rest of the evening staring at the fire, cracking jokes and discussing the goings-on in the locality.

Their mam said little, contentedly listening and dozing beside the fire. It was after twelve when they shook their mother awake and headed to bed.

Sam hugged Aoife on the landing. 'It's good to have you home, love,' he whispered.

CHAPTER 2

The sound of a cock crowing, followed by the bellowing of cattle, and the hum of milking machines jolted Aoife awake. In the city, the noise was perpetual and lost its power to intrude. She slept through blaring car horns, the brutal insistence of pneumatic drills ripping through pavements, and even the cacophony of her alarm clock. Connor joked that she would sleep through Doomsday. Here in the country, the morning sound leached into her sleep and turned her from unconscious owl to reluctant lark in an instant.

Throwing her arms back against the headboard, she stretched until her body ached pleasurably. Then springing out of bed, she ran with rapidly cooling feet into the tiled bathroom. She shivered as lukewarm water trickled from the ancient shower-head. Getting out of the shower, she cursed, realising that she had left her towel in the bedroom. Grabbing a small hand-towel for modesty, she raced into her room to retrieve it.

It was just past nine when she descended the stairs to have her breakfast.

The smells emanating from the little kitchen were enticing. Freshly grilled bacon, and the sound of frying eggs made her mouth water in anticipation. Funny, but she hadn't felt the slightest bit hungry until now.

Her mam greeted her with a beaming smile as she buttered toast at the counter.

'Sam is due in from the milking shortly, so you are just in time to tuck into a nice fry-up. Fetch some cutlery and sit yourself down.'

Aoife got a place ready for herself as Sam came through the back door. He removed his boots in the scullery and washed his hands. He was wearing his farm clothes – a holey jumper and a battered blue windbreaker. His unshaven face made him look scruffy and younger somehow.

They sat down to eat.

Agnes was her usual lively, chatty self but Sam, even for him, was unusually quiet.

'Is there anything the matter, son?' Agnes asked.

'It's Nell – she seems to have gone missing.'

Nell was a fifteen-year-old sheepdog, an ever-present feature of the farm. She wasn't a house dog but dearly loved nonetheless.

'It's not like her to just disappear,' Sam said. 'I hope something hasn't happened to her.'

'When did you last see her?' Aoife asked.

Sam wrinkled his forehead. 'I fed her at bedtime, and she seemed OK. She's getting on a bit, but she wasn't ailing. I hope she didn't get knocked down by some idiot coming home from the pub last night.'

Soberly, they recalled what happened to Bradys' Labrador last winter. Hit by a car, the poor dog had dragged herself home to die.

Now Sam had lost his usual hearty appetite and picked at his food. Aoife hadn't realised how attached he was to Nell. Like most farmers, he was unsentimental about animals. Nell wasn't a pet, she was a working dog, but over time what had started as a respect for her herding abilities had become tinged with genuine affection. Her disappearance had clearly hit him hard.

'Look here,' said Aoife, 'why don't I take a spin round the roads and see if I can find her? She may have gone off for a run and just went too far.'

Sam nodded. 'That would be great. I'd look myself, but I have a lot on this morning.'

He took a final slurp of tea, wiped his mouth with the back of his hand, and went out.

The two women mused over Nell's possible whereabouts as they washed up.

Aoife was glad of her jacket as she walked out into the chilly morning. The sun was high in the steely blue sky. As she drove slowly down the country roads, she realised she had little hope of finding Nell but wanted to try for Sam's sake. Every so often she stopped to call for the dog and asked a few people she encountered along the roads. No one had seen Nell.

ALSO AVAILABLE ON
AMAZON AND POOLBEG.COM